BESTSELLING AUTHORS
IN THE SPOTLIGHT

Dear Reader,

It's time to shine the spotlight on six special authors—bestsellers you wouldn't want to miss!

We've selected stories by some of your favorite authors to give you a chance to meet old friends or discover new ones. These novelists are strong, prolific women who write the stories that you've told us you love, and each is distinguished by a unique style and an uncanny ability to touch the heartstrings of her readers.

If you're not acquainted with the work of Alicia Scott, Sherryl Woods, Barbara Boswell, Kristine Rolofson, Janice Kay Johnson and Muriel Jensen, now's your big chance! And if you are, you may want to have a peek at page six for a more complete listing of books by the author of this volume.

Take a chance on a sure thing, and enjoy all six of our Bestselling Authors in the Spotlight!

The Editors

Praise for the work of
JANICE KAY JOHNSON

"Janice Johnson always delivers fine, strong
writing with an emotional, heartfelt punch."
—Jayne Ann Krentz

"Janice Johnson writes with passion,
power and tenderness."
—Stella Cameron

"Janice Kay Johnson dishes up a sexy hero,
a strong heroine and absolutely superb
sensual tension."
—*Romantic Times*

"Janice Johnson's heartwarming stories will make
you smile and cry and laugh out loud."
—Pamela Toth

BESTSELLING AUTHORS
IN THE SPOTLIGHT

JANICE KAY JOHNSON

Her Sister's Baby

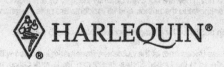

HARLEQUIN®

TORONTO • NEW YORK • LONDON
AMSTERDAM • PARIS • SYDNEY • HAMBURG
STOCKHOLM • ATHENS • TOKYO • MILAN • MADRID
PRAGUE • WARSAW • BUDAPEST • AUCKLAND

ISBN 0-373-83518-3

HER SISTER'S BABY

Copyright © 1995 by Janice Kay Johnson.

All rights reserved. Except for use in any review, the reproduction or
utilization of this work in whole or in part in any form by any electronic,
mechanical or other means, now known or hereafter invented, including
xerography, photocopying and recording, or in any information storage
or retrieval system, is forbidden without the written permission of the
publisher, Harlequin Enterprises Limited, 225 Duncan Mill Road,
Don Mills, Ontario, Canada M3B 3K9.

All characters in this book have no existence outside the imagination of
the author and have no relation whatsoever to anyone bearing the same
name or names. They are not even distantly inspired by any individual
known or unknown to the author, and all incidents are pure invention.

This edition published by arrangement with Harlequin Books S.A.

® and TM are trademarks of the publisher. Trademarks indicated with
® are registered in the United States Patent and Trademark Office, the
Canadian Trade Marks Office and in other countries.

Visit us at www.eHarlequin.com

Printed in U.S.A.

Dear Reader,

I'm delighted to have one of my favorite books reprinted. The story is one I mulled over for a long time before actually starting. If you'll excuse the pun, *Her Sister's Baby* had a slow gestation! Surrogate parenting intrigued me as a writer, but as a mother I couldn't imagine bearing a child and giving it away.

Then I saw the newspaper article. One sister had offered to serve as a surrogate for the other. The idea of a woman willing to give an amazing gift to her dearly beloved sister was one I understood. My heroine would offer the same gift. Only, what if her sister died before the baby was born? And what if the heroine didn't know her sister's husband very well?

I understood the rest of the story, too. I remember how I felt when I was pregnant with my own daughters—the stirrings inside, the wonder, the growing attachment to a baby I'd never seen, but one I knew was *mine*. Maybe that's why *Her Sister's Baby* is so close to my heart, and why, of all the books I've written, this is the one I'm happiest to see have a new life. I can only hope Colleen's story touches you, as well, and brings back treasured memories.

Sincerely,

Janice Kay Johnson

A Selection of Janice Kay Johnson's Titles

SUPERROMANCE

PROLOGUE

THE CEMETERY WAS OLD, with the graves of each generation sprawling beyond the last. Ancient maples, leafless now, followed the lane that curved through the green sward. Even older were the first headstones, gray, sometimes tilting, their carved letters silent testament to long-past tragedies.

But the tragedy that had brought the mourners here today was as raw as the empty stretch of sloping land ready to receive the next generation. Beneath a tarp, dark earth was heaped beside the newly dug grave, where Sheila Elizabeth Delaney was being laid to rest.

In agony, Colleen Deering wrenched her gaze from the braced casket and stared unseeing at the small crowd huddled beyond it.

Oh, God. The pain cramped inside her chest, stealing her breath. She didn't know if she could bear it. Her sister had been only thirty-two, happy in her marriage, looking forward to raising a family. *Why Sheila?* Colleen cried silently. *Why now?*

The minister was talking, his voice soothing, his utterances age-old and perhaps even true. Was everyone else listening? Colleen looked from face to face, struggling to find some link with another soul among this crowd of mourners.

Not unexpectedly she found it in the eyes of the man who faced her across her sister's grave. He truly was a stranger, this tall, broad-shouldered man who had remained dry-eyed throughout the ordeal, a silent, rigid presence. She supposed some of the mourners were his friends, though he stood apart from the others, staring at the gleaming, flower-draped casket atop its supports. His expression was set, unrevealing. Only his hands, curled into fists, gave away the anguish he otherwise disguised.

And then he lifted his head. His blue eyes, shockingly vivid here, where even the sky wore the colors of mourning, met Colleen's. In them she saw everything she felt and more.

She wished suddenly she knew him better, this man her sister had loved. Instead of staring at each other across a rift, they ought to have been able to offer each other comfort. After all, Michael Delaney was—no, *had been*—Sheila's husband.

He was also the father of the unborn child Colleen carried.

CHAPTER ONE

"KIM LIKES her teacher at least," Colleen said, turning on the faucet to rinse the breakfast dishes. "Mrs. Peters. Do you know her?"

"I don't think so." Sheila's tone was distracted.

She sat at Colleen's kitchen table sipping coffee, at first glance looking perfectly at home. She was a beautiful woman, but today she seemed brittle, edgy. She had lost weight, Colleen thought.

Chattering to cover her unease, Colleen said, "Well, Mrs. Peters is one brave woman. Last year she taught kindergarten. This year she's switched to sixth grade. Can you believe it?" She shook her head. "From five-year-olds jumping on desks to a roomful of preadolescent hormones."

Sheila gave an odd, twisted smile. "Don't parents make the same transition?"

Colleen grabbed the kitchen sponge. "Yes, but gradually, thank God."

Sheila neither laughed nor remarked, odd in itself since she had stopped by just to visit. Instead, as she idly stirred her coffee, there was unexplained tension in the way she held herself. She was too pale, with dark circles beneath her eyes. Without her usual smile, the lines beside her mouth were unhappy ones.

Colleen occupied herself scrubbing on the countertop

while she tried to think of a tactful way to ask what was wrong.

Out of the blue Sheila said, "Do you know how much I envy you?"

Colleen turned, the sponge still in her hand. Her first instinct was to make some teasing remark despite her sister's strange tone. But when she saw the way Sheila's mouth twisted, the cloud in her huge brown eyes, Colleen said carefully, "What do you mean?"

"Isn't it obvious?"

"Given the fact that my small store of savings is almost gone and my business is barely breaking even, that Drew refuses to talk to his father when he calls while Kim cries herself to sleep..." Her laugh revealed more frustration than she'd known she felt. "No, it's not obvious."

"At least you have them." There it was again, the anger, the hurt, the envy.

"That's true." Colleen tossed the sponge into the sink and went to sit at the table. She touched Sheila's elegant, long-fingered hand. "Have you given up?"

Sheila's face contorted and then she bent her head to hide the tears Colleen had already seen in her eyes. "I can't go on like this," she said, on a hiccuping sob. "I've tried and tried, but I'm just pretending. I don't even tell Michael any more when my period's late. What's the point? We both know what'll happen. Do you know what he said the last time? 'Why are you doing this to yourself?'" Her hands curled into fists. "God."

"Doesn't he want children?"

"Oh." Her tone was suddenly lifeless. "I don't know." More than the tears, it was the emptiness in her eyes that scared Colleen. "No, that's not true. He always claimed he wanted a family. But of course, it's *my* body that's the issue. We both know that, even though he never blames me. But how can I give up? What would we have left?''

The idea of not having Drew and Kim was unthinkable, but Colleen tried to remember how she'd felt before they came into her life.

"A happy marriage, a beautiful home, a job you enjoy..."

Sheila hadn't even heard her. "*Nothing*," she said fiercely. "That's what. All I ever wanted is a family. I feel betrayed, as though somebody promised—'' She broke off.

When Colleen came to her, Sheila buried her face in her sister's stomach and wrapped her arms around her waist with the intensity of a child who needs to hold on for dear life. Tears wet Colleen's cheeks. She murmured the kind of reassurances that satisfy a child. Sheila was beyond that, but what else could Colleen offer?

Maybe it was enough. At least she was *here*. Until three months ago, when Colleen had moved with her children to this small town in eastern Washington, all she'd been able to do was listen to her sister long-distance and sympathize. Of course she'd known that Sheila wanted children, and that she and Michael were disappointed because of the countless times she'd miscarried. But preoccupied by her own divorce, she hadn't fully understood how devastated her sister was by what she saw as her failure.

Well, things were different now. Colleen had moved to Clayton to be close to her sister. Obviously Sheila had needed Colleen just as much.

Finally Sheila let go of her and lifted her head. Mascara tracked down her cheeks and her peaches-and-cream complexion was blotched. "I want to hate somebody," she said with devastating simplicity. "But the only person I can hate is myself."

"That's ridiculous!" Colleen protested. "It's not as

though you can help it. I can't imagine that Michael holds it against you.''

"No," her sister said drearily. "Of course he doesn't. But I do."

Grasping for straws, Colleen asked, "What about the adoption agency?"

Sheila gave a mirthless laugh. "They've never even done a home study. We've been on their list for four *years*. And it's an average of three years after that before you get a baby. I don't think they're going to give us one. There are never enough babies. Who knows, maybe they didn't like something about us. It would be so easy to trip up and never even know it."

"There must be other agencies…"

"You're supposed to stick with one. They'd drop us from the list if they found out we'd gone somewhere else. Anyway, we'd be starting all over and I hear it's just as bad no matter what agency you're with." She mopped at her tears with a napkin. "I'm sorry, Col. I didn't mean to dump on you. I'm just…I'm at the end of my tether."

"Cry to your heart's content," Colleen declared. "That's what sisters are for."

Sheila's smile trembled and fresh tears washed away the old. "I'm so glad you're here. I've missed you. Since Mom died, I've felt so alone."

"Well, you're not." With a sting of anger, Colleen wondered what was wrong with Michael that his wife was so lonely. But this wasn't the time to ask. Instead, Colleen hugged her sister, brushing her curls back from her wet face. Sheila's hard veneer was gone; she might have been the fifteen-year-old who had cried when her older sister left for college.

"I'd do anything for you," Colleen said passionately. "You know that, don't you?"

"Yeah." Sheila gave another shaky smile. "It's ironic that the one thing I need is something you can't give me."

That was when the notion came to Colleen, simple, almost ridiculously obvious, breathtaking. Slowly, examining it from each side, she said, "Why not?"

"If you mean that you'll share Drew and Kim—" Sheila stopped dead, her eyes widening. "You're not thinking…?"

"Why not?" Colleen said again, recklessly.

Her sister jumped to her feet. "You're crazy."

"What makes you say that?" Instead of regretting her impulsive suggestion, Colleen liked it better the more she considered it. Pregnancy and childbirth had been embarrassingly easy for her.

Sheila shook her head. "Col, we're talking about nine months of your life! Morning sickness, stretch marks, getting as big as a cow! It's one thing to have your own children, but when the baby wouldn't even be yours…"

"Yeah, but I actually *like* being pregnant," Colleen told her. "I can't claim to enjoy childbirth, but I was only in labor with Drew for three hours. No big deal."

She would have willingly embarked on forty-eight hours of labor, even a C-section, if only for the look in Sheila's eyes—the incredulous hope, the dawning wonder.

"You really mean it, don't you? You'd do this for me?"

"Of course I mean it." But Colleen felt obligated to warn, "Michael may not like the idea."

Sheila gave a quick shake of her head. "He won't mind. Why should he? It'd be his baby. And almost mine. At least you and I share the same genes. We even look alike."

Colleen wrinkled her nose. "Well…almost. You've always been prettier."

"Don't be silly." Sheila jumped to her feet. Her cheeks

were pink and her eyes glowed. "You'd really do this for me?"

"In a second," Colleen told her. Then she smiled. "Well, not quite. We'll have to wait until the right time of the month."

Sheila made a face. "I'm an expert on that! I swear not an hour has passed in five years or more when I didn't think about what time of month it was, whether tonight we ought to try again, whether *this* time we'd get lucky…" She let out a long, shuddering breath. "Part of me had given up and part of me never stopped hoping."

Tentatively Colleen introduced a note of practicality. "Do you know…well, how to go about it? I mean—" she was blushing now, too "—getting me pregnant?"

Sheila didn't seem to notice. "I'll bet our doctor would do it. After I talk to Michael, I'll call and find out." She suddenly laughed and snatched Colleen into a hug. "I can't believe this is happening! I've dreamed about it for so long!" In her mercurial way, Sheila suddenly sobered. "Oh, Col, I don't know if I can do this to you. Wouldn't it break your heart to give the baby away?"

"It won't be mine to give away. Consider it baby-sitting." Colleen gripped both of her sister's hands and gazed solemnly into her eyes. "I swear," she vowed, as much for herself as for her sister, "that I will never, even for a minute, think of the baby as mine. It's yours—and Michael's."

Sheila stared at her for a long moment, then sank onto a chair as though her legs had suddenly turned to jelly. "You do mean it."

Colleen's own legs felt a little weak, and she, too, sat down abruptly. Half in amazement at herself, Colleen said, "I really, really do. The only thing is…well, maybe you'd better not talk to Michael yet."

"What do you mean?" Sheila asked in quick alarm.

"I need to talk to Kim and Drew. I can't do something this drastic without giving them some voice in my decision." Colleen bit her lip. "I'm sorry. I should have talked to them before I got your hopes up."

"Don't be silly." Sheila bounced to her feet again, moving nervously, her voice deliberately light. "Of course they should come first. And promise me, if they don't like the idea, you won't put pressure on them. I don't want them feeling guilty. Okay?"

"Okay," Colleen agreed. "I'll call you the second I talk to them."

"And I'd better get to work." Sheila's gleaming auburn hair, worn in a stylish bob, shimmered as she bent to grab her purse. Then she gave Colleen a quick kiss on the cheek. When she straightened, she was unexpectedly blinking away new tears. "Col... I just want to say..." She tried to smile. "Look at me, not able to get out a simple thank-you. But I want to say it now. Even if nothing comes of this, thank you. Just...talking about it made me realize how much we mean to each other. We're lucky, aren't we?"

Colleen didn't even have a chance to answer. Sheila was already slamming the bottom half of the Dutch door and waving before she vanished down the walk. A moment later Colleen heard the throaty engine of her sister's bright red sports car.

Colleen wanted to talk to Drew and Kim *now,* but they were in school and she had to open the store at ten. In fact, she remembered, with a panicky glance at the clock, she'd promised to be there early so that the instructor for the class on appliqué could set up in the back room. Sheila would have to wait.

At dinner Colleen had to hear all about her kids' day at school before she could get a word in edgewise. It wasn't until afterward, when Kim and Drew were both helping her clean up, that Colleen realized the right moment had come. Hands in the soapy dishwater, she was suddenly struck by how many of life's decisions she'd made in the kitchen, how many crises had found her there. She just been drying the last pan the night when Ben had announced he wanted a divorce.

Shaking that particular recollection off, Colleen took a deep breath and said very casually, "I have something I want to discuss with you guys."

Drew had just come back from taking the garbage out to the can. Ignoring her, he complained, "This is a gross job. Why can't Kim do it? I'd rather dry dishes."

"That's not what I heard two weeks ago," Colleen reminded him. At the time he had whined that taking out the garbage only took a minute, while drying took forever.

"Yeah, but I didn't know then how garbage stinks."

Colleen smiled at him. "That probably means we should wash out the trash can. Saturday."

"But—"

Kim elbowed him. "Why don't you put a cork in it. Mom has something to say."

"Don't tell me what to do." Drew's square jaw jutted out just like his father's often had. "You're not my mother!"

Colleen sighed. "Kim, you might have phrased that a little more tactfully. Drew, I *am* your mother, and I do want to talk about something."

He subsided, mumbling, "Yeah, well, she always thinks *she* can give orders…"

Forging on, Colleen said, "You guys know how much your aunt Sheila and uncle Michael would like to have a baby."

Kim shot her brother a dirty look. "Why don't you give

'em Drew? *I* wouldn't miss him. And he's a baby, all right.''

Drew had gotten as far as storming, "Talk about babies! You should have seen *her* yesterday—" when Colleen covered his mouth with a soapy hand.

Giving her daughter a minatory look, she said, "Tempting though the idea occasionally is, I would never give either of you away. I'm actually kind of fond of you both.''

Kim wrinkled her nose. *"Fond?"*

Colleen smiled and removed her hand from Drew's mouth. "Well, okay, maybe a little more than fond.''

Drew scrubbed at his mouth with his T-shirt. "Gross. You didn't have to wash my mouth out with soap.''

"If you'd shut it a little quicker, you wouldn't have gotten soap in there." Colleen was getting a headache. "Can you two just listen to me for a minute?" Reassured by their reluctant nods, she explained, "The problem is, your aunt Sheila can't stay pregnant. There's something wrong with the walls of her uterus." Drew was beginning to squirm—he didn't want to hear any more about girls and sex than he absolutely had to—but she ignored him. "They've tried to adopt a baby, but they've been waiting forever. There just aren't very many babies available for adoption. So I got to thinking…well, that I could have one for her.''

Her children stared at her with identical expressions of horror. Drew was the first to speak. "But who would be the *father?*"

This was the tricky part. The part, in fact, that she didn't like thinking about herself. "Your uncle Michael."

"But he's married to Aunt Sheila already."

Colleen tried to remember how much she had told Drew about sex and procreation. Hoping it was enough, she gave an upbeat explanation of how artificial insemination was done and how the pregnancy wouldn't really affect them that much. "I'd go to the hospital and have the baby, and then come home. Only instead of bringing it with me, like I did you guys, Aunt Sheila would take the baby. He—or she—would be both your cousin and your half brother."

She fielded a barrage of questions. Why *half* brother? What would Dad think? Would anybody *tell* the baby that his mom wasn't really his mom? At last the stream slowed, and Colleen said, "Some people might not approve of my doing this. I would have worried more about that if we were still back in Pacifica, but here hardly anybody would have to know."

"What about our friends?" Drew asked.

"What friends?" Kim muttered.

"You'll make some," Colleen said. "It just takes time. Especially in a new town where everybody else has known each other forever. And, Drew, I don't think the boys you've had over would even notice if I was pregnant. The only reason they ever come into the house is to look for something to eat."

He appeared to contemplate that briefly. "I guess I wouldn't care if one of *their* mothers was having a baby." His curled lip conveyed his opinion of the whole business.

"What do you think, Kim?" Colleen asked quietly. Her daughter was the one who hadn't wanted to move, who clung ferociously to her belief in her father however many times he failed her. Drew wasn't old enough to be traumatized by the snubs that might come his way if the community found out and disapproved of this pregnancy. But Kim was, and not even for Sheila would Colleen hurt her daughter.

After a minute, the eleven-year-old shrugged awkwardly. "It's okay with me, I guess. I think it's cool that you want to do it for her."

Colleen gave each of her children an impulsive hug. "Believe it or not," she informed them, "the time will come when you two are willing to admit how much you love each other, too."

Kim leveled a cool stare at her brother, who returned it in good measure. "Yeah, right," she said flatly.

"She's a *girl*," Drew said.

Colleen laughed. So much for her only serious reservation about the step she contemplated taking. Now it was up to Sheila and Michael.

FROM THAT DAY ON Colleen couldn't bring herself to face Michael. Suddenly he wasn't just Sheila's husband; he was a man. Even though the process of artificial insemination was completely impersonal, Colleen couldn't forget that Michael would be the father of the baby she'd carry. He might never touch her, but still some part of the two of them would be melded into one. They would have come together in the most intimate of ways.

What she should do was resolve her feelings, maybe even talk about them with Sheila. Coward that she was, Colleen avoided him altogether. Whenever Sheila suggested dinner, Colleen pretended she had to be at the shop but offered to meet her for lunch, instead. Drew's soccer game saved her from a Sunday barbecue at her sister and brother-in-law's house; the meeting of the local quilt guild happened to be the evening Sheila and Michael were having friends in for drinks. She could only pray that neither of them had put two and two together and realized why she was making excuses.

Once she narrowly escaped running into him at, of all disastrous places, the doctor's office. She'd just arrived for her second attempt at being inseminated and was dropping her chart into the in-basket at the nurse's station. She turned when she heard footsteps approaching and the nurse saying, "Right this way, Mr. Delaney. I'll just get you a cup..." Behind the nurse was Michael, his dark head bent as he listened to her, his face inscrutable.

Colleen had never moved faster in her life. She whisked out of sight through the nearest open door, her heart pounding and her knees weak. Thank heavens he hadn't been looking her way! What if they had come face-to-face? What would she have *said* to the man who was here to produce sperm to impregnate her, thanks to the doctor who insisted it had to be fresh for the optimum success rate?

Her heartbeat took another dizzying leap when the nurse spoke again, sounding so close that she had to be standing with Michael right on the other side of the door Colleen was hiding behind.

"Why don't I put you in this room?"

With a horrified glance over her shoulder, Colleen discovered she had taken refuge in an examining room. What if the nurse brought Michael in here? A wave of heat washed over Colleen's face.

But the footsteps receded, and a moment later she peeked out to see that he was gone. The nurse was hurrying toward her.

She looked startled to see Colleen emerging from a room. "Oh, Mrs. Deering, I didn't see you arrive. I'm afraid it will be a few minutes. You're welcome to stay in that room if you'd prefer, or I can call you back in when we're ready for you."

Colleen chose the privacy of the room to avoid any chance of meeting Michael as he was leaving, having handed over the precious cup.

For the first time it occurred to her to wonder, if she was embarrassed, what Michael must feel. She'd assumed that Sheila was accompanying him to these appointments, but he had undeniably been alone. How on earth did he get aroused, alone in the sterile surroundings of the clinic, knowing that the nurse waited just outside? Think how dreadful it would be to a man's ego if he had to admit that he just couldn't do it!

But apparently he could, because not fifteen minutes later the doctor was ready to do his part in the procedure that would magically produce life inside her even without the warmth and closeness of lovemaking.

SHE KNEW in a matter of weeks that she was pregnant, but Colleen wasn't about to raise her sister's hopes. Not yet. She waited another week, then closed her shop early one day and went by the clinic. A pregnancy test confirmed her hopes.

On her way out Colleen almost stopped at the pay phone in the waiting room. But somehow a phone call didn't seem adequate for news so momentous. And surely it was too early in the afternoon for Michael to be home. She could stop by to exchange mutual congratulations with Sheila and then run.

Sheila confounded her.

"Don't be silly, the kids will be fine without you. You have to be here when I tell Michael. We're in this together, aren't we?"

"But it's your baby," Colleen protested weakly. "Wouldn't you like to be alone—"

They both heard the sound of the garage door opening.

"Oh, here's Michael now." Sheila jumped to her feet, face glowing. "I can hardly wait to tell him!" She danced several steps toward the kitchen, then stopped theatrically. "Or should I open some champagne and spring the news on him when I hand him the glass? I wonder if we have any… Oh, I can't bear it." She spun toward the kitchen. "I've got to tell him. You don't mind, do you, Col?"

Sheila vanished into the kitchen and Colleen braced herself. For heaven's sake, Michael was her sister's husband! Colleen had known him, if distantly, for years, since she had been Sheila's matron of honor. He hadn't changed just because his sperm had impregnated the wrong sister. And besides, she had volunteered for this, hadn't she?

He was tugging absentmindedly at his tie and undoing the top button of his dress shirt when Sheila drew him through the kitchen doorway. His gaze went directly to Colleen and she saw a muscle twitch in his jaw. But his stillness gave nothing away; he only waited for the news he must surely have guessed.

Sheila's eyes were sparkling when she stopped, still holding her husband's hand, and cleared her throat. "Colleen has something she wants to tell us."

They faced Colleen and waited, Sheila expectantly, Michael with brows raised. Colleen made a face at her sister, but surrendered with as much grace as possible. "I'm pregnant," she said baldly. "Six weeks along. Your baby is due July 20."

The last thing she expected from Sheila, who already knew, was tears, but suddenly she was blinking them away as she smiled tremulously at Colleen. "I guess I still can't believe it. We're really going to have a baby." Her tone was filled with awe.

But what Colleen was waiting for was Michael's reaction. Sheila had talked about her hurt and disappointment at remaining childless as though it was hers alone. Colleen wondered now whether Michael didn't care as much whether they ever had children, or was only a typical male who didn't like to talk about how he really felt.

He was still staring at her, his blue eyes unnerving in

their intensity. Just as the silence became uncomfortable, just as Sheila was turning in puzzlement to look up at him, he smiled.

Michael's smiles were rare, but worth waiting for. The first time she had met him, during a prewedding party, Colleen had watched him unobserved for several minutes before Sheila drew him over. Her first reaction hadn't been positive. He was so handsome she had felt intimidated and—unfair though it was—mildly irked at him for having that effect on her.

She'd just been brooding over whether she *wanted* to dislike her sister's intended when Sheila had pointed her out to him and Michael turned his head. Colleen felt first the shock of his blue eyes. But not until he smiled, with warmth, self-deprecation and real charm, had she understood why Sheila had fallen so hard for this man that she was planning a wedding within weeks of their meeting.

But today's smile, so slow in coming, crooked, a little shaky and completely genuine, reached Colleen in a way his more deliberate ones never had.

"Damn," he said softly. "It worked."

Colleen knew exactly how he felt. What had taken place in the doctor's office couldn't possibly have anything to do with this moment, with the life that would soon be fluttering in her womb. How could it have happened without the sweat and pleasure of two bodies meeting? But happen it had, and the proof was within her.

Colleen flushed, realizing that her hand was instinctively spread over her abdomen. Michael's gaze flicked down to her hand, then back to meet hers. His smile faded, and she felt that odd tension again, that self-consciousness. She was the fifth wheel here, an intruder on her sister's marriage.

She managed another smile. "I really need to get home.

But I wanted to tell you... Well, that's obvious, isn't it? Anyway, congratulations again.''

Michael took a few steps forward, blocking her way. Before she could react, he bent to kiss her cheek. ''The words are inadequate,'' he said roughly. ''But I'll say them, anyway. Thank you.''

Sheila was right behind him, giving Colleen a swift hug. ''Didn't I tell you she was a sister in a million?'' she asked her husband.

He shook his head, his blue eyes lingering on Colleen's face. ''I never doubted it for a minute, but you've got to admit, this is above and beyond the call.''

Colleen made a face. ''You're going to have me blushing, for Pete's sake! Like I told Sheila, I loved being pregnant. I have every intention of enjoying this time just as much, only I can hand over the 2 a.m. feedings to you guys. That'll give you something to look forward to.''

Michael's grin was wry, while his wife had a faraway look in her eyes. Very softly Sheila said, ''You have no idea how much I do.''

CHAPTER TWO

COLLEEN WAS just peeling off her bra and reaching for her nightgown when the telephone rang. She might have felt a thrill of alarm had she not known Drew and Kim were both safely tucked into bed just down the hall. Still, who would call her at nearly ten o'clock at night?

She reached for the receiver with one hand and her hairbrush with the other. "Hello?"

"Colleen?" She almost didn't recognize Michael's voice. With no preamble he said, "Sheila's been in a car accident."

The hairbrush fell out of Colleen's hand, thumping on the carpet. "Oh, my God." She sagged onto the edge of the bed. "Are you at the hospital? Is she...?"

"The state patrol just called. I'm on my way. I thought you'd want to be there, too."

Already she was on her feet, reaching for her jeans. Action of any kind staved off the terror. "Did they say how she is?"

"Colleen—" his voice roughened "—I don't think it's good."

"Oh, no, please no," she whispered.

"If you can't leave the kids..."

"They'll be all right." *Please, please, let Sheila be too.* "I'm on my way."

She awakened Kim and then drove through the rainy night to the hospital, running a red light once at a deserted intersection. Inside the hospital she was directed to a small waiting room. Michael was there, and the moment she saw him, she knew. His face was wet with tears.

Colleen's fingernails bit into her palms. "No. Not Sheila…"

"Oh, God." He bowed his head. His voice was thick. "She was speeding. You saw how wet the roads are. She, uh, she couldn't make a curve."

"No." Grief rose with shocking force, and Colleen, shaking her head vehemently, backed up until she came against a wall. "No!"

He kept talking, as though he had to say it. "She slammed on the brakes and skidded off the road straight into a telephone pole. They say…" Michael took a shuddering breath. "They say she died instantly."

Not Sheila. Oh, God, please…

He came to her then, her sister's husband, and held her. She held him as tightly and cried.

Sometime that night Colleen went mercifully numb. She stayed that way, going through the motions of life, until the funeral. And there, faced with Sheila's casket, Colleen couldn't hide any more.

Across Sheila's grave, Colleen met Michael's eyes. His agony mingled with her own, and she remembered for the first time in days that she was pregnant. That she carried her sister's baby.

But her sister was gone.

SHE WOULDN'T THINK about it, Colleen told herself on a wave of fresh pain. She didn't dare. Not now. She could only deal with so much at a time. Her pregnancy could wait. Thank God that so few people knew and that she didn't show yet.

Colleen kept her promise to herself for hours on end that

day. She just didn't have time to indulge her shock and grief. Instead, she acted as hostess at the reception, accepting condolences, checking in the kitchen with the volunteers from the church who were providing the food, keeping a sharp eye out for Kim and Drew. She had turned into an automaton, a grimace that masqueraded as a smile frozen on her face.

"Thank you for coming," she repeated over and over. "Yes, we'll miss her dreadfully. No, it doesn't seem quite real. How kind of you to offer, but I think we're fine."

Her hand stung from being patted so many times; her voice came to her own ears from a distance, as though it belonged to somebody else.

The first time the crowd parted and she came face-to-face with Michael, he merely nodded. The movement was jerky, as though his neck was stiff. Their eyes met, conveyed weariness and wariness in equal measure, and then Colleen turned away.

The next time, his large hand closed on her arm and he bent his head. "Are you all right?" he asked in an undertone.

Colleen looked down at his hand where it lay, brown and strong, on her forearm. She knew, without understanding why, that she was avoiding his gaze.

"I'm...managing," she said. "What about you?"

Michael withdrew his hand. "I'm fine," he said shortly. "How are your kids?"

But somebody was already claiming her attention, and she was vaguely aware that Michael had been engulfed in a bear hug. As aloof as he was, he must detest the necessity of accepting such physical intimacies from well-meaning people he hardly knew.

Of all the things that were said to her that afternoon,

only one really penetrated—the words of a woman who had worked with Sheila.

Very kindly she said, "Poor Sheila longed so for children, but you must be grateful now that she didn't have any. It's so dreadful when young children lose their mother."

Colleen's hand spread protectively over her stomach and she took an involuntary step back. Nausea rose in her throat and she was momentarily unable to speak.

Something must have showed on her face, because the woman said hastily, "Of course, they would have been a consolation to their father. And to you."

Somehow Colleen escaped without disgracing herself. And endured more gentle pats, more well-meant comfort. All the while, she wept inside. *Oh, Sheila...*

REAL PANIC didn't hit Colleen until several days after the funeral, when she awakened at five in the morning only to have to run for the bathroom with her stomach heaving.

Afterward, she wasn't sure she had the strength to stand. Still kneeling in front of the toilet, she reached up to flush it, her forehead resting on her arms.

When had she last eaten? Really eaten? Over the past few days, she'd fed the kids of course and made a pretense of eating herself, but that's all it was. At best, food was unappetizing; at worst, the idea of putting a bite in her mouth was enough to make her stomach quiver in protest.

But her stomach obviously didn't like total neglect, either.

She had to think about the baby, for its sake if not her own. She'd taken such care when she was pregnant with Kim and Drew, making sure she had so many dark green vegetables a day, so many citrus fruits. Not a drop of alcohol had crossed her lips, and she had avoided anyplace where people might be smoking. This baby, her gift to her sister, deserved as much.

And that was when fear began to trickle through her veins like a drug administered intravenously. Weak at first, then stronger and stronger, until she was panting for breath and blinking away the sweat that beaded her brow.

Dear God, what was she going to do?

She was pregnant. Inescapably, inarguably pregnant. Stuck, a victim by her own choice, trapped in an inexorable process that would carry her along willy-nilly.

And then what?

That was the really scary part. This wasn't her baby, was never *supposed* to be her baby. She was a long-term sitter, that was all. This child she carried was Sheila's.

The baby's not mine! she screamed inside, where only she could quail from the terror. *It's Sheila's! Sheila's, do you hear me? Bring her back!*

The grief tore at Colleen until she could no longer suppress the fear and sadness and sense of aloneness that had swamped her all week. Her hurt came out in huge, wrenching sobs, in the hot, salty taste of tears. Sheila was all she'd had, except for Kim and Drew, and they were children, for God's sake! Children, who needed her to be strong. What about *her*?

Just this once, she let herself be selfish, grieving not so much for her sister as for herself. She cried for her aloneness, for the burden she had taken on so joyfully and now could not lay down. She cried for her divorce, for her children, for the uncertain future.

"Mom?" The small, scared voice came from just behind her.

Colleen jerked around to see her daughter standing in the open bathroom door. Her eyes were wide and she clutched the faded baby quilt she had loved and now used as a throw on her bed, nothing important but always near.

"Mommy, are you okay?"

"Oh, sweetheart." Colleen squeezed her eyes shut and scrubbed at her wet face before she held out her arms. "If you don't mind getting soaked," she said as lightly as her tear-clogged throat would allow, "come here."

At eleven, Kim was too tall to sit on her lap, had been for several years, but somehow they still scrunched together on the bathroom floor.

Her cheek against her daughter's soft brown hair, Colleen said, "I'm just…letting it all out. Mostly none of this has seemed real. I'd lie there at night and part of me didn't believe Aunt Sheila was gone. I've been in shock, I guess. Suddenly this morning it hit me."

Kim turned brown eyes on her. "In the bathroom?" she said doubtfully.

"I was already here." It was on the tip of her tongue to add that she was having morning sickness. After all, Kim knew she was pregnant and why. But something stopped her. It apparently hadn't occurred to her daughter yet to think about what was going to happen with the baby, and Colleen didn't want to start her worrying. Until she herself talked to Michael and they made some decisions, she would just as soon not remind the kids of the inescapable fact of her pregnancy.

It developed that Kim was already worrying, but about something else, because she asked suddenly, "Will we move again? I mean, the only reason we came here is Aunt Sheila."

"Do you wish we would?"

Kim went still. "Not really."

"Even if it meant going back to Pacifica?"

There was a long pause before Kim muttered, "It's okay here." Not an answer, but an answer all the same.

"Well—" Colleen pressed a kiss to the top of her daughter's head, inhaling the scent that was still little girl "—I won't promise we'll never move again, but I'm sure not planning on it. For one thing we can't afford to. You know I sank everything we had into starting the business."

There was silence for a moment. Colleen's back had begun to ache because of her awkward position on the floor. But she didn't move a muscle.

"What if...well, if not enough people around here want to quilt?"

They had talked about this in some detail. After all, the risk was one they shared as a family. But if there was ever a time when even adults needed reassurance, it was right after a sudden death, when the uncertainty of life was brought shockingly home. So she said patiently, "Then I'll get a job. A regular, working-for-somebody-else, nine-to-five job. You know the kind."

"But you'd hate it."

"Hey." Colleen gave her daughter a small shake. "Most people have one, you know. I like owning my own business. But the world isn't going to end if it doesn't work out."

Kim nodded. After a minute she said, "Uh, Mom?"

"Yeah?"

"This is kind of uncomfortable."

Colleen groaned and collapsed, ending up on her back with Kim sprawled on top of her. Kim was giggling, the pinched look her face had worn this last week easing for the first time. Colleen knew she must look as wonderful as the leftovers she had a habit of forgetting in the back of the refrigerator, but she, too, felt a welcome easing inside.

Unfortunately it didn't last long. She tucked her daughter

back in bed for a last hour or two of sleep before the alarm sounded. She'd no sooner kissed her softly when she saw, in her mind's eye, Sheila, sitting at the kitchen table.

At least you have them.

And the anguish roared back. It wasn't fair. Why had Sheila been cheated yet again, and finally, of the chance to hold her own child?

COLLEEN USED the simple mechanism of denial to survive the next two weeks. The waistbands of her jeans and skirts were getting a little tight, but nothing she couldn't ignore. The kids were absorbed in their own concerns, and she had plenty to occupy her at the quilt shop.

Should she cancel classes that didn't completely fill or run them at a loss to build her customer base? What about a "fabric of the month" club, as many quilt shops had, in hopes of bringing in a little more money? But each new project took time, leaving her less for the kids, more weary.

Her increasing tiredness was something else she wouldn't let herself think about. Because if she did, she would also be forced to think about the pregnancy.

Which Michael was trying to make her do.

Except for Sheila's blithe communications, scarcely a message had been left on Colleen's answering machine since the move. Ben knew the kids weren't home during the day or after school; he called—when he bothered—in the evening. Kim hadn't made any friends yet, and Drew's skidded their bikes up the driveway on their way to the playing field, instead of picking up the phone. So when Colleen came home to the blinking red light for the third time that week, she looked at it as distrustfully as she would have a tarantula on her kitchen counter. She was in no hurry to push the Play button.

Michael's last two messages had been increasingly peremptory, both with the same theme: they had to talk. If this was him again, she didn't want the kids to hear what he had to say.

But Drew, coming into the house behind her, had already thudded up the stairs, and Kim hadn't followed her mother in at all. The fourteen-year-old boy next-door was shooting baskets in his driveway, which might have something to do with it. Kim insisted that all boys were jerks, but she thought of plenty of excuses to hang around the yard casually when Jerry was outside.

Maybe the talent at making excuses was hereditary, Colleen thought wryly. She'd made more than a few herself these past two weeks.

Reluctantly she pushed the flashing button. Michael's voice, deep but somehow remote, had unnerving immediacy, despite the fact it was recorded.

"Colleen, is there some reason you're not returning my calls? I know that this isn't the best time to think about the future, but we'll both feel more settled once we have it over with. Call me."

Colleen sank into one of the kitchen chairs. Well, she supposed that was reasonable enough. All Michael was doing was making it clear he was a decent man who was aware of his responsibility. She'd have more reason to be anxious if he *wasn't* calling her.

"So why don't you want to talk to him?" Colleen asked herself aloud. Then she made a face. "Dumb question. You know perfectly well why you don't want to. So put the groceries away, okay?"

As she nudged the refrigerator open and tried to find room for the gallon of milk, her memory popped up with something her ex-husband used to say.

You can run, but you can't hide.

In this case it was all too true. She wanted very badly to

hide, at least for a while. She wasn't ready to make the kind of decisions that had to be made.

But hiding wasn't going to work. She was beginning to show, would have to wear maternity clothes soon. People would ask about her pregnancy. What would she say?

"Oh, the baby's not mine. Really, it belongs to this man who used to be married to my sister. I don't know him very well, but I'm sure he'll be a good father."

Impatiently she blinked away the moisture in her eyes. Damn it, the baby *was* his. And she had promised, hadn't she? Right here in this very kitchen, she had sworn she would never, even for a minute, think of the baby as hers.

But that was before Sheila died. Now Colleen was the only mother this baby would have. So what was more important? Michael's rights and her promise? Or the infant she carried within her?

COLLEEN ACCEPTED the bolt of cotton fabric from the customer. When she saw the tiny stylized flower on the deep rose background, she said, "Oh, I love this one. I couldn't resist buying a couple of yards myself. How much do you need?"

The woman tilted her head, considering. "Oh, Lord, why don't I ever write these things down? This is supposed to be the backing and binding for a crib quilt. I'm making it for my granddaughter."

"What pattern?" Colleen asked with interest.

"Tumbling Blocks. I've always wanted to try it, even though those set-in pieces can be tricky. Does three and a half yards sound like enough to you?"

"That should be plenty," Colleen assured her, and began measuring the rose calico. "What other colors are you including?"

She continued to chat with the woman, a regular customer, meanwhile using her rotary cutter to slice smoothly through the fabric. Folding the piece, she rang up the purchase.

"Why don't you bring it in when you're done? I've love to see the finished product," she said. "In fact, I was thinking of having one of my monthly, miniquilt shows just for crib quilts. What do you think?"

"That's a wonderful idea," the customer exclaimed. "At the rate my kids are producing grandchildren for me, crib size is about all I have time to make anymore."

Colleen already regretted the subject. Crib quilts made her think of cribs—and babies. She had a sudden picture of Kim as an infant, just tucked in. She lay on her tummy, knees pulled up, thumb buried in her rosebud of a mouth. Over her was the quilt Colleen had lovingly pieced and quilted, the one that was now faded and worn and loved.

This baby should have her—or his—own quilt. The idea was bittersweet, as would be the task.

Colleen was accepting the woman's check when the bell over the front door tinkled. With an automatic smile of welcome, she glanced up. But at the sight of the tall, dark-haired man closing the door behind him, her pulse took an uncomfortable jump and her smile faded.

Michael. He had run out of patience.

His gaze found and moved swiftly over her, as palpable as a touch, before he inclined his head and then glanced around the front room. Sheer masculinity made him out of place here among the row upon row of shelves that held bolts of cotton fabric in colors that flowed from one to the next, from lavender to deep violet to purple-blues, from the palest of creams to rusts and earthy browns. It was a feminine place, celebrating an art form that was woman's own, a way she'd had to express her creativity in a man's world that denied her other outlets.

This place was both challenge and refuge to Colleen, who saw all the colors and textures and patterns as possibilities—incomplete alone, but ready to play roles in the quilts that were as unique as the women who would make them.

But Michael's interest was cursory, not appreciative. He was here to pin her down, to limit her possibilities. She couldn't blame him—and yet a knot of resentment clogged her throat.

She was briefly rescued by a young woman, who had been browsing for the past half hour. Now she appeared from one of the inner rooms and asked, "Can I possibly get some advice?"

"You bet," Colleen assured her. She glanced at Michael as though he were only another customer. "If you don't mind waiting?"

"Not at all," he said imperturbably, and strolled over to a table spread with a display of quilting books. He picked one up as Colleen left the room.

All the while she discussed which shade of teal would work best next to a warm brown, inside she was panicking. Why was he so determined to corner her now? The baby wasn't due for six months. What was it that he wanted "settled"?

If only she knew him better, Colleen thought futilely; if only he didn't have that air of rigid control that had always struck her as cold.

If only she knew what was right: for him, for her and for the baby.

Why hadn't he let her hide just for a little longer? Why did he force her to remember?

Eventually Colleen had said everything there was to say about shading and contrast and why she thought one teal fabric, with a swirling design, was the most effective. The customer continued to stand there, staring indecisively at the several bolts of fabric fanned out on a table.

At last the young woman made an exasperated sound. "Fiddlesticks. I just can't make up my mind. I don't know what's wrong with me today. Listen, I think I'll just come back tomorrow. Maybe I'll bring my thirteen-year-old, if she's willing to risk being seen with me. Her taste in everything but boys is dependable."

Colleen laughed as expected, but refrained from mentioning, as she might otherwise have, that she had an eleven-year-old daughter who was already showing signs of the rebellion to come. Instead, she assured the woman that tomorrow was fine, and no, she didn't need to put the bolts away, Colleen would take care of it later. She followed her customer out to the front room and with the tinkle of the bell over the door, was left alone with Sheila's husband.

Only, of course, he wasn't anymore, which was another of those things Colleen didn't like to think about.

She curled her fingers so tightly into fists that her nails bit into her palms.

She was dimly aware that Michael had said something, but he had to repeat it. "We need to talk. Can I take you out to lunch?"

She retreated behind the cutting table. "The lunch hour is one of my busiest times."

He raised a dark brow and glanced around. "Then what about right now?"

"We might be interrupted."

"Tonight?"

"I don't want Kim and Drew..." She flushed at his expression and closed her eyes for a moment. Opening them, she gave him a twisted smile. "I'm sorry. Now is fine, as long as you don't mind if we're interrupted."

He looked at her for a moment, half frowning, then shoved his hands in his pockets and hunched his shoulders. He spoke in an oddly gruff tone. "It won't take long. I just wanted to make sure you knew that, as far as I'm concerned, Sheila's death doesn't change any of the arrangements about the baby. I still expect to pay your medical expenses and to take him after the birth."

He sounded so businesslike, talking about "arrangements" and "expenses." But what popped out of her mouth surprised even Colleen. "What if it's a her?"

Michael looked at her in bafflement. "What?"

"What if the baby's a girl?"

His dark brows drew together. "Did I say I didn't want a girl?"

She sounded truculent and didn't care. "You said 'him.'"

"Good God." He rubbed the back of his neck and spoke tersely. "You know what I meant. I won't deny that the English language is sexist. 'Him' was merely convenient shorthand. I don't give a damn whether the baby is a girl or a boy."

The fight abruptly left her. She knew she'd been petty, and she didn't even altogether know why. Michael was the baby's father, and his intention today presumably had been to reassure her she wasn't to be left holding the bag.

Colleen looked down at her hands, which all on their own had taken to lining up and squaring the objects beside the cash register: a pincushion, a book with the enrollments for quilting classes, some notes to herself and receipts on a spindle. There was undoubtedly something Freudian about this sudden need for tidiness, for order.

She looked up to see that Michael, too, was watching her hands in their obsessive task. With difficulty Colleen said, "I'm sorry. I...I'm not usually so combative. This has been a difficult few weeks."

"Granted."

Either she hadn't looked hard enough or he had just let his veneer crack, because she saw suddenly that his eyes were bloodshot, the lines carving his cheeks and between his brows so deep, he was no longer handsome. The hands he took out of his pockets had a tremor that explained why he had hidden them.

His chest rose and fell with a long breath. "I suppose I'm handling this badly," he said stiffly. "Somehow we never got to know each other very well. Considering the circumstances, I regret that. My intention today wasn't to upset you. I just thought we should...discuss it."

There he went again, being so reasonable that in comparison she felt even pettier. Worse yet, she knew herself for a coward.

"I'm sorry," Colleen said again, knowing he deserved at least that much. "You're right of course."

"I didn't intend—" Michael broke off. After an instant he grimaced. "Hell. We could apologize forever. Let me just say it again—as the bills come in, save them for me. You are seeing the doctor, aren't you?"

"Yes, of course." It was her turn to sound stiff. "But I think for the moment that I'd prefer to take care of the bills myself. I haven't said anything to my insurance company, and they do cover pregnancy..."

"We've talked about that. They shouldn't have to." He was frowning again. "This pregnancy is on my behalf..."

"It was for Sheila," she whispered, then more loudly, "I did it for Sheila!"

A spasm of pain twisted his face, and his voice was hoarse. "Do you think I don't know that?"

"I'm sorry." She whispered the words again, uselessly, but he didn't even acknowledge her regret.

"You're not thinking you'll keep the baby?"

"I'm not...thinking at all."

"Good." His words were clipped. "Don't."

The bell tinkled and the door swung open to let in two women who were laughing, but it was a moment before Colleen could wrench her gaze from the anger and pain riveting her. When she did at last, he left without another word, pulling the door shut behind him so hard the glass shivered.

She was shaking as she stared after him. In her heart Colleen knew she had behaved irrationally, but what had he expected? The baby was his only by the accident of fate that had made him Sheila's husband. It wasn't fair that he was here to claim it when she wasn't! *Sheila* was the one who had wanted and needed this child, who would have given anything for it. *Sheila,* not him!

You're not thinking you'll keep the baby?

Seeming not to notice Michael's abrupt departure, the two women had latched avidly onto a class list and were twittering as they pointed to one offering or another. They wavered in front of Colleen's eyes, not quite coming clear. They could have been new customers or her oldest. She wished they would go away.

But she smiled, anyway, and said in a voice that sounded only a little odd to her ears, "May I help you?"

MICHAEL HAD DRIVEN half a mile before he realized that he was heading home, instead of back to work. Home, he thought grimly. What a joke. It was an emotional mine field, that place, every room, every piece of furniture, every small collectible, holding memories. And every damn one of them was painful right now.

Some nights he was tempted to move out, just check into a hotel. Maybe six months from now he could go home again, if such a thing was ever possible, decide what he wanted to keep, what he had to get rid of to get on with his life.

But something drew him back day after day, made him wander through the house, running a hand along the cool surface of the tile countertop in the kitchen, fingering the rough-soft texture of the quilt that had been Colleen's wedding gift to her sister, picking up one by one the tiny thimbles Sheila had collected, God knew why. At last he would pull out photograph albums and thumb through them until his eyes blurred and he couldn't see the pictures anymore.

The something that drew him was guilt. He was here and Sheila wasn't.

And six months from now, he would be doing a hell of a lot more than stumbling through the front door of a house that had been packed in mothballs to preserve it until he was ready. He would be a father, bringing home his newborn baby. A baby who would need to understand someday why he had a mother, but didn't really.

The wave of pain was expected, even obligatory, giving Michael time to pull off State Avenue onto a tree-lined residential street. He steered the car to the curb, set the hand brake and leaned his forehead against the steering wheel.

He couldn't afford to cry, had to go back to work, and he looked bad enough already, gaunt, hollow-eyed, shambling. He didn't want to subject the people he knew to any more of his grief. It was his, not theirs. He didn't like talking about any emotion that ran deep, had always been private.

Right now he was taking in air with great gasps, sweating as though he'd run three miles. Deliberately he wrenched his thoughts from the empty house to his wife's sister.

In pictures she looked so much like Sheila he'd been uncomfortable with the very idea that there existed such an almost perfect copy of his wife-to-be. Auburn hair, pale creamy skin, eyes a green-brown that made him think of forest pools and moss growing on tree trunks. Both women were medium height and slender.

But that first time he hadn't recognized Colleen across the crowded room, despite the uncanny resemblance. In life it didn't exist, or it was only the trappings, not the substance. Sheila was like a butterfly: beautiful, dainty, quick-moving, somehow elusive. He'd always felt the need to touch her to be sure she was there.

But Colleen Deering was nothing like Sheila. She moved gracefully, but without the fluttering effect his wife had given. Her eyes were more direct, and yet she was grave, even reserved. She was the steady one, the patient one, the one you knew just knew would never lie or evade. Colleen wouldn't necessarily turn men's heads the way Sheila had, and yet she had some indefinable quality that would reward the looking, a stillness, a serenity, which he thought would be more peaceful than Sheila's restless fluttering.

Those early years of his marriage, he had been halfway jealous of Colleen, because she and Sheila were so close. The phone calls, the letters, never fully shared with him, the joy in their brief visits, the sadness in their partings, had made him conscious of his own fumbling attempts at intimacy, his silence when Sheila needed words, his dry eyes when she wanted tears. He could not be what her sister was to her, and he eventually gave up trying. Nor did he have that kind of closeness with his own parents or much older brother.

Yet the jealousy had died, envy become resignation and finally indifference. Much between him and Sheila had been killed by their failure to have children, the one thing she wanted most from him. How ironic that in the end it was her sister who gave her what he could not. His own role seemed minor, a mere bit part; he'd given seed for the sowing, but even the sowing was taken from him.

And yet he *knew*, on some visceral level, that this baby was his. He'd agreed to do this for Sheila, but from the moment Colleen had announced her pregnancy, his feelings for the baby had never had anything to do with Sheila. He was a man who had made a woman pregnant. The knowledge was uncomfortably sexual. He hadn't been able to look at his wife's sister, the mother of his baby, the same way again.

He'd been glad that she stayed away, so that he could pretend it wasn't so. She was a caretaker, a means to an end, a foster mother, a surrogate for his wife. The act of procreation that had taken place between him and her meant nothing, was a feat of modern medicine. The sperm could have come from any man; the womb belonged to any woman.

But it didn't. The seed was his. The body that cradled his unborn baby was hers. And the knowledge tormented him.

CHAPTER THREE

IT WAS FOR SHEILA. I did it for Sheila! Colleen's voice was raw, her eyes blazed accusation, even hatred.

With a ragged cry, Michael lurched to a sitting position, fighting the covers tangled around him. "The baby's mine, damn you, mine!" he shouted.

When he looked around and saw only darkness and patterns of moonlight, Michael buried his face in his hands.

Sleep had become a time of nightmares.

Sometimes it was Sheila's death he saw. He was sitting in the passenger seat of her sports car, telling her to slow down, his foot convulsively pressing the floor where he wanted the brake to be. But she didn't seem to see him, didn't hear him; he was invisible to her. The tires skidded in a turn, but Sheila accelerated out of it. She had the radio on and was singing along. She was so happy she was snapping her fingers and bebopping to the music, only a minimal amount of her attention on the road.

Michael knew the curve where she would die, saw it coming. She quit singing when she had to slam on the brakes, when the long skid began. In his nightmare, it wasn't the telephone pole he saw, but her face; it wasn't the crash he heard, but the music, which the police had told him was still playing when the next motorist came upon the scene.

Other times he dreamed that Sheila was still with him and that she was pregnant. He kept asking where Colleen was, but Sheila never answered. She would look at him in puzzlement, as though she didn't know who he was talking about. And then he would wonder if this wasn't really Colleen, not Sheila at all. Of course she would be perplexed by his asking where she was. And so he would look closely, but he couldn't tell which sister he was with. He always woke up before he knew, and sometimes he would lie awake and strain to remember the woman in his dream so that he could decide once and for all. But in the frustrating way dreams had, the clear images would slip away.

And now he had a new nightmare designed to make the dark hours hell. Michael groaned and kicked off the covers, swinging his legs off the bed. This dream wasn't slipping away as conveniently, perhaps because he had been reliving something that had really happened. His mind had warped it, of course; he didn't think Colleen had looked at him with hatred. What he remembered seeing on her face was pain, but would she have said what she had unless she wanted to hurt him? Did she blame him somehow? Resent him because he was alive and Sheila wasn't? Or had Colleen always disliked him, and hidden it for her sister's sake? If so, how must she feel to be pregnant by him?

He swore under his breath and headed to the bathroom for a shower. The blast of hot water washed away the last ghostly images of his nightmare, but left his thoughts grim.

Colleen Deering wasn't just grieving; she sounded like a woman who was getting cold feet. If she hadn't yet considered changing her mind about their arrangement, he greatly feared she was working her way around to it.

He and Sheila and Colleen had sat down together and tried to think of every consequence, every misstep that could be taken on this unusual road to parenthood, but one possibility they hadn't anticipated: that Sheila would die before the baby had been handed over. Because the sisters

were so close, because this pregnancy was a gift of love
and not a cold-blooded contract, nothing had been put in
writing. Colleen was pregnant with his baby, and he had
no way of proving she had promised to hand the child over.

He didn't think she was a liar, but how well did he really
know her?

Michael was thinking coldly now as he toweled himself
dry. If she would let him pay even one of her bills for a
prenatal visit to the doctor, that would be evidence an
agreement existed. And she *had* agreed that he should pay
them. So now was the time to continue some gentle pressure before her intentions solidified—if they were going to.
God only knew she couldn't *want* to be pregnant on her
own.

In the meantime he would continue to behave as though
nothing had changed—even though his world had become
an unfamiliar place.

"MO-OM!" DREW BELLOWED from the front room. "Uncle
Michael's here!"

Colleen groaned and closed her eyes momentarily, leaning her forehead against the refrigerator. Just what she
needed. It was five-thirty, she had just walked in the door,
exhausted and starved, to discover she had forgotten to defrost the chicken she'd planned for dinner. And now Michael, apparently not satisfied with their talk, had to drop
in unannounced. Wonderful.

But she straightened, blew her bangs off her forehead
and headed for the front door. Before she got there, she
pinned a pleasant smile in place, as much for Drew's sake
as for her brother-in-law's.

"Michael. What a surprise."

Damn. Those blue eyes did it every time, leaving her
feeling she'd been stripped—though not in a sexual sense.

Instead, she was pretty sure he saw every ache, every moment of discouragement she'd suffered today, every bout of nausea or tears.

In the past his face would have given away nothing comparable, but that was no longer true. The lines were even deeper today, the skin stretched more tightly across cheekbones that were almost gaunt. He couldn't be sleeping any better than she was.

Colleen felt a pang of guilt. Maybe Michael wasn't trying to put pressure on her. Maybe he was looking for some comfort himself, from the one person he knew shared his grief.

"I'm sorry," he said with restraint, his gaze still on her face. "Is this a bad time?"

Why was it so hard for her to be casually friendly to him? "No, it's fine," she said, trying to convince herself, as well. "Really. Today was just one of those days. Come on in."

He didn't move over the threshold. "Actually, I stopped by to see if I could take you all out for a pizza. I didn't want to go home—" He stopped abruptly and hunched his shoulders in what she now recognized as a symptom of discomfiture. "It was just an impulse. If you already have dinner on..."

Colleen made a decision without conscious thought. "No, that sounds wonderful," she admitted. "I was just staring hopelessly into the cupboards. I think the can of chili was beating out the box of macaroni and cheese."

"Gross," Drew exclaimed.

"So my son, at least, will be eternally grateful." Colleen smiled at Michael. "Why don't you come on in while I try to round up Kim."

Which wasn't hard, since Colleen knew exactly where her daughter was. Kim was sulking out on the back-porch swing because some girl at school, who had been casually friendly, mentioned that she took horseback riding lessons at a stable outside town. Kim had immediately decided that if she had something in common with the other girl—namely, riding lessons—they would become bosom buddies. Coldhearted Mom hadn't even called the stable for prices before informing her daughter there was no way the budget would stretch that far.

What Kim didn't realize was how much it hurt Colleen to have to say no. For the hundredth time she wondered if she was being selfish in sinking everything they had into a business designed to give *her* satisfaction.

At least the prospect of going out for pizza cheered Kim up slightly, since right now Colleen couldn't afford even that very often. Better yet, at the pizza parlor Michael produced several dollars' worth of quarters so that Kim and Drew could play video games. For once the best of friends, they took off for the game room, leaving a peaceful oasis behind.

"Thank you," Colleen said quietly.

"They are my niece and nephew."

"True. It's just that I don't think of you…" Colleen stumbled to a halt, flushing. Oh, Lord. She must be tired to let something like that slip.

A glint of humor in his eyes, Michael lifted a dark brow. "What is it you don't think of me as?"

Resigned, Colleen admitted, "An uncle. A brother-in-law." She let out a breath. Would it help to put into words her unease with him, or would it add to the unspoken tension between them? "I'm not sure why, but I've just never felt like I knew you very well. Relatives are supposed to be…comfortable. Familiar."

The smile faded from his eyes, leaving something nameless in its wake. "Yeah, I know. It's been mutual."

So she hadn't imagined his stiffness toward her.

He was still talking. "Strange, too, when you look so much like—" he paused, the muscles along his jaw clenching "—her."

Colleen ignored the burning feeling in her nose that usually presaged tears. "Do you know, Sheila always said how much we looked alike, but I never thought we did. Even clothes didn't look the same on us." Colleen had a flash of remembrance, in which her fifteen-year-old sister paraded in front of the mirror in Colleen's sweater with a panache she herself would never have. The image faded just as the first tear fell. Starkly Colleen said, "Sheila sparkled."

Michael handed her a napkin. After Colleen had blown her nose he said abruptly, "Yes, she did. You know how I used to think of her? A stream running over rocks. The way sunlight glints off it, and the little trills it makes..." He swallowed and bowed his head. His eyes had a damp sheen when he lifted them to Colleen, and there was something almost angry in his voice. "When you were together, you and Sheila, I thought about that stream. She was the rapids and you were the deep pool below."

Colleen stared at him. Idiotically she said, "You mean, the one with the trout?"

His gaze was locked on her face. Only after a long, taut moment did he blink and give his head a small shake. "Yeah," he said, sounding oddly far-off. "The one with the trout and all the shades of green. Cold and clear, but somehow shadowy, too."

What an extraordinary conversation, Colleen thought. She couldn't quite decide whether she ought to feel flattered or insulted. What was most astonishing was how apt the analogy was, considering he didn't know her well.

From the time Sheila was born, she'd been in motion,

chattering, dancing, at the playground swinging higher than everyone else, at parties the center of an admiring crowd. People had always been drawn to her glittering orbit, as though life could be lived more intensely in her presence.

Colleen had often been grateful she was the older of the two, because if their birth order had been reversed, she would have been fated to live in her sister's shadow. As it was, teachers and swim instructors and even her mother's friends had known her first, so there was no disappointment.

Colleen was well aware that she was different: quieter, slower to commit herself, more thoughtful. She had never laughed as easily, never effortlessly charmed anyone, didn't *feel* as passionately. Yet she was content enough with who she was, had her own strengths. Sheila might have chosen vivid, memorable colors and fabrics had she been making a quilt, but she lacked the patience to set the thousands of tiny stitches to create a masterpiece. As sisters and friends, they had balanced each other well. Perhaps that was why Colleen felt now as if Sheila had leapt off the other end of a seesaw, dropping her with a painful thud to the ground.

"I miss her," Colleen said, and balled the napkin in one hand.

Michael's mouth twisted. "She always drove too fast." A mere observation, it was also an epitaph, symbolic of her entire life—and of its end.

They might have been in a bubble, she and Michael, separated from the noisy families and teenagers by its fragile, transparent walls. Colleen had never felt closer to him than she did now. Perhaps that was why she blurted out her single greatest regret. "Why couldn't Sheila have lived long enough to hold the baby?"

Michael sucked in a breath as though she had struck him, or perhaps she had only surprised him. He opened his mouth as though to say something, swallowed and managed to say huskily, "At least she knew you were pregnant."

Colleen had to blow her nose again. "I'm sorry. I'm not helping matters, am I?"

He seemed not to hear her. He was staring down into his mug of beer. "She's not the only one who wanted a child, you know."

Startled, Colleen met his gaze when he lifted it to look almost fiercely at her. Slowly she said, "I wondered sometimes."

"I always wanted one, even though I learned to accept that children wouldn't be part of our lives. Sheila couldn't. It was an obsession with her. Sometimes I thought... Oh, hell." His voice had thickened and he closed his eyes for a moment to regain control. "I thought she was so full of life herself it was an especially cruel irony that her body wouldn't let her create life."

Before Colleen could answer, she saw her kids wending their way through the tables toward her. Michael must have seen them, too, because he handed her another napkin.

She quickly swiped at her wet cheeks. "Oh, Lord, all I do is cry these days."

Michael shoved back the bench and stood. "That's our number being called." He set a course to intercept Drew and Kim, and when he spoke briefly to them, they turned to follow him.

Colleen was grateful for the couple of minutes he'd given her to compose herself. She hated to cry so much in front of her children. As many changes and upsets as they'd had in their lives the past few years, it was important that they had at least one parent who gave them a sense of safety, of certainty. She had to mourn, of course, but she knew they'd be frightened if they had any idea how scared and alone she really felt.

Her eyes were probably still red, but she hoped the dimness of the pizza parlor disguised that when she smiled at her daughter, who arrived with a tray of drinks. "So, did you set any new records on the video games?"

Kim gave her a searching look, but only shrugged. "I'm not very good."

"There are more important things in life to be good at."

The eleven-year-old rolled her eyes. "You don't have to tell me again. I know, I know. School's more important."

"It's boring," Drew said, handing out the plates.

Michael's gaze met Colleen's over her son's head. His mouth twitched. "School gets better as you go along. You can't say that about many things."

Kim's lip curled just enough to express her opinion. "I'm in fifth grade, and it hasn't gotten any better."

"Well, now, that's not quite true," Colleen reminded her. She reached out to break the string of cheese that stretched from her plate to the pizza. "Think back to Miss Fisher in kindergarten."

"I remember her yelling all the time."

"Do you also remember how you pretended you were sick so you could stay home?"

"Not really, but…"

"First grade was no picnic, either. You cried every Monday morning."

"Well, yeah, but…"

"Come on, be honest." Colleen raised her eyebrows. "Fifth grade's not really so bad, is it?"

Kim wrinkled her nose in an expression that made her look unsettlingly like Sheila at that age. "Okay," Kim conceded. "I guess it's getting better."

"It can't get any worse," Drew muttered, shoving the last bite of his pizza in his mouth. "Can I have some more?"

Michael gave him another piece. "Come on," he said, "you must like some subject."

"Well..." Drew screwed his face up as if the question required painful thought. "Science is cool," he finally said. "Miss Cole has a black widow spider in an aquarium. She's gonna have babies."

"Miss Cole?" Michael asked with a straight face.

"No! The spider. Thousands and thousands of them."

Colleen set down her pizza. "Dare I ask what Miss Cole is going to do with them?"

Her son shrugged. "I don't know. Some of the kids are scared to sit on that side of the room, but I don't mind. Friday I pretended I was going to knock over the aquarium. Nicole screamed."

"Gee, I wonder why," Colleen murmured.

Surprisingly Michael grinned. "You know what I did when I was your age? Caught a rattlesnake in the apple orchard by the school and chased girls with it."

"Cool," Drew breathed. "You didn't get bit?"

Kim was gazing, horror-struck, at her uncle. Colleen shook her head. "Give him ideas, why don't you?"

"Actually, it was dumb as hell," Michael admitted. "I wore leather gloves, but I could easily have gotten bitten on my arms. I knew better, but I seem to recall that Timothy Chandler had called me yellow-bellied."

"How come?" Drew asked.

"Don't remember that part." Michael shook his head. "All I do remember is spending the rest of the school year on detention. Not to mention being grounded at home."

"Wow." Drew chewed in silence for a minute, an unnervingly thoughtful expression on his face. At last he asked, "Did you go to my school?"

"Uh-huh. Doubt if you'd still find a rattlesnake in town

anymore, though. It's a wonder the orchard is still there. School was on the outskirts in my day.''

"You've lived here your whole life?" Kim asked.

"Not quite. I went away to college and worked in a bank in Seattle for a few years. That's when I met your aunt Sheila. After we married I decided to take a job here in Clayton.''

"How come we haven't met your parents, then?" Drew demanded.

He smiled easily at the boy. "Because they've retired to Florida. They got tired of our winters, I guess. My brother took over the wheat farm. You've met him, I think.''

"Is he our cousin or something?"

Colleen forgot to eat as she listened to Michael explaining that technically his brother wasn't related to Drew or Kim at all. The conversation progressed to first cousins and second cousins once removed, Michael quizzing them until Kim giggled. Nobody seemed to notice Colleen's silence; Michael continued to banter with the kids, and both of them, Drew especially, responded in a way that made her wonder whether they didn't miss their father more than she had guessed.

If she was suspicious, she'd think that Michael was making a special effort with her children in an attempt to demonstrate to her that he really was cut out to be a father. She certainly didn't recall him ever doing more than nodding hello or goodbye before.

And yet he related to them so easily. Didn't his brother have two girls? But Colleen didn't remember Sheila mentioning the nieces often, which surely she would have if she and Michael were a big part of their lives.

Colleen wished she knew what Michael was thinking. Under other circumstances it wouldn't have mattered why he was teasing Kim or listening to Drew's account of his escapades. But as things stood, it did. It mattered so much she couldn't trust her instincts. If she was to give up the baby, she had to be very sure that Michael would love him or her as much as Sheila would have. As much as she herself would.

Under the table, Colleen touched her stomach in an absurd need for reassurance that the gentle swell was still there, that she really was pregnant, that the baby was safe.

She had five and a half months to decide, she reminded herself; until then, nobody could make her give up her child.

Her doubts hadn't been erased by the time Michael dropped the kids and her off, but her general feelings toward him were positive.

Even so, she didn't leave an opening for him to insinuate himself into her home. When he reached for his door handle, she said quickly, "I'd better say good-night now. The kids have homework, and I usually try to put in an hour or two of quilting."

"Mom," Drew whined. "I don't have that much to do…"

Colleen silenced him a look. "Did you thank Uncle Michael for the pizza and all those quarters?"

Both children did so, then raced each other for the front door. Colleen was instantly aware of Michael in a way she hadn't been when Drew and Kim were bickering in the back seat. Her days were spent with women in the feminine world of her quilt shop. Since her divorce, she had become unused to men. In the close confines of the car, Michael seemed very large, his gaze disturbingly perceptive if guarded.

"Do you make quilts for sale?"

"On occasion." Colleen hoped he couldn't see through her outward composure. "In this case, a woman came to me with a quilt top that was a family heirloom, but it had never been quilted. It's very old and lovely, and I'm excited to have a chance to finish such beautiful work.''

''I'll bet you're not charging enough.''

In surprise Colleen asked, ''What makes you think that?''

His smile was a little wry. ''Sheila talked about your generous impulses. Was this one of them?''

Flustered, Colleen said, ''I figured a job like this was good advertising. Mrs. Neely—do you know the family?—seems to be involved in everything going on in the community. If she's pleased and shows the quilt off...''

''Everyone else will figure they can take advantage of you, too.''

''What a pessimistic outlook!''

''An occupational hazard.'' Michael nodded at her stomach. ''How are you feeling?''

''Just fine,'' she said. ''Michael, thanks for dinner. You were a lifesaver tonight.''

Her evasion didn't work.

''Are you seeing the doctor regularly?''

''You asked me that already,'' Colleen said a little tartly. ''I've done this before, you know.''

''What does he say?''

''*She* tells me that everything is going exactly as it should be. There's not a whole lot a doctor can offer at this point. I'm not old enough to need amniocentesis, and my doctor doesn't believe in ultrasounds unless there's reason for concern.''

''Then what does she do?''

''Are you afraid I'm not getting my money's worth?''

He chose that moment to turn his head away and gaze out the windshield. ''It ought to be *my* money's worth, but let's not make that the issue.''

"Then what is?" she snapped.

He didn't answer immediately. When he did Michael still wasn't looking at her. "I'm...curious," he said, his tone stiff. "Unlike you, I haven't done this before. If Sheila and I'd had a baby in the usual way, I might have been going with her to appointments."

Shame washed over Colleen. Why was she so determined to think the worst of him? Of course he was interested; the baby was his, too. She kept forgetting that. This wasn't—yet—a competition between them.

"I'm sorry," she said past the lump in her throat. "I wasn't thinking. I take for granted stuff that seemed pretty amazing the first time around. Like the fact that the doctor will probably be listening to the baby's heartbeat by the next visit."

His eyes, so very blue, swung back to her and held her pinned. "She can hear the heartbeat? So soon?"

Colleen nodded. "Somehow that makes it seem real, doesn't it? To think that there's already another heart beating inside of me..." Just saying it brought back the awe she felt at the wondrous, mysterious business of creating life. There were no words powerful enough to describe it. "Well," she finally said, and cleared her throat. "If you wanted to come sometime... I'm sure you could listen."

He looked at her for a long moment. "You'd let me do that?"

Colleen floundered, "I...if you wouldn't feel embarrassed..."

"Does this doctor know why you're having the baby?"

Colleen bowed her head, staring down at her fingers, which twined nervously together. "There hasn't been any reason to tell her."

Michael's voice was hard now. "The plan was that you'd hand the baby over to us immediately in the hospital. I think it's fair to expect that the nurses and the doctor should know that ahead of time.''

Anger flared. "I've only been to see the doctor once since the initial appointment. My sister had died the week before. The *plan* was the last thing on my mind.''

Answering anger flickered in his eyes, then died. He turned again to stare ahead through the windshield, his hands wrapped so tightly around the steering wheel his knuckles were white. "You're right. It's my turn to apologize.''

"Accepted," Colleen said very crisply. Opening her car door, she added, "Now, if you don't mind, I'll say goodnight.''

She slammed the door without allowing him a chance to respond. Hurrying up the walk, Colleen began to feel a little guilty for not thanking him again for dinner. On the other hand, he'd given her even more reason to suspect that this evening had been an investment on his part. He was obviously afraid she had changed her mind about giving the baby to him and figured he should remind her of his rights.

Was that so bad? Colleen wondered. Why didn't she just reassure him? A single parent already struggling financially, she wasn't really thinking she would keep this baby and raise it alone.

Was she?

YES, BUT HE DID HAVE rights, Colleen reminded herself, taking one side of the dialogue—or was it an argument?—she'd been silently conducting for the past week. She had implied—okay, *said*—that he would be welcome to come to her next appointment.

She remembered again the leap of interest, hope, in his eyes. This baby was his; he would be the one to carry the swaddled bundle out of the hospital, to buckle it gently into a car seat. The one to stumble out of bed in the dark hours, to sleepily stand by the microwave waiting for the formula to heat, the one to kiss the soft, fuzzy top of her child's head, breathing in the scent of baby and knowing the joy of cradling this tiny person.

She should have felt better because she could so easily picture him doing all that. Instead, her heart was squeezed in the grip of a sense of loss so profound she couldn't face it. Her mind yanked a curtain in front of the hurtful images, letting her deal rationally with the irrational.

His baby, she reminded herself. Never hers. He had a right to be part of the excitement and the choices made while the infant was still part of her.

Her hand reached for the telephone, hesitating yet again before lifting the receiver.

Maybe he was the father, but he wasn't in a relationship with her. She didn't *want* him there when the doctor lifted her shirt and gently palpated her abdomen. She didn't want Michael bending down with a stethoscope to hear the tiny thud, thud, of the baby's heartbeat.

But she had promised. *His baby,* that internal voice whispered.

On a long sigh, Colleen picked up the phone and dialed. Once she had identified herself, his secretary assured her that Mr. Delaney was in. A few clicks later, Michael said, "Hello, Colleen."

"Hello. I, um, called to let you know that my next doctor appointment is tomorrow. If you're really interested in coming—"

"What time?"

"Two o'clock. At the women's clinic on Second."

"I'll look forward to it."

Colleen hung up and took a deep breath. Her heart was racing as hard as if she had just committed herself to going up in the next space shuttle. Really, this was no big deal. If she'd still been alive, Sheila would have been going with her. Colleen ignored the sudden knot of pain and told herself she would think of Michael as a stand-in.

That was harder to do when the time actually came. Michael was already there when she arrived five minutes early at the clinic. She had the same sense of unreality she always did when she first saw him. In a dark, well-cut suit, he was formidably handsome, so effortlessly magnetic she felt both drawn and repelled. He was not the kind of man she'd been used to.

Her hesitation was brief. Feeling his eyes on her, she checked in at the front desk. When she went over to Michael, he set down the *Time* magazine he'd been thumbing through.

"You're here," she said. Brilliant. She could almost hear her son's favorite response. *Duh.*

She half expected some slightly more sophisticated sarcasm from Michael, but he only inclined his head. Before Colleen could take a seat or make some other intelligent remark, the nurse called her name.

Colleen felt unusually self-conscious during the familiar ritual, especially the weighing-in. She couldn't see Michael behind her, and she could only hope he had the good manners not to watch. Fortunately she hadn't gained an excessive amount. All she needed was to be chided in front of him.

In the examining room the nurse checked her blood pressure and pulse, then said cheerily, "The doctor will be with you shortly," and exited, closing the door behind her.

Colleen hadn't realized until now how tiny the examining room was. In trying to think of something to say, she became very conscious of her social inadequacies. They were made worse by the fact that Michael clearly wasn't in a chatty mood. He answered her feeble conversational forays with monosyllables. The wait seemed interminable, although it couldn't have been more than five minutes.

Just as the silence was becoming unendurable—and as Colleen was wondering whether Michael might actually be nervous—the doctor breezed in. A no-nonsense, middle-aged woman with a faint Scandinavian accent, she didn't look surprised to see Michael. "Ah, the father."

Colleen hadn't figured out what she would do if the doctor had said, "Ah, your husband." Fortunately she was saved. Of course maybe Michael would feel compelled to explain the situation. But their eyes met, very briefly, and then he stood and held out his hand. "Michael Delaney."

Dr. Kjorsvik shook it, then turned to Colleen. "How are you feeling?"

"Just fine." Not for anything would she have admitted it if she *wasn't* fine, not in front of him.

"Well, let's take a look." Colleen lay back when she was told to. Dr. Kjorsvik's deft fingers lifted her blouse, exposing the pale swell of stomach. She felt her way around for a moment, her gaze unfocused. Then she lifted the stethoscope to her ears and bent forward, pressing the cold diaphragm to Colleen's abdomen. "Hm," she murmured, and moved it. "Um-hm…ah." She lifted her head to smile at Colleen. "Clear as a bell."

No matter that she had been through this twice before, Colleen still felt the thrill. "Really?"

"You sound surprised," Dr. Kjorsvik said indulgently, then turned to Michael. "Would Dad care to listen?"

It should have been hugely embarrassing, but somehow wasn't. The wonder in his eyes erased any awkwardness. For nearly the first time, Colleen felt a connection between them, stripped to its essentials. He stayed very still and listened for the longest time. "Amazing," he murmured,

and his reluctance was obvious when he gave the stethoscope back to the doctor.

She stuffed it in the pocket of her white coat. "Indeed
it is. Tiny as the fetus is right now, he or she is already
growing hair, even eyelashes. And fingernails and toenails.
We're getting somewhere.''

And then she breezed out, tossing over her shoulder a
few instructions for Colleen.

Colleen didn't hear them. She had just discovered that
her cheeks were wet with tears. Hurriedly she pulled her
blouse down and rolled to one side to sit up, an operation
she wouldn't be able to accomplish with much dignity in
just a few more months. Her back to Michael, she surreptitiously wiped her cheeks.

The weird thing was that she had no idea why she was
crying. Something had happened just now, deep inside her,
as disorienting as the shifting of a fault in the earth's crust,
but she couldn't yet describe the movement, even to herself.
All she knew was that it had to do with this baby, this tiny
being who would be laid in her arms, who would be born
knowing how to root for her breast, who would recognize
her voice and turn instinctively to her, the mother. It had
to do with Michael, who had let her see how badly he
wanted this baby and how much it would hurt him never
to hold it. But there was more; there was her own father,
whom she'd barely known, the husband who had walked
out. There was the close circle of her mother and sister and
her, and the aching loneliness she felt now without its warm
embrace. Like a jigsaw puzzle, all the pieces had been jum-
bled, but not yet fitted together into a whole.

She breathed in slowly, deeply, and decided she wouldn't
think about it right now. Later, she promised herself.

Cheeks dry, a lump in her throat, Colleen slid off the
examining table. It took courage to face Michael and to

accept her purse from him. Even her voice sounded odd to her. "Ready?"

He opened the door, but still blocked it. "Are you taking the vitamins she recommended?"

The question was so mundane, so far from her disorganized thoughts, she stared at him blankly before she took it in. Then she said, "Yes, of course."

"You're not worrying about your weight too much, are you? I read somewhere that the baby's birth weight is higher if the mother gains at least twenty-five pounds."

"I'm well on my way," Colleen admitted, her cheeks warming.

"Good." He hesitated, then stepped aside.

She hurried past, holding herself stiffly to avoid brushing against him. In the waiting room, the receptionist looked up and smiled. "Would you like to make your next appointment?"

"Yes, thank you." To Michael, who had paused, too, Colleen said, "You go ahead. There's no reason for you to wait."

"All right." Those blue eyes met hers squarely. "Thank you," he said in a low voice.

Colleen gave a jerky nod and turned away, although she was preternaturally conscious of the door opening and closing behind him. It took only a minute to make the appointment for the following month.

Colleen was closing her purse when she remembered something. "Oh, shoot, I meant to bring you a claims form. Can I stick it in the mail?"

The receptionist waved an elegantly manicured hand. "Oh, we don't need it. Your husband already took care of the bill."

For a shocked instant, Colleen stared at the young

woman. No wonder Michael had gotten here early. And left so willingly.

She managed to nod. "Thank you."

His BMW was easy to spot. He was just backing out. Colleen cut across the parking lot, telling herself she had a right to be angry. It felt good, healthy. In some part of her mind, she knew she *wanted* to dislike him. Had wanted to all along.

He saw her coming in the rearview mirror and braked. Just as she reached the car, his window glided down. "Is something wrong?" he asked.

"How dare you?" she said in a voice that shook.

His dark brows drew together. "What the hell...?"

"You knew perfectly well I'd resent your going behind my back to pay the doctor."

Michael's mouth thinned. "We have an agreement."

She was almost blind with her anger and her need to lash out at him. Very distinctly Colleen said, "You mean, my sister and I had an agreement. You and I never did."

CHAPTER FOUR

EVEN THROUGH HER HAZE of anger, Colleen was chilled by the icy set of Michael's expression. But she was driven by a force too powerful, too instinctive, to allow reason to govern her behavior. She was a mother protecting her young, unable to convince herself this man was not the enemy.

His voice was dangerously soft. "Are you trying to tell me something?"

"You're darn right I am. Quit pressuring me!"

Pure rage flickered in his eyes. "I'll quit pressuring you the day you sign a contract confirming *our* verbal agreement. I know you were doing this for Sheila and not me. But she's gone, and I'm still here. And this baby is as much—no, damn it!—*more* mine than hers. By God, you're not stealing it from me."

His window glided up with the force of a door slamming, and the BMW shot away, tires squealing. Colleen jumped back. She was left standing in the parking lot, shaking, nauseated, angry.

And scared. Had she really threatened to keep the baby?

"Oh, Lord," she whispered. Startled by the honk of a horn, she collected herself enough to get out of the way of an oncoming minivan and go to her own car. She waited there until her hands quit shaking before she even attempted to start the engine.

Colleen managed—almost—to block the ugly scene from

her mind. How else could she get through the day? In between waiting on customers, she spent the afternoon hanging a display of 1920s- and 1930s-era quilts borrowed from the local historical society, which didn't have the space to show them all.

Handling them would have been undiluted pleasure had her emotions not been in such turmoil. Most of these quilts had been treasured, probably seldom used, and the colors were as fresh as the day they'd been stitched together. They were bright and cheerful, with the gaiety of a flower garden full of annuals. Here was none of the subtlety of contemporary quilts, or the faded tints of nineteenth-century fabrics. The patterns were traditional: two Wedding Ring quilts, a Log Cabin, a Fence Rail and a Grandmother's Flower Garden. The stitching was fine, reflecting a skill nearly forgotten until the revival of the past decade.

And the texture... She would have loved quilts even if she'd been blind, Colleen thought, savoring the close-quilted layers between her fingers. There was comfort in the feel of a quilt, somehow stiff and soft at the same time, warmth that embraced a baby even as it had the strength to endure the centuries.

It was time she began a quilt for the baby. *Her* baby. The doing would comfort her, and if she started soon, her labor of love might not be tainted by knowledge of the future. Right now, for this brief time, the baby was a possibility, not a reality. Boy or girl, redhead or brunette, blue-eyed or brown, this oddly conceived child could be anything. Although the ache of loss played in the back of her mind, Colleen didn't yet have to face handing over her baby to the near stranger who was the father. Whatever the future held, the quilt would be her gift of love.

She knew without second thoughts what pattern she would use. Carousel Horses, intricately pieced in jewel colors, would chase each other among the clouds, puffy and white and layered. No border, she thought, nothing to confine them.

In quiet moments before closing, Colleen chose several fabrics, including a cloud print in a bluish white, knowing even as she concentrated on the details that it was a form of self-protection. This process was natural for her, and as long as she immersed herself in it, she could pretend that this pregnancy was just like her others.

At home she cooked dinner, helped Kim with homework on fractions and did flash cards with Drew. After they were in bed, Colleen cleaned up the kitchen and worked on Mrs. Neely's quilt, stretched in her quilt frame. Keeping her hands busy, however mindless the task, prevented her from thinking. She was safe.

Until she showered and, while rubbing her hair dry, glanced up to see herself reflected in the long mirror on the door. The sight was familiar and yet not; her skin was pale and she was still slender, but there were changes, subtle but unmistakable. Her breasts were fuller and her belly gently swelling. With the symmetrical oval of her face, she might have been a Renaissance madonna, the embodiment of the mysteries of womanhood.

Colleen gave her head a firm shake and looked again, more realistically. Botticelli wouldn't have liked the tiny lines traced beside her eyes, the freckles sprinkled on her nose, the sags here and there. His madonna was young and innocent, not the mother of an almost teenager.

"I must have been crazy," Colleen said aloud. But in her heart she knew she would do it all over again. For Sheila.

Curled in bed, staring at the faint light coming in the window from streetlamps, Colleen relived the scene in the parking lot.

My sister and I had an agreement. You and I never did.
She was still a little shocked at her own defiance. She
was already the single mother of two children; she was
already cutting every corner that could be cut just to scrape
by financially from month to month. How could she add a
baby to her burdens? Never mind the fact that he or she
would be another mouth to feed, another child entitled to
swimming lessons and Little League and band, all of which
had to be paid for. No, it was the cost of day-care that
made the whole idea ludicrous, impossible.

Michael, a banker, could afford the best of everything
for this baby. He could hire a nanny, buy a piano and a
show horse and lessons to go with each, add a red Corvette
for his child's sixteenth birthday. He could pay for an expensive private college. All of which would have sounded
meaningless, except that she also knew he'd give something
more important yet—love. She had seen it on his face today
when he'd listened to those miraculous heartbeats, the beginning of his child's life.

And hadn't she promised her sister she would never,
even for a minute, think of this baby as hers? Hadn't she
said the baby is yours—and Michael's? How could she go
back on her word now?

Colleen knew what she was doing. With all the precision
of a quilt-maker, she was piecing a relentless, painful pattern excluding herself and her own hunger to hold this baby
and never let go. She was employing cold reason to dam
the flood of emotion.

Her bitter regret told her she'd succeeded, at least for
now.

MICHAEL WAS WRESTLING with the coffee machine when
Colleen called the next morning. He wasn't a gourmet-
coffee drinker; caffeine came more conveniently in a

spoonful of dark granules. But Sheila had to have this damned, elaborate, high-tech coffeemaker, so he'd bought it for her for Christmas. The Christmas barely past, the one full of shining promise, thanks to Colleen.

The stupid machine sat on the gleaming tile countertop, too big to shove into hiding, reproaching him day after day. Just a week before, cursing, he had finally used it. Now, frowning, he was stabbing buttons when the phone rang.

Absently he reached for the receiver and grunted, "Yeah?"

"Michael? This is Colleen."

He forgot the coffeemaker and braced his hands on the countertop, hunching one shoulder to hold the receiver to his ear. "Colleen," he said neutrally.

Her voice was constrained. "I, um, lost my temper yesterday. I want to apologize."

He waited, knowing he should say something about losing his own temper, too, maybe express regret for driving away as he had, but his vocal cords seemed paralyzed.

After a moment she went on, sounding still more repressed, even lifeless. "I want you to know I wasn't implying I intend to keep the baby. I just…resent being coerced. Maybe more than I should, because I understand your worries. But I'm a little…raw emotionally right now."

His voice came out hoarse. "I'm the one who should apologize. Sheila had complete faith in you. I guess I'm showing a character flaw by being a suspicious bastard."

There was a small silence. Then, "I haven't given you very many reasons to trust me."

"God!" he said explosively, squeezing his eyes shut. "Your pregnancy is a gift. A decent man wouldn't demand a receipt along with it."

"Is that what you want? A bill of sale?"

"Apparently," he admitted. "An occupational hazard."

Either that, or the insecurity of a man never very sure of his parents' love, or even his wife's.

"Well, I can't give you that, not yet." He thought he heard a sniff, and her next words were choked. "I won't promise, but I do know the baby is yours. I know you have...rights."

"I won't ask for anything else now," Michael said quickly. What she'd offered wasn't enough—he wanted promises signed in blood—but he recognized a concession when he heard it. Whatever else happened, Colleen was the mother of his baby, and he was increasingly certain she would continue to be. That he wouldn't be able to walk away, the sole possessor of his son or daughter. That he wouldn't be able to pretend the woman who had borne his child didn't exist.

He didn't even know if he wanted to.

"Well—" she definitely sniffled "—that's all I had to say. I'm sure I'll be talking to you."

"Colleen."

"Yes?" She sounded wary.

"Thank you."

She didn't ask what he was thanking her for, didn't say, "You're welcome." Instead, he heard the quiet click of the connection being cut.

It was a moment before he restored the receiver to its cradle, a moment during which he wondered where he now stood. Was he supposed to wait, doing nothing, while she made up her mind? Had Colleen meant only that she acknowledged his paternity, or that she knew she would have to hand over the baby? Would calls or visits be welcome or at least tolerated, or would both qualify as coercion?

Michael settled for a quick bowl of cereal and took his mug of strong, dark coffee with him in the car. It was getting harder, instead of easier, to live in that house, permeated with Sheila's personality. With more time and interest than he had, she'd chosen the furniture, papered the walls, curled her toes into the thick carpet. The colors were hers, the dishes, the brands he bought from habit at the grocery store.

He always had the feeling she'd walk back in any minute. No, not walk; she hardly ever moved so sedately. Danced, twirled, hurried. She'd been restless, tending to choose colors and furnishings that were stunning but unsettling, as though she hated being soothed.

Would the baby have changed her, brought her long-lasting contentment? She could be so fickle, her interests intense but short-lived. Even her friendships seemed transitory. Only her closeness to her sister and her desperate need for a baby had endured.

He recognized his thoughts for the criticism they were. They brought familiar, sharp-edged guilt that he didn't analyze. He was in no mood to contemplate his own lacks, which undoubtedly were responsible for the emptiness Sheila had sought so hungrily to fill.

He didn't know how good a mother she would have been; what counted now was how good a father he would be. Whether he liked it or not, he might well be in competition with Colleen, should their battle reach the courts.

MRS. NEELY RAN her fingers over the soft folds of the magnificent Basket of Tulips quilt. When she'd brought the top to the store, she'd told Colleen how it had been appliquéd by her grandmother, then folded away in a trunk and never layered and quilted. Colleen had finished quilting and binding it only yesterday; the moment she called, the woman had hurried over.

Mrs. Neely was blinking back tears when she lifted her head. She groped in her purse for a tissue. "Oh, dear. I'm being silly. It's just that I can't help thinking how happy my grandmother would be to know her quilt has been finished. And so beautifully.''

"Maybe she does know," Colleen suggested. From the beginning she felt an odd connection to the quilt's maker. She had never even seen a picture of her, yet she knew so much about her, this woman who had cut and appliquéd hundreds of tiny pieces with such care, and chosen colors so exuberant. Colleen had almost felt herself being watched as she worked, filling the background with a crosshatched design that gave the quilt texture and emphasized the beauty of the appliqué.

At her comment, Mrs. Neely had an arrested expression. "What a lovely thought. Do you know, I have the funniest feeling she does know. Oh, my dear, thank you so much. The money is totally inadequate—"

"Nonsense," Colleen interrupted with a smile. "The pay was not only generous, I'm grateful for the chance to finish such an exquisite quilt."

"Your own are just as beautiful," the older woman said. "Have you started a crib quilt yet?"

"A crib quilt?" Stupidly, she didn't understand.

"You are expecting, aren't you?"

Colleen felt the heat rush over her cheeks and the anguish tighten her throat. "I...yes, I..."

"Oh, dear. Was I prying?"

Somehow Colleen produced a smile of sorts. "No, no. I just didn't realize I showed yet. And...well, I'm planning a mini-show of crib quilts, and I thought for a second you were referring to it."

Even to herself, her explanation sounded weak. But Mrs. Neely was kind enough to say only, "When you reached up to the shelf for the quilt, I saw you in profile and felt sure you were pregnant." She smiled mischievously. "But I'll keep it quiet. Tell me, is your husband pleased?"

Like a projector clicking to the next picture, Colleen saw with her mind's eye Michael, bending over to listen to the baby's heartbeat, so close to her bare stomach she'd been able to feel the warmth of his breath. Colleen was disconcerted to have thought so automatically of him. Why hadn't the idea of a husband conjured up Ben?

She was flustered enough to blush again, but she returned some answer that wasn't quite a lie. Whatever it was satisfied Mrs. Neely, who caressed her quilt one more time before stuffing it back in the bag and taking her departure, leaving the much-needed check on the counter.

Alone for a precious few minutes, Colleen splashed cold water on her face in the tiny bathroom and gazed blankly at her image in the mirror. She should have anticipated this, planned what she would say. Of course people would start noticing soon! And while men in an office might not comment, her women customers surely would.

In the back of her mind, Colleen had intended to tell the truth. Sheila had popped into the shop often enough so that regular customers had met her. The community was so small, some had already known her.

But it was different now; everything was different. Colleen didn't even understand her own chaotic feelings. How could she tell people she was giving this baby away to a man she scarcely knew just because he could afford it and she couldn't, and because of a promise to her sister who was now laid to rest in the cemetery?

Would these women sympathize with her? Or condemn her?

She took care in the next few weeks to make sure nobody else noticed. It was easy to wear clothing that disguised her shape, baggy cotton sweaters over leggings, a loose, drop-waisted jumper over a turtleneck. She would need maternity clothes soon, and of course she hadn't kept hers from her previous pregnancies. Ben hadn't wanted more children—hadn't really wanted the ones they had. And once the divorce was final, she had firmly closed the door on her vague longing for another baby. So the maternity clothes had been sold at a garage sale, along with the other detritus of her married life.

She would make some, she decided, and as she looked at patterns at the local fabric store, she thought ironically about how domestic she suddenly was. She might be any other woman anticipating a baby.

But the pain that squeezed her chest reminded her that she wasn't. What she intended to do—and must do—would hurt for the rest of her life.

Michael was silent for these short weeks, allowing her to block from her mind as much as possible the threat he represented. And yet she felt guilty, remembering his ravaged face that day in her shop. Was he grieving alone without the comfort that reminders of his unborn child would bring him?

Ridiculous! He must have friends, and he had family of his own, a brother here in Clayton. He knew her as little as she knew him, he had admitted as much. She was the last person he would come to for comfort.

And yet she was curiously unsurprised when after dinner one evening she heard a knock on the door and opened it to find Michael on her front porch. He had changed after work to well-worn jeans and a blue chamois-cloth shirt with the sleeves rolled up. He was too handsome, really, to be standing here. He stole her breath for an instant, before she thought practically, *Well, at least the baby ought to be beautiful.*

"Hello, Michael," she said. "Come in."

That was when she noticed that his hands were shoved in his jeans pockets and that his shoulders were hunched just enough to give away his diffidence.

"If this is a bad time…"

Colleen stepped back. "No, the kids are doing homework and I was thinking about paying bills. I'd rather talk to you."

His mouth twitched. "The devil and the deep blue sea?"

She made a face. "Oh, dear. I didn't mean that quite the way it sounded." Although the analogy was all too apt, she thought ruefully.

Kim called from the kitchen, "Mom, is somebody here?"

"Uncle Michael," Colleen called back before asking him, "Would you like a cup of coffee? Or tea?"

"If you don't go to a lot of trouble."

"I never do," Colleen admitted. "I can't taste the difference. But Sheila was such a connoisseur, I know she spoiled you. Maybe I should offer you a glass of apple juice, instead."

His grin was startling and completely disarming. "To tell you the truth, I could never tell the difference, either. I lied to her."

"Coffee it is," she said, smiling back despite herself. "Have a seat in the living room."

In the kitchen she filled the kettle and turned on the burner.

"What's he want?" Kim asked.

"I suppose he's checking up on me," Colleen said dryly. She turned from the stove to find that Michael had followed her and now stood in the kitchen doorway. His eyes met hers; a muscle jumped along his jaw, and then he disappeared.

Kim lifted her head. The chair scraped as she swiveled toward the doorway.

"Did he hear you?" she whispered.

"Yup." Colleen grimaced. "That'll teach me."

Michael was now in the living room, standing with his back to her, studying a collage of photographs—herself when she graduated from college, her mother with Sheila and her children, Ben with five-year-old Kim on his shoulders, Drew riding a two-wheeled bike for the first time. Those pictures were the story of Colleen's life, symbolic moments preserved forever.

He must have sensed her presence, because he spoke without even glancing over his shoulder. "You and Sheila looked less alike as children."

"Perhaps because of the years between us. If you compare baby or school pictures, you'd have a hard time guessing who was who."

He made a sound of acknowledgment, only then turning to face her. Bluntly he asked, "Would you prefer I stay away?"

She flushed, lifting her hands in an apologetic gesture. "What I said in the kitchen was terribly rude. I'm sorry."

His mouth twisted. "Is it so hard to believe my motives aren't completely selfish?"

"No." Colleen bit her lip. "I meant it when I said I feel raw emotionally. I'm...not at my most reasonable. I just..." She groped for words. "I'm confused. I guess I need to think all this through on my own. But as long as you don't pressure me, I'm glad to see you. Sheila would have wanted us to be friends."

Friends. It was not a word she could connect with him. She could imagine a woman lusting for him, even loving him as her sister had, but friendship? Never. He was too remote, too distrusting, too reserved emotionally.

And yet, she suddenly remembered him at the pizza parlor. *You know how I used to think of her? A stream running over rocks. The way sunlight glints off it, and the little trills it makes...* And his peculiar addendum: *You were the deep pool below...the one with the trout and all the shades of green.*

She'd been startled to find him so poetic. But the comparisons he'd drawn were more; they were revealing and unexpectedly introspective. They were the words of a man she didn't really know, a man she shouldn't jump to conclusions about.

If he agreed that Sheila would have wanted them to be friends, he didn't say so, although it seemed to her his shoulders lost their rigid set. He nodded toward the window. "Is that your quilting frame?"

Grateful that her frame didn't hold the Carousel Horses, Colleen crossed the room. "Yes. I just started this quilt. I finished the commissioned one—I mentioned Mrs. Neely, didn't I? This one I'm planning to sell."

He was suddenly uncomfortably near, although he was looking down at her work. "Did you design the pattern?"

"No. This is a traditional one called Burgoyne Surrounded. See?" She touched the small white squares that were in sharp contrast to the rich blue background. "This is the Revolutionary army surrounding General Burgoyne's forces at Saratoga. Or so the story goes. Actually, I've never heard of an example of the pattern any earlier than the 1850s or '60s, so heaven knows how it got its name."

Michael lifted his head to look at her, and she was lost, inescapably trapped by the vivid blue of his eyes. They were so penetrating she felt stripped of the pretense that had made her chatter. Curiously, she was able to note quite clinically in another part of her brain that his eyes were the precise shade of the quilt. Had she been thinking of him when she chose that fabric?

Like an idiot, she blurted, "I wonder if the baby will have your eyes."

Michael blinked, and some emotion flickered across his face. "Or your hair." He sounded gruff and cleared his throat. "You have beautiful hair."

When he lifted his hand to touch it, carefully winding a tendril around his finger, Colleen quit breathing. She was shockingly conscious that his hand was inches from her breast, and she was humiliated by her own awareness.

As much for herself as him, she whispered, "Sheila's was exactly the same color."

The hair slipped off his finger and his hands curled into fists as he withdrew them and shoved them into his pockets. She saw his face twist as he turned away.

"Yes," he said hoarsely.

Colleen touched his arm. "I didn't mean to remind you."

What she prayed was that he would never guess she had needed to remind *herself* that it was her sister he was thinking about. Not her.

"I don't need reminding." His voice was like skin scraped over gravel. When he turned to look at her, his face was still contorted. "I never forget."

"Mom!" Kim yelled from the kitchen. "The water's all going to boil away!"

"Oh, no," Colleen said guiltily. "I forgot about the coffee. If you'll excuse me a minute..."

"Let's skip it." His tone was distant now, his rigid control back in place. "Maybe this wasn't such a good idea."

"This?"

"Coming here." Michael rotated his shoulders as though to relieve tension. "Visiting." There was something ironic in the way he said the last.

Puzzled by his withdrawal, Colleen studied him. "Would you rather we don't talk about Sheila?"

Muscles bunched in his jaw. "It's not…easy for me."

"Do you have anyone else you can talk to?" She stopped. "I'm sorry. That's none of my business."

They both ignored another yell from Kim. Michael frowned as he looked at Colleen. "Why are you afraid of me?"

"Afraid?" she echoed. "Don't be silly." But he only waited, and she was edgy enough to give an unconvincing laugh. "I told you I've never felt really…comfortable with you, but that's a long ways from fear."

"Maybe 'afraid' is too strong a word." He gave his head a shake. "Never mind. I seem to have that effect on people."

"You're just…hard to get to know." Though his expression had closed, Colleen felt a need to soften his harsh analysis of himself. She pressed her lips together and tried again. "Maybe I never really tried. It would've been different if I hadn't been divorced. But three's such an awkward number…."

"Yeah. But we're not three anymore." He didn't even wait to see the expression on her face. "Hell. I'm sorry."

She tried to smile. "You don't need to be."

Michael swore under his breath. "I was right. This wasn't a good idea. One memorial service was enough."

"I'm not so sure about that," Colleen said. "I was numb during the funeral. I'm more ready to mourn now than I was then. If you want to talk about Sheila…"

"I don't."

Colleen was taken aback. "Well, if you change your mind…"

"I didn't come here to cry on your shoulder." Abrupt,

unemotional, he was the stranger again. "Colleen, if you need anything, including money, call."

It would have been easy to be hurt by his withdrawal. But why should she be? Everyone dealt with grief in individual ways. And it wasn't as though she'd ever expected to feel close to her sister's husband.

"I'll remember that," Colleen said. "And if you ever want to talk, you know where I am."

Michael gave a nod and was gone, leaving her dry-eyed and emotionally wrung out. Refusing to analyze her feelings, she went to the kitchen.

Her daughter looked up from her math book and said self-righteously, "I turned the burner off. I didn't want the house to burn down."

With a certain amount of restraint, Colleen said, "Thank you."

"Did Uncle Michael leave?"

"Uh-huh. I'm going to work upstairs. Yell if you need me."

On the way, she stuck her head into her son's room. He leapt out of hiding to deal her a mortal wound with his plastic sword.

A practiced mother, Colleen staggered and clung to the door molding. "Have mercy!"

"You die better than Evan does," Drew told her cheerfully.

She straightened. "Thanks. Time for your bath."

"Mo-om."

"Pretend I bled all over you," she suggested. "Warriors need to clean up after battles, you know."

Drew considered her point. "Oh, all right."

Her quilting frame took up so much of the living room Colleen had been forced to squeeze a good-size sewing table into her bedroom. Inching past her bed, she remembered the real-estate agent throwing open the door.

"This is the master suite," she had announced breezily.

It was neither a suite, nor contained room for a master, but Colleen managed in its limited space, which was all she could ask for. She and Ben had sold their house in California, but the equity divided two ways had left her with just enough to open the shop. Buying a house was out of the question. She'd been grateful rents were so much lower here in eastern Washington and glad to find a house that let the kids have separate bedrooms.

Colleen plugged in her iron and sat in front of her sewing machine, automatically reaching for two triangles. The pieces for the crib quilt were all cut out and neatly arranged to remind her of what went where. She lined up the edges and fed the first two triangles into her machine, then the next and the next, never lifting the feeder foot. When she had sewed everything that could be, she began snipping the thread between pieces and gently pressing seams to one side.

As Colleen half stood to lay the newly formed rectangles and squares out on the table so that she knew which seams to sew next, she felt an odd quiver deep inside her, a muscle protesting her position or a murmur of hunger or—

She froze, even quit breathing. There it was again, the tiniest of flutters, but unmistakable. She laid a hand on her belly and gently rubbed, as though this loving touch could be communicated through her skin and muscle and womb. A wondering smile trembled on her mouth even as she had to blink away tears.

There, again... It was as if a small fish were leaping inside her, as if a butterfly was breaking free of its cocoon, spreading its wings, tickling her. There was life inside her.

Not even the heartbeat had convinced her, not in the way these first minute movements did.

Her womb was a cradle now, sheltering this tiny being. Soon, soon she would feel fists and toes, and this baby, amazingly growing inside her, would hear her voice and Kim's laughter and Drew's mock roars.

She wouldn't think about the time beyond that, the time when her womb became walls surrounding a space that was too small, when the baby fought to enter the new world outside.

The time when she could no longer protect her baby.

CHAPTER FIVE

KIM SET A PILE of dirty dishes by the kitchen sink. "Can I call Dad?"

Damn. Why now? Colleen asked silently, unanswerably.

If she—and Kim—were lucky, tonight Ben would succeed in sounding glad to hear from his daughter, interested in her life, reasonably regretful at the distance separating them.

Unfortunately those occasions were rare. Most often Kim's father was mildly annoyed at her interrupting his work or a favorite TV program or an intimate dinner with a "friend." Almost worse was when he wasn't home at all, because then Kim left a message on his answering machine. After that, for days she would leap up eagerly every time the phone rang. But the eagerness would fade, the brightness dim, because he usually forgot to return her calls.

"Of course you can," Colleen said matter-of-factly, turning on the water to rinse off a plate. "He's your father. You don't have to ask my permission."

Although she pretended not to listen, Colleen eavesdropped as she cleaned up the kitchen.

Ben was obviously there, because Kim said, "Hi, Dad. It's me." She hopped up on a bar stool at the counter. After a brief pause, she told him, "Nothing special. I just... wondered how you are."

Colleen ran water into the sink and missed the next exchange. She turned it off in time to hear Kim say, "I don't have any friends here. Well, maybe one. Our teacher moved us around in class Monday, and I'm sitting next to this girl. She's really cool, smart and popular and everything. But she acted like she doesn't mind sitting with me, and she said maybe I could come to her birthday party.''

Colleen quit worrying about Ben and started worrying about this ''really cool'' girl. If she raised Kim's hopes of finding a friend and then smashed them, Colleen was going to…well, do something dire. Steal the black widow spider from the science room and drop it on the girl's desk.

Her instinct was so instantly protective, so fierce, that she made a face. Her kids had to fight their own battles, hard as it sometimes was to stand back. No matter how much Colleen wished she could help, Kim had to adjust to this new school alone and make her own friends. If only it was as easy for her as it was for Drew!

''Nothing's ever new,'' Kim was saying gloomily. ''Well, except for Mom being pregnant.''

Colleen's fingers tightened on the sponge. Oh, Lord. Why had she put off telling Ben herself?

''You didn't know she was pregnant?''

Colleen turned slowly to meet her daughter's eyes. Kim scrunched her face up in a look of contrition. ''I'm sorry,'' she mouthed to her mother.

''Don't worry,'' Colleen said softly.

Through the receiver she could hear Ben saying something when Kim interrupted, ''Um, do you want to talk to Drew?''

Colleen didn't quite have time to plug her ears before her eleven-year-old bellowed, ''Drew! Dad wants to talk to you!''

His answering bellow was almost as loud. ''I don't want to talk to him!''

Kim put the receiver back to her mouth and said quickly,

"I guess he's doing homework or something. Well, I guess I'll talk to you later." She listened. "Oh. You want Mom?" She held out the phone. "Dad wants to talk to you."

"I wonder why," Colleen muttered. She watched her daughter beat a cowardly retreat, then took a fortifying breath and said, "Hi, Ben."

"What's this about a pregnancy?" Things could have been worse. He sounded more curious than accusatory.

Colleen sighed. "You want to know the truth? It's a mess."

"Messy affairs aren't your style."

Perversely, she half wished she could unfold a sordid tale of illicit love. If he hadn't been her children's father, she might have been tempted to manufacture one.

"I was acting as surrogate mother for Sheila. You know how many miscarriages she had." He would know, that is, if he'd ever listened when Colleen passed on her sister's news. "Michael is the father, but it was my egg."

There was a long silence. At last Ben said, "Good God."

"That pretty much says it all."

"So, has Michael left you holding the bag?"

Just once she had to say it. "No, but I wish he had."

Another silence. Ben knew her too well. "You're the mother. You can fight him for custody."

"But I promised..."

"You could lie. Say we reconciled and it's mine."

Occasionally she remembered why she'd married Ben. The ethics of his suggestion were a little shaky, but his intentions were good.

"Thank you for the offer." Colleen smiled crookedly, even though he couldn't see her. "But they can do tests these days that establish paternity."

"Oh. Yeah. Well, hell, you *are* the mother. Why wouldn't the court award you custody?"

"Money, for one thing. He's a banker. I just started a business that isn't breaking even yet."

Her ex-husband said, "I won't offer to pay child support for this one."

Colleen was able to laugh. "I won't ask you, I promise. Although if we'd pretended we had that reconciliation..."

"Dumb idea."

Her second laugh was more genuine. "Well, I'll let you know how it goes."

"You do that." He was silent for a moment. "I take it Drew doesn't want to talk to me."

Kim had become good at making excuses. Colleen hadn't needed to, because Ben had never directly asked her. Now she didn't even hesitate.

"You take it right. He's feeling betrayed by you."

A pause. "I guess I'm not the world's greatest father."

"It wouldn't take a lot of effort to change that," she pointed out. "If you just called more often, the kids would feel like you're interested in them."

"Yeah. You're right. I'll do that."

Sure, Colleen thought cynically.

"Listen," Ben said, "if you get really hard up for money, I could probably help out."

Just like that, she felt like crying. "Thank you." She blinked hard. "That's nice of you. But I'm okay right now."

"Good, good." His agreement was a little too quick and hearty. "Say hi to Drew."

"Sure." Not that their son would be interested.

Colleen thought about Ben as she finished cleaning up the kitchen. His announcement that he wanted a divorce had been a shock. During the struggle since to manage on her own, she had surrendered to the temptation to alter her memories of Ben. She wanted to dislike him; a kernel of anger gave her strength where sadness would only have weakened her.

But once in a while she remembered the man she married, handsome in an engaging, boyish way. She thought about how he'd made her laugh, the fun they'd had dancing and going to the theater, trying out new restaurants in San Francisco, walking on the beach. Colleen had a sudden picture of Ben jumping onto a moving cable car, holding out a hand to her, grinning in a way that dared her to take chances. It was all so vivid: the crowded sidewalk, the Victorian row houses along the steep street that plunged toward the bay, the breeze ruffling his light brown hair, the sparkle in his hazel eyes and the creases in his cheeks.

Colleen dried her hands on the dish towel and hung it up, then wandered into the dark living room. She ran her fingers over the quilt stretched taut in the frame, but didn't turn on the lamp or reach for her thimble or needle.

She and Ben *had* been happy once upon a time. Their marriage had been a good one until Kim was born. No, that wasn't true. The pregnancy itself had changed everything.

It was an accident, but a welcome one as far as Colleen was concerned. They'd had several wonderful years of marriage, but gradually she had come to feel something was missing. She convinced herself most of the time that what she really needed was a new job, but other times she would see a display of baby clothes, so tiny, the fabrics so soft, or a mother jiggling a newborn against her shoulder, cooing gently, and Colleen would be stabbed by a primitive need to have a baby of her own to hold.

When she tentatively raised the subject with Ben, he dismissed it. Their condo was too small; they couldn't afford a house big enough for a family; day-care cost the world and she would get bored stuck at home. He always had an array of practical reasons why now wasn't the time. In retrospect she doubted that any time would ever have been right.

Once she was pregnant, Ben resigned himself to fatherhood. In his own way, she supposed he even loved Kim and Drew; after all, he'd agreed to the second pregnancy. But he didn't like the changes children brought, the nights he and Colleen couldn't afford to go out, her preoccupation with diapers and Kim's play group, the bright plastic toys that littered the living room, and even her friendships with other young mothers.

She had taken the class that started her new career when she was pregnant, with the vague idea of making a crib quilt. In the piecing and stitching of that first small project, Colleen learned a new passion, one that in some mysterious fashion gave her a sense of connection to past and future. She had never made something that would outlive her; she had never realized what a legacy had been left by women who had otherwise made little imprint on their world.

Ben resented her quilting, of course, along with her intense involvement in motherhood. Now she could understand his feelings. Suddenly he wasn't the center of her life; he must have felt as if he barely clung to the edges of it.

Well, her story was an old one, long ago concluded. Ben was what he was; somehow Kim and Drew would have to come to terms with that and realize it had nothing to do with them. But they would adjust; after all, she and Sheila had never known their father, either, and Colleen didn't remember feeling any lack. She had been mildly curious about him, that was all. Her mother had drawn a loving circle around her daughters that had made them feel safe. They hadn't needed a father.

Colleen laid her hands over her belly and felt the familiar stirring inside. This one, at least, had a father who cared. But was that enough? How would a child feel to know that his mother had given him away, not out of desperation or for his own welfare, but because he had been conceived for someone else?

"I don't know if I can do this," she whispered. "I don't know."

MICHAEL INTENDED to stay away, both for his sake and for Colleen's. They were grieving enough without egging each other on. Mostly he was numb now, done with the worst of it. He was empty inside, feeling almost nothing, which he knew was unnatural, but better than what had come before.

It still hurt like hell when some reminder of Sheila slipped past his guard. Like this morning, when he'd opened a drawer and there was her hairbrush with a few curling auburn hairs still clinging to the bristles. Part of her. His hand was shaking, but he hadn't been able to stop himself from touching that hair. As in his nightmare, however, he was seeing double: Sheila, shaking her short, stylish hair as she laughed, and Colleen, who had stared at him with huge, unreadable brown eyes as he fingered a lock of her hair. Alike, yet not alike.

He'd meant to stay away. So why was he sitting in his car right outside her rental house, trying to work up the guts to go knock on her door? Did he imagine that if he ingratiated himself with her, she'd willingly hand over his baby when the time came?

But he knew his reasons were more complicated than that. He felt...not protective, though that was the word that came to mind. Obligated, maybe. Colleen was carrying his baby. It was a physical and financial burden she shouldn't have to handle by herself.

He kept thinking of how alone she must feel. Colleen had moved to Clayton because of Sheila, and now Sheila was gone. Their mother had died a few years back; the father was out of the picture. Colleen was divorced, and from what Michael had seen, her husband had been damned worthless, anyway. Did Colleen have a single other friend in town? What if she got sick? Needed a loan? Just needed to talk?

"Yeah," he muttered, "and what makes you think she'd choose you to talk to?"

God knows, Sheila hadn't talked to him, not really, not the way she'd talked to her sister. He hadn't noticed at first. They'd had passion and good times and laughter. But later Michael could remember how often he passed the open bedroom door and saw Sheila sprawled on the bed, talking on the phone to Colleen. He would stand unnoticed in the hall for a moment, listening as she said things to her sister she never said to him, things he hadn't known she felt.

He still looked at other men sometimes, the ones who seemed to have happy marriages, and wondered if they lay in bed at night and talked to their wives. Could they say things in the darkness they couldn't in the daylight? Did other wives rub their cheeks against their husband's chests and murmur confidences?

Michael sometimes suspected Sheila had tried early on. He remembered times they'd made love, and she wanted to talk afterward. Her voice had poured over him, the topics all so ephemeral, so *feminine*—how she felt about something minor that had happened at work, or whether this friend seemed secretive and that one unhappy—that he had no clue how to answer. He hadn't known—how could he have?—that she was testing him, dipping her toes into the water, and finding it too cold.

God. On a burst of frustrated energy, Michael jumped out of the car and slammed his door, striding up the walk before he changed his mind.

Colleen answered the doorbell. Surprise showed openly on her face. "Michael."

For a moment he was speechless at the sight of her. She hadn't been obviously pregnant the last time he saw her. Even at the doctor's office, her stomach had been nearly flat. But now...now her breasts were fuller and the gentle curve of her stomach pulled at the T-shirt she wore over leggings.

At the direction of his gaze, she flushed and tugged at her shirt. "I'm sorry, if I'd known you were coming..."

He shook his head abruptly. "No. I shouldn't stare. It's just..." He cleared his throat.

"I know, I know. I'm pregnant." She made a face. "In another month or two I'll look like a horse. Come on in. Can I get you—"

"I haven't had a cup of coffee here yet."

Her grin made her look younger, a pretty girl who couldn't be carrying her third child. "There's always a first time."

"Yeah." His hands felt awkward dangling at his sides, and he shoved them into his pockets. "Listen, I, uh, just wondered how you are."

Their eyes met, hers shadowed, more brown than green in this light. Her lashes fluttered and pink stained her cheeks.

"I'm...fine," Colleen said so softly he had to strain to hear. "Come on in."

He followed her to the kitchen, where Kim was hanging up the telephone. The girl's face glowed and she said wonderingly, "Lisa wants me to come to her birthday party. It's at the stables. We're going riding."

"Is that the really cool girl?" Colleen asked.

"Yes!" Kim jumped up and down, then flung herself into her mother's arms. "Oh, I can hardly wait!"

Laughing, Colleen hugged her daughter, then said pointedly, "Did you notice that Uncle Michael's here?"

"Yes, yes, yes!" Kim sang. Her feet barely touching ground, she danced to him, curtsied, said, "How do you do, sir?" and twirled out of the room.

Bemused, Michael watched her go. She flew up the stairs, singing in an uncertain soprano, her voice trailing away until it was cut off by the slam of a door.

Behind him Colleen said dryly, "I can hardly wait until she's a teenager."

"She's—" he did some quick mental calculations "—eleven?"

"Mm." She leaned a hip against the kitchen counter and shook her head. "Going on sixteen."

"Were you that skinny at her age?"

A secret smile played about Colleen's mouth as she gazed into the past. "Both of us were." She didn't seem to realize what she'd said. "I was so skinny my knees were knobby. All the other girls started getting figures, and I was still flat as a board. I was this height by the time I turned twelve. I hated P.E. The other girls looked like women. I looked like a flagpole without the flag."

Michael crossed his arms and leaned against the kitchen doorjamb. God, she was beautiful right now, her face soft, her reminiscent smile reminding him of how generous her mouth was. Even in the flat kitchen light, even pulled back in a severe ponytail, Colleen's hair shone with a rich fire. She had extraordinary eyes, too, the same color as Sheila's, but different somehow, not sparkling, more...serene. And right now her body was damned womanly. Ripe. Mysterious. Sexy.

God, she was beautiful.

Hell. How could he be attracted to her? His wife's sister. Michael swore viciously to himself and half turned away, leaning his head back against the doorframe and closing his eyes.

"I'm sorry," Colleen said contritely. "I don't know why I was babbling on. Here, I'm putting water on to boil right now. See?"

He opened his eyes to find that her slender back was to him as she suited action to words.

His voice sounded a little scratchy as he said, "I, um, didn't mind your babbling."

Colleen went still for a moment, then turned slowly. Her eyes were huge in the pale oval of her face. "You didn't?"

"No." Michael moved his shoulders uneasily. This was the kind of thing that was hard for him to express. "It made me see you— And Sheila."

"She was always prettier."

"Humbug." It came out more forcefully than he'd intended, and Colleen looked surprised. Michael tried to smile. "You know, it's funny. Sheila always said the same thing. That *you* were prettier. She said she was always the little sister, skipping to catch up. But never—" he had to swallow. "Never as though she minded."

Colleen bowed her head. Her voice was next to inaudible. "I think she minded that I had children and she couldn't."

"Damn it, Colleen!"

Her head came up sharply, like a startled doe.

"You did the most incredible thing for her that any sister could. So don't start torturing yourself."

She pressed her lips together, blinked several times. Then

she gave a tremulous smile. "You're right." The kettle behind her hissed softly. She didn't seem to notice. "Somehow we always end up back on the same subject, don't we? But I suppose that's inevitable. Sheila's the only thing we have in common."

"Not anymore."

She cast a quick look down at her stomach, then said in a stifled voice, "You're right. Of course."

"The pregnancy's going okay?" Put like that, it sounded impersonal, somehow outside her, like a special project he'd assigned at the bank.

"Yes." Letting the bald answer stand alone, Colleen turned away and busied herself spooning instant coffee into cups, pouring the boiling water, reaching into the refrigerator for milk.

"It's not getting in the way of work?"

With the milk carton in her hand, Colleen stopped dead. "Am I *that* huge?"

"No, I didn't mean to imply... Hell." Thank God, she looked amused by his stumblings. "It's just that I don't know that much about pregnancy," Michael tried to explain. "How uncomfortable you are."

"Well, I'm not going to take up ballet..." She rose on her toes in a surprisingly graceful imitation of her daughter's performance. Colleen dropped back to her heels and shrugged. "But otherwise, it's business as usual. Do you want milk or sugar?"

"Black's fine." Michael accepted the mug from her, careful that his fingers didn't touch hers. "When does a woman get..."

"Enormous?" she suggested. "Grotesque?"

"I wouldn't put it that way." A little uncomfortably he said, "You look...beautiful pregnant."

Her eyes shied from his and pink touched her cheeks again. "Thank you. I wish..."

"That Sheila were here?" Strangely, he was able to say it without pain.

"That she could've been pregnant like this."

"She wouldn't have been like you," Michael said ruefully. "She'd have chafed at being slowed down, worried about her figure..."

"And gloried at the attention a pregnant woman attracts."

"Do you attract any yet?"

Another flutter of those thick lashes, calculated, he guessed, to hide her reaction. "Attract attention? I'm... starting to."

He took a deliberate swallow of coffee. "How do you handle it?"

"If you mean, do I tell them the circumstances, no, I don't."

Her tone warned that the subject was not a welcome one. Michael figured that he'd pushed it about as far as he dared. He said conversationally, "I'll bet men don't ask if you're pregnant."

"Sit down." She brought her coffee and sat at the round oak table, waiting until Michael did the same. "It's funny, I was thinking the same thing the other day. Women get personal quicker, anyway, and pregnancy is one of those shared experiences that gives us instant intimacy. But I find it a little peculiar to be comparing labors with some strange woman in line behind me at the grocery store."

"Is it—labor—very bad?" That wasn't what he'd meant to say.

Colleen looked down at her coffee mug, which she was cradling in her hands. She spoke quietly. "Not for me. Not really. There's a purpose to it all, you see. It's…different than pain from an injury."

He nodded, not knowing what to say.

"Don't worry."

"Is that what I was doing?"

She smiled. "Yes. And thank you."

The way her eyes met his, the sweetness in that smile, tugged sharply at something in his chest. Michael didn't like the feeling, didn't want to acknowledge the reason for it. So he changed the subject.

"Tell me how your business is going."

Later he wondered whether she had been as relieved as he was to discuss something relatively impersonal, or whether his earlier guess that she had nobody to talk to was right. Whatever the reason, Colleen poured out her worries, helped along by a few pointed questions from him.

They might have talked longer if they hadn't been interrupted by her son, who needed help with a homework assignment. Guessing that she would be involved with the kids until bedtime, Michael bowed out.

When Colleen repeated, as he opened the front door, "You know, you really don't have to run off," he shook his head.

"I've overstayed my welcome already." He hesitated, his hand on the doorknob. "Don't forget, if you need anything…"

"Thank you."

Michael turned to look at her. Her expression was still friendly, but also more reserved than a moment ago. He felt a sudden, fierce, almost angry longing for another smile of such sweetness, for her to mean it when she told him not to run off. He wanted…

Damn. He didn't know what he wanted. His own house

not to be so empty, so cold compared to hers? Sheila to be waiting for him there? Some warmth somewhere in his life?

A moment later he started the car, ignoring his confusion, pushing it down where he'd pushed all his other emotions lately. He would have the warmth he craved once the baby was born. He'd have the kind of love he saw in Colleen's eyes when she looked at her children, and in theirs when they looked at her.

Seeing her so unmistakably, honest-to-God pregnant had done what even hearing the heartbeat hadn't—it had made the crazy business of fatherhood real for him. It had gotten him thinking.

He and Sheila had talked a little about names, but come to no conclusions. He tried to remember her favorites: Catherine for a girl, or Rachel, and for a boy...Cam. Cameron. Yeah, that was it.

Michael tried it out loud. "Cameron Joseph Delaney." Not bad.

Instead of looking for a day-care center, he'd hire a woman to come to his house days to take care of the baby, Michael decided, pulling away from the curb. That way some semblance of a real home would be waiting for him after work. Maybe he could find somebody who would also take over the housework and put dinner on. He'd like to open his front door and smell pot roast.

It was a little early to advertise, but soon, he told himself as Colleen's house diminished in his rearview mirror. He wouldn't want to wait too long.

"Catherine Delaney," he murmured. "Or is it Cam?"

COLLEEN WAS PINNING the last blocks of the Carousel Horse quilt together when the baby started hiccuping. Her stomach bounced and she glanced down, startled. Then it bounced again and she laughed. This was one of the aspects of pregnancy she'd forgotten. Kim had had hiccups all the time, often just as Colleen was falling asleep.

"Not again," she said aloud, a smile curving her mouth.

"Who are you talking to?" Drew asked from the doorway.

Colleen carefully set down the quilt top, bristling with pins. "Myself. Who else?"

He advanced into the room, looking unusually serious. His short, dark blond hair was damp from his bath, and he wore red-striped flannel pajamas. Surprisingly, he was carrying his baby quilt, made from an old pattern with many names. The funny thing about the pattern was that, created in the mid-nineteenth century, it looked like beach balls. So that was how Colleen had made it: red and green and blue beach balls bouncing on a pale yellow background. Drew still slept with it—except when he had a friend over—but he'd never clung to his baby quilt as Kim had to hers.

"Feel this," she said, and laid his hand on her stomach. When it jolted, Drew jumped back.

"Hiccups," she told him.

He wrinkled his nose. "Hiccups? *Inside* you?"

"Yup."

"Cool."

"So what's up?" she asked.

He moved thin shoulders. "I'm ready to be tucked in."

"Is it bedtime?" As she stood, Colleen glanced at the clock. "Oh, no! I'm glad you came in. Where's Kim?"

"Reading. Does she ever do anything else?" He nodded past her toward the sewing table. "Is that the baby's quilt?"

"Yeah. What do you think?" She held it up.

The Carousel Horses were done in jewel tones, vibrant turquoise and teal and gold, with white flowing manes and black saddles. Under their feet flowed the clouds. The horses looked as though they might gallop right off the edges any moment.

He studied it with his head tilted, then nodded judiciously. "I like it."

"Good." Colleen laid the top over the back of the chair and gave Drew a quick hug. "Bed."

They went through their usual ritual: she lifted the covers of his bed, waited while he climbed in and tucked them around him, spreading his quilt over the top. Then she bent down, framed his face with her hands and kissed him.

"Sleep tight. Don't let the bedbugs bite."

"Mom."

She paused on her way to the door. "Yes?"

"Do we get to help name the baby?"

A blade of pure pain pierced Colleen's chest. "I don't know," she managed levelly. "Let's worry about it later, okay?"

"Do you worry now?"

She tried to smile. "Yeah. I worry about everything, you know that. Hey, that's what moms and dads are for."

"Dad never worries."

"That's not true. Sometimes parents worry the most when we know we haven't done the right thing."

"Well, I don't care about him, anyway." Drew's voice was flat. "Just don't name the baby after him, okay?"

If she hadn't felt so sad, Colleen might have laughed. "I can promise that much. The baby won't be named Ben."

"Good," he murmured drowsily.

Colleen had told Kim to get ready for bed, and a moment later she tucked her in, too. Then she went back to her sewing station. She picked up the quilt top, but let it fall onto her lap.

Memories washed over her and she closed her eyes. She

saw the moment when the nurse first handed Kim to her, the small face red and scrunched up, tiny fingers curled into fists and big dark eyes looking so blindly at this new world. And oh, how it had felt, having her baby latch eagerly onto her breast, the small body curving so instinctively to Colleen's it was as though Kim had been created for no other purpose.

A few weeks later, Kim had smiled for the first time. Colleen had been up feeding her in the middle of the night, and suddenly Kim drew back from Colleen's breast, gazed up at her mother's face and smiled with unreserved love and delight.

And Drew, different from the moment he was born. He would smile at strangers when Kim would have frowned suspiciously. As soon as he learned to walk, he was toddling off to explore whenever his mother turned her back. He had nursed with the same intensity he brought to every task. When he was about a year old, the day came quite abruptly when he lost interest. He could carry a bottle with him on his explorations. At his mother's breast he had to be still, so why bother?

Colleen remembered her sharp regret. She knew that there wouldn't be another baby, that she would never again know this incredible closeness with another human being.

But now she could. Part of her desperate need to hold on to this baby was selfish, because she loved being a mother. But part of it was instinct that ran as deep as a baby's ability and drive to suckle at its mother's breast. Colleen had always known she would unhesitatingly die in place of one of her children. She discovered now that no promise on earth could supplant that fierce need to protect them.

Whether the decision was right or wrong, she knew suddenly she could not betray the baby she carried, the baby who was a part of her. Intellectually Colleen knew that Michael would be a good parent, but emotionally she knew only that *she* was the mother.

Colleen opened her eyes and felt the tears that soaked her cheeks. But she was at peace for the first time in months.

Whatever sacrifices had to be made, she would keep this baby. *Her* baby.

CHAPTER SIX

MICHAEL HAD a bad feeling from the moment his secretary's voice came through the intercom. "Mr. Delaney,
Colleen Deering is here to see you."

He punched the button. "Send her in." By the time he
rose to his feet and circled his desk, Roberta had ushered
Colleen into his office. His first, assessing glance took in
her rounded belly; she hadn't had a miscarriage, then, his
instant and worst fear.

But her expression wasn't reassuring. It was strained, her
face pale, and she clutched her purse tightly, holding it in
front of her like a shield.

Michael nodded at his secretary to close the door before
his gaze went back to Colleen. "Come and have a seat,"
he said, touching her arm lightly.

"Thank you."

He saw her settled before returning to his own leather
swivel chair behind the mahogany desk. "What's up?" Michael asked.

"Thank you for seeing me." She was perched stiffly on
the edge of the chair, her back straight. "I should have
called, but I knew if I did you'd ask what I wanted to talk
about, and I thought this was something I should say in
person."

Muscles all over his body tightened, and he had to force
himself to stay seated. "What is it? Are you okay?"

Her usually direct gaze shied from him. "I..." Colleen

drew a deep breath. "Yes. I'm fine. It's not that." With seeming effort she met his eyes again. "Michael…"

He wouldn't listen, was already shaking his head. "Colleen, don't do this. Damn it—"

"I have to!" she cried, her eyes huge and beseeching. "It's not you. I know you'd be a good parent. It's me. I just couldn't live with myself if I give away my baby."

"You were going to give him to your sister."

She squeezed her eyes shut and said in a low voice, "That was different."

Anger filled the great, searing hole in his gut. He stood and planted his hands on his desk, leaning forward. "You agreed," he said harshly. "A promise doesn't have to be in writing to stand as a legal contract. Or are you going to try to deny the baby is mine?"

She flinched, but held her chin up and met his gaze. "No, of course not. I know how much this baby means to you. The decision wasn't easy…."

"You've been making it since the day Sheila died."

"Maybe that's so, I don't know, but I didn't want to hurt you. I never wanted that."

He refused to acknowledge the pain in her voice. His own was gritty. "Don't think it's this simple. Morally, legally and biologically, that's my child you're carrying. By God, I couldn't stop Sheila from dying, but I can stop you from taking our baby!"

Colleen sucked in a long, quavery breath and stood. "You're right, Michael. Sheila's gone. Now *I'm* this baby's mother. That doesn't mean you can't be its father. We can talk about…about visitation or some kind of joint custody. Surely there's a way we can compromise…"

"Would you *compromise* with Drew and Kim?" He spat out the word. Her expression gave him his answer. "I didn't think so. Well, I don't want every other weekend, either. I've waited a long time to be a parent. You had no damned right to hold out hope and then snatch it back again because you don't feel like keeping your word!" He was shouting and didn't care. "I'll see you in court, and I'll fight with every weapon I have."

Michael was as sickened by himself as he was by her breach of faith. But there was no way back without losing the one thing that had kept him going—the certainty of taking his baby home with him.

Colleen was colorless, her freckles standing out in sharp relief. Her cheekbones were too prominent and she had her lips pressed together in a pale line.

"Very well," she said quietly. "I hoped we could keep it from that, but if there's no other way, I'll see you there."

"*Hell*. Colleen, think this through," he said urgently.

"I have. Believe me." Every word ached. "That's all I've done, night and day." With that she marched out. The whisper of his office door shutting behind her held devastating finality.

Michael's head dropped and he swore, long, obscenely, bitterly. He'd liked her, even trusted her.

I didn't want to hurt you. I never wanted that.

Maybe not, but she'd done it, anyway. Right now he felt as if his chest had been ripped open. Every breath was a fresh laceration.

He slumped down in his chair and buried his head in his hands. His fingernails bit into his scalp as he clawed for purchase in a world slipping out from under him.

God, oh God, oh God. How could he survive this? What if he lost in court, lost the one tiny promise of love and warmth and closeness? Would he spend the rest of his life watching other people from somewhere outside, always shut out, wondering how it would feel to have his son's first step be toward him, or hear his daughter's first giggle as he swung her in the air, terrifying her and thrilling her in equal measure. Or to have his toddler run to him when he hurt, because in Dad's arms was security, or his teenage daughter flirt with him, just for practice, because she knew with all her being that he was safe.

After Sheila's death, Michael's brother had reminded him that he was young, he would get married again, there would be another chance to have children. But his brother didn't know how alienated Michael had already felt from Sheila, how aware that he had failed her and himself. Michael couldn't imagine trying again, knowing his own shortcomings.

But he had fathered a child. That baby, *his* baby, was his one chance at happiness. He would not, could not, give that up so that Colleen could satisfy her maternal urges. Damn it, she *had* children; he didn't!

Swearing again, Michael straightened, ran his fingers through his hair. He had himself under control again.

You usually do. He could hear Sheila's acid comment so clearly it was as though she were standing there. He grimaced. If she could see him right now, what would she feel? Betrayed by her sister? Or glad that someone had finally found a way to get to him?

The last time she'd miscarried, Sheila had flung her pain at him in bitter words. "Doesn't it ever hurt? Do you feel anything? Did you ever feel anything, or was I just a suitable choice for a wife?" Her laugh had scalded him. "Not so suitable, as it turns out. Barren wasn't what you had in mind, was it?"

Dear God. Even then, in the face of her agony, he hadn't been able to tell her how much he did feel. No, he'd said something despicable, something like, "Why are you putting yourself through this?" when actually he understood.

God, he understood. They needed something to fill the emptiness.

And then Colleen had offered it, a gift of such magnitude, such unselfishness, he'd been stunned. His first reaction had been painfully mixed, gratitude swamped by the little boy inside crying, *Why hasn't anybody ever loved me this much?*

But somewhere in there he had accepted that he, too, was the lucky recipient of her generosity, if not her love. He'd never forgotten that the love wasn't for him, but he had cautiously begun to believe that the gift was.

Now she'd slapped his hand and snatched back her gift. But the little boy was still rebelling. You couldn't give something away and then take it back.

Michael, the man, flipped through his Rolodex, found his lawyer's number and picked up the phone.

THE LAWYER Colleen consulted was optimistic. "We're old-fashioned on this side of the mountains," he told her. "You'll still find that judges here believe in motherhood. Generally speaking, the fact that you were willing to be a surrogate in the first place would be frowned on, but because your motive was your deep affection for your sister rather than profit, I think we can present it in a favorable light. Now, you say you're divorced?"

They went over her background one more time, with him nodding at last in satisfaction. "No skeletons in the closet. That's good."

Colleen had hoped for somebody a little older, even grandfatherly, but Joe Warren had come highly recommended. The fact that he'd stayed in eastern Washington for college and law school was approved of around here. One of her quilt-shop customers had told her, "If you just want to make a will or something, you can go to anyone, but if you need an attorney to represent you in court, he's the best in Clayton.''

Colleen was made a little uneasy by the lawyer's enthusiasm. She had a feeling he *wanted* to go to court, that he wouldn't mind making headlines with this unconventional custody battle. A settlement didn't interest him. But when she hesitated, all she had to do was remember Michael's shouted *I'll see you in court, and I'll fight with every weapon I have!*

''Thank you,'' Colleen said at last, rising. She was reaching a point where getting out of chairs required some effort. ''I was afraid you'd tell me my cause was hopeless. I feel better.''

''I can't make any promises.'' He stood, too, a tanned, blond man, sleek in an expensive suit. But his grin reminded her a little of Ben's; it was almost boyish, exuberant. He was a man who loved what he did. ''But I'll be surprised,'' he continued, ''if any judge in our town can look you in the eye and order you to hand your baby over to this man, just because he happened to have been married to your sister.''

Colleen had a twinge of guilt at the description of Michael. He was more, much more. Sheila had loved him. And he had loved her as much, or he would never have agreed to father this child Colleen carried. But she couldn't let guilt stop her from doing what she knew in her heart was right.

If only there was a way they could compromise! Even though Michael had rejected any such possibility, she might have suggested it again, if she could have thought of a solution that would satisfy both. But what?

She'd never thought much of true shared custody, where a child spent half his time with one parent and half with the other. There was no way he could have a sense of security and trust when his life was so fragmented. And, even if Colleen had custody, the more conventional ways of allowing a father to see his children frightened her. What if Ben had insisted on having Drew and Kim every summer, for example? How could she kiss them goodbye and put them on a plane to see their father, knowing how much they would miss her? And Drew wouldn't want to go; how could she make him?

Right now, if he had custody, Michael would probably be scrupulous—even generous—in allowing her visitation rights. Weekend visits sounded reasonable enough, but the future could hold almost anything. He might move to Seattle or Denver or New York City. He would surely remarry. A man changed when he had a new wife. What if they had a baby together and she resented the child who reminded him of his first wife? How much power would Colleen really have to fight him if he chose at some point to exclude her from their child's life?

Besides, Michael had made it plain that he wouldn't settle for visitation rights any more than she would. He wanted custody, and so did she. He wanted to raise their child as his; she wanted to raise it as hers. Unlike a divorcing couple, they had no past to bind them, no once-upon-a-time commitment to love and raise their baby together.

Colleen sighed and started her car. Back to work. She couldn't afford to leave the shop closed any longer than necessary. Especially since she now had a lawyer's fees to pay.

That evening she put off, yet again, explaining the situation to Kim and Drew. Eventually she would have to, but right now they were remarkably incurious about her pregnancy. Neither had asked whether the baby would still go to Uncle Michael. The closest either had come was Drew's question about naming the baby. The whole subject was a box of pins she didn't want to spill yet if she could possibly avoid it.

Unfortunately she discovered only a few days later that, in not telling them, she'd been asking for trouble.

It started innocuously enough. A crew of ladies swept into the shop at just after four-thirty, excitedly planning to pick out fabric for a class two evenings later. No way was less than half an hour enough time for them to make their selections, her to cut the fabric from the bolts and each to individually pay. There was also no way she was going to tell them, sorry, she was closing, and they could go to House of Fabrics down at the mall to do their buying.

As soon as they were all momentarily out of earshot, Colleen picked up the phone. Sounding breathless, her son answered.

"How are things going?" Colleen asked.

"Neat!" Drew said. "I was shooting hoops with—"

Colleen had to cover the receiver and smile at one of the women. "Yes, all the brown fabric is twenty-five percent off today. It's a good chance to stock up." Into the phone, she said, "Listen, I'm going to be late. You tell Kim, okay?"

"Yeah, but, Mom—"

"Can it wait until I get home?"

"I guess so, but—"

She rolled her eyes. "No buts. I'll see you in about forty-five minutes."

It was a full hour before she pulled into the driveway. She didn't pay much attention to the pickup parked in front of her house. Three young guys shared the house next door, and they had a constant stream of friends visiting.

So Colleen was completely unprepared when she walked into the kitchen from the garage. Drew was sitting on the counter, bumping his heels into the oak-veneer cupboard door below him, telling some story. She heard the rumble of a man's laugh and only then saw, with shock, a man sitting at her kitchen table.

The door swung shut behind her. "Drew?"

He turned his head, then hopped guiltily off the counter. "Oh, Mom. Cool. See who's here?"

She saw. "Michael."

He stood to face her, the amusement wiped from his face. "Hello, Colleen," he said quietly.

She looked back at her son. "You know you're not supposed to let anyone in when I'm not home."

Her son stuttered, "B-but, Mom, this is Uncle Michael!"

She drew in a breath to tell him sharply that when she said anyone, she *meant* anyone, but stopped herself in time. This was her fault for keeping secrets. "Yes, of course," she made herself say. "Where's Kim?"

"She went to find our Monopoly game. Uncle Michael said he'd play with us."

"Only until your mother came home," he said, sounding stiff. "She and I have something to talk about, and then I'd better be going."

"Scoot," Colleen said, nodding toward the door. Drew made a face but went. Crossing her arms, Colleen looked back at Michael. "What do you want?"

If he hadn't pushed his hands into the pockets of his slacks, she wouldn't have guessed that he felt her hostility. His expression remained impassive, and he spoke formally. "Only to find out how you are."

"You mean, how your baby is."

"No, that isn't what I meant. Believe it or not, I do care about your well-being. You're Sheila's sister."

"Excuse me," Colleen snapped, "if I find it hard to believe it was out of deep affection for me that you coerced my kids into letting you in."

So much for impassivity. He scowled at her. "I didn't coerce anybody into doing anything. They invited me in. I stayed because Drew told me he didn't like being home alone."

Colleen gritted her teeth. "He wasn't alone. He has a sister. And I don't appreciate being condemned for my parenting practices by somebody who doesn't know the first thing about children!"

Just as coldly Michael said, "I know that's my child you're carrying, and I wouldn't want him left alone with an eleven-year-old girl."

Colleen dropped her purse with a thump on the counter, mainly to remove the temptation of swinging it at him. "For your information, she'll be twelve by then. But as it happens, I wouldn't dream of leaving the baby with her. That's a little different from leaving kids the ages of Drew and Kim alone for an hour. Now, are you satisfied?"

"No, damn it, I'm not!" He swung away to pace the narrow width of her kitchen, then back to face her. He was still frowning, dark brows meeting, the creases in his cheeks deeper. "I understand that your kids are home alone because you can't afford to pay someone to be here with them. Colleen, you have to know that you can't take care of this baby, too."

She couldn't help flinching, but she lifted her chin and said with quiet dignity, "Money is nice. Fortunately for the vast majority of families, it's not essential for good parenting. You may convince some judge that it is, but I hope and trust that you'll eventually find out differently."

His jaw muscles bunched, and he looked away. "Money's not the issue."

"You've certainly tried to make it the issue," she fired back. Inside, she was shaking, but she was determined not to let him see that. "Do you imagine that you can buy this baby?"

"Is that what you think of me?"

"What should I think?" she asked uncompromisingly.

His mouth twisted. "I didn't want to be enemies."

"That's what happens when you take somebody to court."

She saw the spasm his hands made tightening into fists, buried though they were in his pockets. In a low voice he said, "We both think we know what's best for this baby. Does that mean we have to hate each other?"

Meeting his eyes across the kitchen, she felt the sudden burn of tears. "I want to hate you!" Colleen cried, shocking herself with the passion of her words. She scrubbed at the tears. "Don't you understand?"

Suddenly he was right in front of her, handing her a paper towel she hadn't seen him reach for. "Yeah," he said huskily. "I understand. I've tried to hate you, too."

Colleen blew her nose on the coarse paper towel, then wadded it up. Keeping her gaze fixed on the ball of paper in her hand, she said almost inaudibly, "This wasn't an easy decision for me, you know."

"Has anything between us ever been easy?"

Colleen gave her head a small shake.

Roughly he said, "I wonder if anything ever will be."

"I...I don't know," she whispered.

He reached out and with devastating gentleness wiped a tear from her cheek. "However this comes out, we're stuck with each other."

She nodded.

"I just...wanted to be able to visit you sometimes." He sounded awkward, nothing like the assured, handsome man she remembered at her sister's side. "I seem to, uh, be drawn here. You've probably noticed."

Another nod. She couldn't make herself lift her head and meet his gaze.

"I knew it would upset you, but I hoped—" Michael stopped abruptly. "Never mind. I shouldn't have come. I'm sorry, Colleen."

In that moment, she felt incredibly selfish. She had so much. He had so little. She'd lost her sister, but she still had her children. Who did Michael have?

The baby chose that moment to stretch, wriggling restlessly. Sheila, more of a believer in such things than Colleen, would have said it was a sign.

Colleen took a deep breath and said hurriedly before she could change her mind, "Would you like to feel the baby move?"

Lifting her head, she saw the blaze of some incredible emotion in his blue eyes. "Do you mean...touch you?"

Her throat tight, she nodded.

He slowly lifted a hand toward her stomach, but stopped with it an inch or so away. She stared down at it, large, dark and blunt-fingered, scarred in a few places, such a contrast to her own hand, which was much smaller, paler, softer but for the calluses on her fingertips from the quilting needle. It took more courage than she'd thought she possessed to lift her shirt and take his hand in her own, placing it carefully over the swell their baby made.

Her skin shivered in reaction to his touch, and something heated and frightening, almost sexual but not quite, tightened inside of her. And at such a small thing—his hand spread over her belly.

For a moment they stood there, so still she wasn't breathing, and then the baby wriggled again, poking at Colleen hard enough to make her jump, before somersaulting into a new position.

She looked up to see incredulity on Michael's face and

the same wonder he'd displayed at the doctor's that day. But something else was in his eyes, something unsettling. It matched her own shocking awareness.

Then his expression closed as completely as if a shutter had dropped; very carefully, Michael lifted his hand from her belly and stepped back. His fingers flexed before he shoved his hands in his pockets.

He cleared his throat. "That's...pretty amazing. It must feel strange."

"Even a little exasperating sometimes." She didn't sound any more natural than he had. "The baby sleeps when I'm active during the day. I guess it must feel like...well, like I'm rocking him." In some part of her mind, Colleen noted her use of the masculine pronoun. For no discernible reason she had started thinking of the baby as a boy. Even as she pondered the oddness of that, she continued, "So at night when I'm trying to sleep, the baby wakes up. He, or she—" this last took conscious effort "—figures it's playtime. I think he's going to be a gymnast. But being so active always gives him the hiccups. All of which makes it hard to sleep."

"You must have really loved Sheila."

His unthinking comment should have reintroduced tension between them, brought Colleen's grief to the forefront of her mind. But maybe, just maybe, her sister had been gone long enough now that Colleen didn't have to mourn every time she heard Sheila's name. When she could think and feel about Michael in ways that had nothing to do with her sister.

So instead, Colleen smiled, if ruefully. "Well, pregnancy is an adventure."

He looked away from her. "Right now, you probably wish it didn't have to end."

There was no need to add, *Because when it ends you'll*

lose your baby. The sadness that clutched at her chest reminded her. And it reminded her that he was the one who wanted to take her baby. *He* was the threat, the enemy.

Her expression must have given away her thoughts, because Michael retreated, emotionally and physically.

"I'd better go, let you get on with dinner. Thank you, Colleen." He inclined his head.

"You're welcome." The traditional response sounded silly, but what else could she say?

She heard a scuttling in the hall, but the kids had made their getaway before she and Michael emerged from the kitchen. At the front door, he said in that same formal tone, "I won't bother you again."

Colleen felt suddenly very tired. It would have been better, easier, if she could have hated him. But as he'd pointed out, when had anything between them ever been easy?

"If you want, you can come again," she said, her tone matter-of-fact, as though she offered nothing meaningful.

Light flared in his eyes, momentarily mesmerizing her. Then he managed to shield his reaction, giving it away only by the rough timbre of his voice. "That's...generous of you."

"Even if I'm not generous in the one way that counts?"

His cheek twitched. "I told you, I tried to hate you. It didn't work."

He didn't wait for a response. As she watched him cross the small front lawn with his long strides, heading for the pickup truck, Colleen was crowded with a chaotic mix of emotions. Foremost, and most confusing, was the way her body reacted to him. Why now? She'd never even been altogether sure she *liked* her sister's husband. She'd certainly never been attracted to him.

"Damn it, Sheila," Colleen said under her breath, "why

didn't you just marry some jerk who'd be happy to have me raise his kid?''

Sighing, she eased the front door closed and turned to face the music. "Okay, guys," she said resignedly, "you can come out now."

First Kim, then Drew, appeared in the living room doorway. Kim's dark eyes were big. "Mom, what did you mean, that's what happens when someone takes you to court?''

Colleen made a face. "I guess it's time I tell you what's going on."

They didn't really understand of course. How could they? But Colleen thought perhaps Drew and Kim had been worrying about the future more than she'd realized, because she had the impression they were reassured to know she intended to fight for the baby.

"How come you're so...so polite to him?" Kim asked, nose wrinkled.

"Maybe," Colleen suggested wryly, "you should wonder how come *he's* so polite to me! After all, I'm the one who is breaking my word."

"Yeah, but Aunt Sheila's dead. The baby was for her."

"This baby is your uncle Michael's, too. I think he cares as much about it as I do."

"He's just a father," Drew said, shrugging. "It's not the same thing."

Colleen looked at her son in dismay. He'd made similar remarks before, but she'd attributed them to unresolved anger aimed at Ben. This time he sounded only puzzled, even indifferent. How dreadful that a boy who would grow up to be a man, perhaps a father, really believed men didn't love their own children.

And she had convinced herself that his failed relationship with his dad didn't matter.

Colleen reached out and tilted his chin up so he had to look at her. Gently she said, "Sweetie, all men aren't like your father."

"How do you know?" He jerked away. "You said you didn't have a father, either."

"Well, you do." She sounded sharper than she'd intended. "Lately he's been trying harder than you have."

"Yeah," Kim chimed in. "I keep telling you he misses us. Dad wants us to visit."

Colleen seriously doubted it. Or did she *want* not to believe it?

"Sweetie—"

"Don't keep calling me that." Her son averted his face.

"All right. Drew." Colleen bit her lip, then continued reasonably, "I know you've had friends who have fathers who care a lot. Remember how Andy's dad coached your soccer team? And Colin lived with his father. He used to take you fishing. Have you forgotten that?"

Drew gave a sulky shrug, still not looking at her.

"Anyway," Colleen went on, too briskly, "we'll still be seeing your uncle Michael sometimes. Talking to lawyers is part of the way we're trying to figure out how we can both be good parents once the baby is born. Right now we don't agree, but that doesn't mean we're enemies."

"I heard you say you *wanted* to hate him," Kim said. "So how come you're telling us now that you don't?"

"That was a private conversation," Colleen said. "You guys had no business listening."

She might as well not have wasted her breath. The discussion degenerated into an argument about whether the fact that she hadn't told them what was going on justified their eavesdropping.

Drew lost interest first, and Kim was eventually distracted by a reminder that tomorrow was the birthday party at the horse stable. Lisa's mother was picking up all four girls at school and taking them directly there. Colleen was to come for Kim at five-thirty on her way home after closing the quilt shop. She'd arranged for Drew to go home with another boy.

She had no trouble finding the place the next day; it was hard to miss miles of crisp, white, board fencing and long green barns, trimmed with white. A discreet sign announced Whispering Winds Arabians.

Colleen could have sworn she smelled money, instead of manure, when she got out of the car. This, of course, was where Kim had wanted to take riding lessons. She hadn't mentioned them lately, but today's outing would no doubt change that, Colleen thought ruefully.

Inside huge sliding doors, she found a long aisle lined with stalls. Dainty gray and brown muzzles poked between the bars as she went in search of the party. She couldn't resist stopping to stroke a few; searching lips told her she should have brought some carrots.

Eventually she came to a central intersection; ahead was a tack room and showers where two teenagers were soaping up young horses even her uneducated eye recognized as gorgeous. To the left was a huge, covered arena.

Her timing was perfect; Kim was just slipping off a pretty bay, helped by a man in boots and cowboy hat. She saw her mother and hurried over, without a word passing the other girls who were dismounting.

No hello. "I'm ready to go home."

Puzzled, Colleen asked, "Did you have a good time?"

"It was okay," Kim said shortly.

Hiding her perturbation, Colleen nodded back at the arena. "You'd better go thank Lisa for inviting you."

Kim's facade cracked. "Do I have to?" she whispered.

Colleen managed a smile at the woman who handed the

reins of one of the horses to a girl and came toward them. "Yes, you have to," she whispered back. "Is that Lisa's mother?"

Kim's head bobbed. Colleen gave her a firm push in the small of her back. Out of the corner of her eye, she watched her daughter cross the arena, scuffing her feet in the sawdust. One of the girls was a miniature version of her mother, down to the dark curls she flipped nonchalantly over her shoulder as she waited for Kim.

Kim said woodenly, "Thanks for inviting me, Lisa."

Colleen didn't hear any reply, because the girl's mother had reached her, saying brightly, "I'm so glad Kim could come. She seemed excited about the horses."

"She'd love to take lessons," Colleen said, smiling. She wouldn't have admitted at gunpoint that she couldn't afford them. "It was nice of you to have her."

She was excruciatingly aware of the way the other girls bunched together and whispered when Kim started back toward her. She wanted to kill them. Instead, she smiled again, thanked Lisa's mother and steered Kim down the aisle.

Kim held up until she got in the car. The second she slammed the door, she burst into tears.

Colleen gathered her daughter in her arms. Cheek against her straight, brown hair, she said, "Tell me about it."

The eleven-year-old wailed, "Her mother made her invite me because I'm new! One of the other girls told me. Lisa just *ignored* me. It was horrible!"

"But I thought she was friendly at school."

Kim's voice was muffled. "Sometimes she is. Sometimes she pretends I'm not there."

"Why do you want to be friends with her, then?"

Her answer was a fresh sob. "She's the most popular girl at school!"

Colleen held her away. "There have to be nicer girls you could make friends with."

"You don't understand!"

Oh, she understood, all right. Colleen remembered a girl who'd moved to her own hometown in seventh grade, immediately becoming the object of adoration for both girls and boys, including the boy Colleen had a crush on. How she'd hated her! But she'd have forgotten all her envy in a second if only the girl had drawn her into that magical circle of the most popular kids.

Now she contented herself with, "I'm sorry. Here, blow your nose. We have to pick Drew up on the way home, and you don't want him to see you crying."

That was enough to galvanize Kim, who wasn't about to give her brother a weapon in their ongoing battles. But just as Colleen was getting out of the car to go and collect Drew, Kim said passionately, "I wish we'd never left Pacifica! I had *friends* there!"

She was quiet all evening. When Colleen kissed her good-night, Kim said, "I want to go home, Mom. There's no reason we have to stay here, is there? I mean, Aunt Sheila's dead. And I hate it here! I really hate it!"

The mattress gave as Colleen sat on the edge of the bed. "Oh, honey," she said regretfully, "there are all sorts of reasons we can't go. You know that. We've talked about it. There's the shop, and Drew's made friends now, and Uncle Michael will want to see the baby often once it's born."

Her daughter flared back, "You mean, I can't see *my* father just so this...this *baby* can see his? Well, it's not fair!" She turned her face away.

Colleen touched Kim's shoulder, but her hand was shaken off. "Honey, you know there are other reasons."

Kim didn't say anything. Colleen sighed. "I understand

that you miss your dad, but the move's been good for all of us. You'll make friends here, I know you will. But I am sorry about today. Now, good night. I love you.''

She sounded more sure than she felt. Colleen lay awake herself, going over and over again the decisions she'd made and the few options left. Had she been foolish to pull up roots so ruthlessly out of some vague need for family? Would the kids have been happier if they'd stayed in Pacifica?

But she knew in her heart that neither had been all that content there. Kim was forgetting how often her father had canceled visits at the last minute, how hard on all of them it had been to have Colleen commuting to San Francisco, working long hours. Kim had detested the before- and after-school care, and her closest friend had moved away last year, anyway.

Sleepless, Colleen told herself that Kim would get over this. Something like this could have happened just as easily back in Pacifica. Kim *would* make friends. She was a nice girl. If only summer vacation wasn't looming so close! The hills around town were green with the new shoots of wheat, and in town daffodils and tulips bloomed in every garden. As a child, Colleen had loved summer vacation, but it was different for her kids. They would have to go to day camp, which would make it harder yet for Kim to meet other girls her age since the kids at camp tended to be younger.

Kim was still subdued the next morning. Colleen dropped both kids off at school and watched as Drew raced off to join a group of boys wrestling on the playground. In contrast, Kim trudged up the front steps, looking terribly alone in the middle of a crowd.

Colleen was depressed and weary all day. Closing time had never been more welcome. But she walked in the door at home to the sight of her two kids glaring at each other.

"Don't tell me what to do!" Kim yelled.

Colleen groaned inwardly. What now?

"Okay," she interrupted. "What's going on?"

Drew answered, but she didn't hear him. All her attention was on Kim, whose eyes glittered and whose mouth was set in defiant lines.

"I talked to Dad," she said, tossing her head. "And he says I can come and live with him."

CHAPTER SEVEN

COLLEEN'S PURSE slipped out of her fingers. She felt peculiarly distant, detached, but still aware of a knife blade of pain. Both the kids were staring at her, but she couldn't seem to think of anything to say.

She'd worried sometimes, when first divorced, that one of them might someday choose to live with Ben, but in her heart she hadn't believed it. Drew wanted nothing to do with his father, and Kim and she were so close. So now her first thought was that her decision to keep the baby was the cause of this. Had she chosen one child at the cost of another?

"Mom, are you all right?" Drew asked.

"Yes, just—" Colleen gave her head a shake "—let me sit down."

Kim stood aside, still defiant, but looking scared, too.

Colleen sat heavily at the kitchen table. She closed her eyes, took a deep breath and said, "Okay, tell me again."

"Dad says I can go live with him."

"You're crazy!" her brother told her. "He doesn't want us. Anyway, remember what weekends with him were like?"

Colleen saw only her daughter. "Your father actually said, in so many words, that you could come and live with him?"

"Well, he said..." Kim bit her lip. "I don't know what he said! But Dad meant I could come."

"Yeah, sure," Drew muttered.

His sister spun to face him. "Are you calling me a liar?"

"Yeah, I'm calling you a—"

Colleen covered her ears. "Stop!" She so seldom yelled they both looked at her in shock.

"Drew." She tried to speak calmly. "This is something Kim and I need to discuss privately. Why don't you go up to your room and do your homework?"

"I don't have any."

"Then you can turn on the TV."

"Can I watch 'Guts'?"

"I don't care what you watch."

"Wow." He shot out of the kitchen, leaving thick silence in his wake.

Colleen nodded toward the table. "Sit down."

Kim silently obeyed. Her chin was thrust out, but Colleen saw her lower lip tremble.

"I'm sorry you're so unhappy here."

"I'll *never* make friends!" Kim burst out.

Colleen stood and swiftly circled the table. She crouched by her daughter and enveloped her in a hug. "Oh, honey, I know it's hard. I haven't been much help, have I?"

Kim was crying now in huge gasps. "Why won't you let us move home?"

Colleen pressed her cheek against Kim's soft hair. Holding back the tears, she said, "Because I can't. And because I'm not so sure Pacifica *is* home anymore."

"We all had friends…"

Colleen held Kim at arm's length so she could see her daughter's tearstained, red-splotched face. "Do you remember what loose ends you were at after Theresa moved?"

"At least I *knew* other kids."

"But you didn't have a good friend any more than you do here."

Kim ducked her head. "Dad was there."

"So he was." Colleen brushed the fine brown bangs back from Kim's eyes. "I'm sorry you can't see him more often. That's the one bad part about moving. But—" she had to force the words past the lump in her throat "—has it occurred to you that if you lived with him, you wouldn't be able to see Drew and me very often, either?"

Kim's face contorted with another sob. "But I'm so unhappy!" she wailed.

Somewhere in the middle of holding her daughter, Colleen remembered that Kim was still a little girl. She remembered how impulsive an eleven-year-old was, how unthinking. And her own hurt receded.

"Honey, I can't let you go live with your father. If you were sixteen years old and positive that was what you wanted to do, I might agree once I'd talked to him. But you're not sixteen, you're eleven. I promise to help you adjust here as much as I can. Maybe this summer you could visit your dad for a couple of weeks if he agrees. But," she concluded firmly, "you're not going to live with him."

"Oh, Mom!" With a new torrent of tears, Kim flung herself back into her mother's arms and wailed, "I was afraid you'd say yes!"

Patting her daughter's back, Colleen thought it would have been funny if it didn't hurt so much.

Once the tears subsided she sat back on her heels. "Goodness, look at you. Here, let me get you a tissue." She carried some in her purse, and in a moment she'd grabbed several and handed them to Kim, who mopped her cheeks and blew her nose.

"All right," Colleen said, "let's get down to brass tacks.

Why did you announce you were going to live with your father if you didn't really want to?"

Kim sniffed. "I thought I wanted to until I told you. And then suddenly I was really scared."

Colleen sighed. "Is he waiting to hear from me?"

"Well—" Kim nibbled uncertainly on her lower lip "—I'm not really sure…" She drew the last word out.

Colleen fixed a stern expression on her face. "Does your dad know you were planning to move in with him?"

Kim hunched her shoulders and spoke in a rush. "Well, I said I hated it here and he said it was too bad we'd moved and why didn't I visit this summer. So I said I didn't want to wait that long, that I wished I lived with him, and he said we could talk about it. So I thought…well, that he was saying okay." She looked beseechingly up at her mother.

Colleen knew damn well that Ben didn't have the slightest desire to have a preadolescent girl living with him. But he had never liked to say no. He'd always foisted the unpleasant task off on her. Just as he had this time.

But nothing on earth could have made her tell their daughter that her father didn't really want her. So Colleen said only, "I'll call him later. Maybe we can set the date for a visit with him this summer if he can get some time off."

Kim gave a jerky nod.

Colleen kissed her and then picked up her purse to plop it on the table. With forced good cheer she asked, "How does French toast sound for dinner?"

"Drew doesn't like it."

"Drew doesn't like anything. I'll open him a can of chili."

Kim waited until her mother was wearily contemplating the contents of the can cupboard. "Mom?"

"Uh-huh?"

"Are you mad at me?" Kim asked in a small voice.

"Mad?" Colleen turned quickly. Her heart almost broke at the sight of the apprehension on Kim's face, and she hurried to hug her close again. "Sweetheart, of course not! I want you to be able to talk to me about anything, anything at all. Don't hide stuff that's bothering you just because you think you might hurt my feelings. Will you promise me that?"

After a second Kim's head bobbed against Colleen. Then she heaved a huge sigh. "I guess I didn't like Lisa that much, anyway."

Colleen squeezed her shoulders. "That's the spirit, kiddo."

DESPITE COLLEEN'S invitation, Michael had no intention of abusing the privilege of being able to visit. He made himself wait for two long weeks before he picked up the phone.

"Can I take you all out for pizza again?" he asked.

"Do you like spaghetti?" Colleen countered. "I owe you a dinner. Why don't you join us, instead?"

"I don't want to barge in on you," he said gruffly. "Why don't I just stop by later in the evening?"

She was polite enough not to ask why he wanted to come at all. Instead, she challenged, "Afraid my cooking will be as bad as my coffee?"

He was cornered. "Name a time."

Michael arrived at her place at five-thirty on the nose, just as Drew popped a wheelie on his bike and slid to a stop in the driveway. Blocking Michael's way, the boy stuck his chin out and asked almost belligerently, "Does Mom know you're coming?"

Last time he was here, they'd been best friends. Why the change? Michael wondered, afraid he knew. He said only, "She invited me."

"Oh." Drew scuffed his feet on the pavement and thought about it. "Well, I guess you can come in, then."

Michael would have been amused if he wasn't already so conscious of being an intruder. "Thank you," he said gravely.

Drew dropped his bike on the lawn and led the way in. They followed the aroma of Italian cooking to find Colleen in the kitchen.

Michael's instant response to the sight of her was sexual, which dismayed the hell out of him. Her vibrant hair was bundled in a loose knot from which tendrils curled on her long, slender neck. She was slim, fine-boned, her creamy redhead's complexion flushed from the heat of the stove. But it was her pregnancy that jolted him like a fist in the stomach. The swell of her belly was visible evidence of her fertility, her femininity. God help him, Michael was reminded on a physical level that his seed was in her, that their bodies together had created the baby she carried, though he had never touched her. Her pregnancy gave her a softness, a mystery, the more potent for his part in it.

The realization shot to hell the excuse he'd fabricated to let himself off the hook: if he reacted sexually to Colleen, it was only because she looked like Sheila. But right this minute Colleen didn't. And he wanted her, anyway.

Oh, God. What if she ever guesses?

Think about it later, he told himself.

"Uncle Michael's here," Drew announced. "He says you invited him."

Colleen's head turned and her startled gaze flew directly to Michael's.

"Yes, I did," she said, sounding just a little breathless. "He's having dinner with us. Hello, Michael."

"You mean, we're not having macaroni and cheese again?" Drew asked.

Michael pretended not to notice the look she gave her son. "You'll have your uncle thinking we never eat anything else."

"Yeah, well, sometimes it seems like..." The kid subsided under her stare.

"Go wash your hands and then come set the table," she told him before smiling at Michael as prettily as if he was a truly welcome guest. "I'm sorry I'm running behind. Although I don't suppose you're used to eating this early, anyway. But with children you find yourself making changes..." Colleen puffed her bangs off her forehead and threw up her hands. "I can't seem to say the right thing to save my life! Let me try again. Would you care for a glass of wine? I'm afraid it's not very good wine, but—"

He interrupted. "If I can't tell exotic brewed coffee from instant, what makes you think my taste in wine is any better?"

This time Colleen's smile was grateful. "Coming right up."

Michael was careful to keep the conversation light, leaning one hip against a counter and sipping a mediocre burgundy while Colleen dropped the spaghetti in boiling water and checked the garlic bread in the oven.

"Business is picking up," she was saying as she carried the food to the table. "But not as much as I'd like. The fabric store at the mall is part of a chain. They can undercut me on prices, and I know even some of my regular customers only come to me for the kind of fabrics they can't get there."

"So you need a bigger customer base. Play on your selection, the fact that you carry unusual fabrics. An easy way of getting at a large audience is those coupons that are distributed in the mail," Michael suggested. "I hear they're effective."

"I assumed they were expensive."

"I don't believe they are, and the return can be very high." Kim appeared in the doorway, and Michael smiled. "Hello."

"Hi," she mumbled with one of those shrugs kids do so well. She wandered over to her chair and slumped dejectedly into it.

Michael glanced with raised brows at Colleen, and she rolled her eyes. "Later," she mouthed, and he nodded.

She called Drew to the table, where they all bowed their heads and said a brief grace before passing around bowls. Kim brightened a little at the sight of the spaghetti.

"Cool. I thought we were having hot dogs tonight."

Colleen's cheeks turned pink again. "Obviously," she said lightly, "I need to vary the menu."

Before Michael could say anything, Drew turned to him and asked in a conversational way, "Uncle Michael, are you taking my mother to court?"

"Drew!" Colleen exclaimed, dropping one of the bowls with a clunk. "For heaven's sake! This is something Uncle Michael and I need to figure out. It's none of your business." To him, she said, "I'm sorry. I...well, I had to explain."

The boy ducked his head. "I just wanted to know what court *is*."

Kim's lip curled. "Gol, don't they teach you little kids anything?"

In measured tones Colleen said, "Kim, you don't talk to your brother that way. Drew, we'll discuss it later."

The coward in Michael wanted him to take the out she'd offered. But he was suffering enough guilt where she was concerned. So he shook his head.

"No, that's okay. Drew, one kind of court is when somebody is arrested by the police for a crime, like stealing."

He explained about trials and juries as simply as he could manage. When Drew nodded, Michael continued, "In a case like your mother's and mine, there's no jury. But somebody has to decide who our baby will live with once he—" Michael glanced at Colleen "—or she is born. If we can't, we'll go to court and both tell our stories to a judge, who will then decide for us."

Drew's forehead crinkled. "But what if you don't like what he decides?"

Michael's eyes met Colleen's. The one look was enough to tie a knot in his gut. Then her gaze shied away and she said very steadily, "One of us probably won't like what the judge decides, but we'll both have to accept it. Unfortunately I can't always have my way, any more than Uncle Michael can."

"I wish you wouldn't talk about it!" Kim burst out. "I don't want to think about the baby!"

Drew stuck his tongue out at her, but Colleen reached over and squeezed her hand. "I'm sorry, honey. We'll change the subject now."

Michael couldn't seem to tear his gaze away from her slender hand, wrapped around her daughter's. He was torn between two powerful forces: terrible hunger for a touch that tender—God help him, for *her* touch—and bitter envy. If just once in his life he'd been able to reach out that readily, he might not be so alone now.

Colleen gently disentangled her fingers, breaking the spell, but when Michael lifted his gaze he found her watching him. Some knowledge of what he felt was in her eyes, and for a shattering moment their gazes held. At last, by sheer force of will, Michael looked away.

Neither of the kids seemed to have noticed anything, although how they could have missed the tension between their mother and him, he couldn't imagine. He was damned careful not to look at Colleen again for a few minutes, until Drew had told them enthusiastically and at great length about soccer sign-ups.

"I brought home a paper about it, Mom," he told her eagerly, at the same time stuffing garlic bread into his mouth. "It's only twenty dollars: I can play, can't I? Ian's gonna. He says his dad might coach, except he coached his sister's team last year and he might again. I don't know why he'd want to coach *girl's* soccer."

Kim snapped, "What makes you think *boys* are so much better?"

"Guys!" Colleen exclaimed. "Can't we have peace until we finish eating?"

Kim subsided into unhappy sullenness, and, once assured by his mother that, yes, he could play soccer, Drew began to gobble his spaghetti. Michael watched him out of the corner of his eye. Did all boys his age eat that much? Or was their usual diet so depressing, he was grabbing what he could while the chance was there?

Colleen managed to make the rest of the meal more pleasant than the beginning, although she couldn't possibly be as relaxed as she seemed. She probably wished he'd go to Timbuktu, Michael thought ruefully.

If so, she was too good a hostess to show it. After dinner, she set the kids to clearing the table and made coffee for Michael and herself. They carried it into the living room.

The living room was cramped. Colleen's quilting frame took up a large space in front of the picture window, while a handsome sectional overfilled the rest of the room. Michael assumed it was from her more prosperous married life, like the maple coffee table and end tables. They didn't fit with the slightly shabby, builder's-grade tan carpet, or the outdated, avocado green drapes.

Once he'd sat down, Colleen settled about as far from him as possible.

With her legs curled under her and her long hair slipping out of its knot, Colleen had no resemblance to Sheila. That should have let him relax. Oddly enough, the fact that he wasn't having to deal with his unresolved feelings for his wife made him more conscious of Colleen, not less.

He didn't want to be so aware of her every breath that he waited for the faint rise and fall of her chest. He didn't want to find his gaze wandering from her face down the length of her throat to the hollow at the base, where he imagined her pulse beating.

Michael looked away. He hoped to God she hadn't noticed his reaction to her. Of course, he found that she was watching him over the rim of her coffee cup.

She said abruptly, "It seems as if we always talk about me. How are things going for you, Michael?"

He couldn't decide whether she really wanted to know or was grabbing for the first topic that occurred to her.

"Fine," he said, hoping she didn't push it. "How are you feeling, Colleen?"

"Back to me, huh?" Her extraordinary eyes were steady and unsettlingly perceptive, her tone tart. "Amazingly enough, I'm fine, too. Now we've shot two subjects. What do *you* want to talk about?"

"How about Kim for starters?"

His choice was a smart one, because Colleen grimaced and looked down at her coffee. Away from him, thank God. She said, "It's tough at her age. She hasn't made a single friend yet, and she's feeling awfully lonely."

Michael frowned. "What about Drew?"

"Oh, he's fine, which doesn't help matters. We have a little jealousy working here, too. The trouble is, it's easier for a kid Drew's age, especially—at the risk of sounding sexist—for a boy. They seem to do things in crowds, and they're perfectly happy to add one more. On the other hand, the fifth-grade girls go in pairs. As Kim puts it, they all have best friends already.''

"And it's almost summer vacation. What are you going to do with them once school's out?''

Colleen sighed. "Probably the YMCA day camp. Kim's really too old for it, but she's not old enough to stay by herself all day. What else can I do?''

If the last was a plea, he couldn't answer it. Instead, he studied her, for the first time in weeks, months, shedding his own preoccupations to wonder about her motives. He'd thought about her plenty, but mostly in relation to himself. Realizing that, Michael felt selfish as hell.

"Why did you move?'' he asked. "Was it just to be near Sheila?''

Colleen set down her coffee cup and smiled a little sadly. "We came to Clayton because of Sheila. I had lots of reasons for moving.''

"What were they?'' he asked quietly.

Layers of complex emotions shadowed her eyes, reminding him that she had depths he had never seen. Her response wasn't quite what he'd expected, any more than most of what she did was.

"Let's make a deal,'' Colleen said, lifting her chin in an unmistakable challenge. "I'll tell you why I moved if you'll tell me how you really are.''

Not by a twitch did he show her how little he wanted to open the door she was knocking on.

"Why?''

"Because I don't know you.'' She shrugged gracefully. "Because I never will if we don't get past 'fine.'''

Michael wanted to tell her to forget it. He had no desire to talk about sleepless nights and emptiness so vast it echoed. He didn't want to talk about guilt, or why he was hanging around her house like a hopeful stray.

But she was the one person he couldn't keep evading. They shared something too basic: their unborn baby. She had a right to learn enough about him so she could trust him with their child.

He let out a long breath. "All right."

"Well." Suddenly she wasn't so anxious to meet his eyes. "There were lots of reasons. The kids and I kept the house after my divorce, but I got so I didn't want to live with memories. And it didn't really suit us on our own."

"Too big?"

"Too expensive," Colleen said. "Plus, I slowly realized it wasn't the kind of house I'd have chosen on my own. Sort of like this couch." She ran a hand over the plush surface. "After a while, you start thinking about things like that."

He already had. But Michael wasn't ready to admit that, even if he'd wanted to take the chance of interrupting her musings.

"Originally I figured I should stay where the kids could see Ben often, but...oh, it didn't work out all that well." She pushed her hair back from her face. "Ben had a habit of forgetting he'd made plans with them. Or they'd spend the weekend with him, and he'd either be absorbed in paperwork the whole time or he'd hire a baby-sitter so he could go out. It was one disappointment after another. I thought it might be good for them to be far enough away that they didn't have any expectations of him anymore. I thought it would be easier if they *couldn't* visit him than to have him not bother."

When she lapsed into silence, Michael nodded his head toward her. "What about you?"

"Me?" Looking surprised, Colleen returned from wherever her thoughts had taken her.

"Do you miss anything you left behind?" Michael asked. He didn't usually get that personal, but he found he was very curious to know how she felt about her ex-husband.

Like a bird studying something intriguing, Colleen tilted her head to one side. "You mean Ben, don't you?"

He shrugged, pretending disinterest. "Your job, city life, friends."

"Not city life. Not Ben." Her wrinkled nose gave her ex-husband the same status as something moldy in the back of the refrigerator. Michael was oddly gratified. Colleen went on, "Friends, of course. But Sheila was here," she added simply.

As she'd observed once, all roads led to Sheila. Michael chose not to follow this one. "I should let you get back to the kids."

She saw right through him. "Not on your life. It's your turn."

"I meant it when I said I was fine. What do you want me to say?"

All the humor was suddenly gone from her eyes; instead, they held compassion. "You don't look fine."

"I don't sleep very well," he said on a surge of anger. "So what? There's nothing unusual about that."

Still she wouldn't let it go, though her voice was soft. "Do you miss her?"

"No!" he snapped. "Yes! Hell, I don't know."

Crinkles formed between her brows. "Are you mad at her for dying?"

"Damn, you don't know when to stop, do you?" He hadn't even been aware of rising to his feet. All he knew was that he was standing now, glowering down at her.

Colleen tilted back her head to look at him. Other than that, she didn't move at all. She sure as hell wasn't scared of him. He'd have felt like the lowest crud on earth if she had been.

"Well, are you?" she asked again.

His voice was raw. "No. I feel guilty. Here I am, left with everything she ever wanted on earth. Why didn't I die, instead? Hell, I drive over the speed limit sometimes, too. So why her? Why?" He was shouting, but still Colleen didn't quail.

"Sheila wanted *you*," she said, uncoiling to stand in front of him. He was shocked to feel her hand laid gently on his cheek, even more shocked to realize he was crying. "If you'd died, she wouldn't have had you anymore."

"She didn't want me." Michael shook his head blindly. "Not anymore. Maybe not ever. She wanted to be married. She wanted children. I just happened to be there."

Colleen's hand stilled; she slowly pulled back. Looking perturbed, she searched his face, her eyes huge, pools he could drown in if he didn't get a grip on himself.

"That's not the way Sheila talked about you."

He cursed and shoved his fingers into his hair, backing up until he bumped into the coffee table. "Don't listen to me. All I do every night is lie in bed and think. I've thought fifty times about every moment of our lives. If you do that, after a while you start imagining things."

"I did wonder sometimes from the way she talked..." Colleen began slowly.

Michael tasted acid in his throat. "Forget it. I'm tired, that's all. There's a reason I didn't want to go past 'fine.'"

"You should talk about how you feel."

"No." He shook his head. "I'd say things I didn't even mean. Listen, I'd better go. Tell Kim and Drew—" Michael stopped.

One second she was with him, the next Colleen's attention had turned elsewhere. Inward. When she focused on him again, she smiled. "Come here," she said, her voice velvet. "Talk to your son."

He couldn't resist. A minute ago she'd been Pandora opening the forbidden box, but now she was holding open the gates to heaven. He crouched in front of where she'd sank back down on the couch. She took his hand again, just as she had the night in the kitchen, and set it on her belly under her shirt.

Her skin was smooth, warm, the nicest thing he'd ever touched. His entire being was focused on that one point of contact. But it wasn't enough. The moment in the kitchen when he'd realized he was attracted to *her,* not to the memory of his wife, had changed everything. He wanted to move his hand, caress her. He wanted...

Something poked at his hand. Michael looked at her in shock. "What the hell was that?"

Her lips still had that tender curve, and her eyes were soft. "A foot or a knee. Maybe he just elbowed you."

"He?"

Colleen made a face at him, but her eyes still had that dreamy quality. "For some reason I think it's a boy."

"Yeah. Me, too."

"Really?"

"Uh-huh." Michael moved his hand over the tight, silken surface of her stomach, felt the baby shifting within her. It was the damnedest thing. Only reluctantly did he finally remove his hand and stand up. "Amazing."

"It is, isn't it?" Her gaze touched his and skittered away. Somewhere in there, she, too, had become self-conscious.

Michael escaped as quickly as he could after that, knowing he'd been a fool to come at all, but unable to regret the evening.

And knowing damned well that by tomorrow he'd be counting the days until he could visit again.

MICHAEL RAN the sandpaper back and forth again and again over the wide plank of oak. At this stage, he could have used his belt sander, but some no doubt primitive instinct insisted he use his bare hands as much as possible to build this toy chest. The pull on his shoulder muscles, the gritty texture under his fingers, were satisfying.

So was the feel of the wood when he ran his fingers over it. Different woods had different textures. From long practice, he could tell with his eyes closed whether he was working with cherry or oak or maple.

This shop was the one part of the house that was entirely Michael's. His stamp showed: racks and pegboards provided a place for every tool; screws and nails were sorted and labeled in tiny, plastic drawers; the room was spotlessly clean.

Sheila had called him obsessive. He could never convince her that he organized tools so that he could put his hand on what he needed when he needed it. Every tool was rust-free, well oiled and in its place.

He hadn't decided yet whether to paint the toy chest or just finish it with linseed oil. Little kids liked bright colors, but then the beautiful grain of these slabs of oak was wasted. Maybe he'd paint part of it—say, the sides—and use a clear finish on the top. Or just paint the letters of his son or daughter's name. They were going to be carved out of the solid oak lid, not tacked on. Cameron. Or maybe Catherine. He wouldn't finish the chest until he knew.

It wasn't as if he wouldn't have time after the baby was born. He hadn't memorized a developmental timetable yet, but even he knew that babies couldn't roll over for a few months, much less dig a stuffed animal out of a toy chest.

Michael's hand slowed as his thoughts drifted. As ignorant as he was, the idea of bringing the baby home and having sole responsibility was a little scary. He didn't even know how to change a diaper.

"To hell with the environment," he muttered. "I'll buy paper diapers." How wrong could you go with them? All he had to do was watch a few Pampers or Huggies commercials on TV. Free lessons.

Anyway, he wouldn't be the first parent who'd had to learn on the go. Probably most had to. For all her hunger for parenthood, Sheila hadn't even baby-sat as a teenager.

"I tried it once," he remembered her saying, her nose wrinkling in the same expression of distaste he'd seen on Colleen's face when she talked about her ex-husband. "This little monster wanted to run after his parents when they left. Every time I turned my back, he unlocked the front door and took off. I spent the entire evening with one hand braced on the door. That was it for baby-sitting. I told Colleen she could have it. *I* worked at Joe's Burgers, instead."

Of course, as a new mother she would have had a sister to call at every minor alarm. Colleen would have coached her through any crisis. Michael tried to imagine himself picking up the phone at midnight to ask Colleen what to do with a baby who wouldn't quit screaming. It would be all but admitting he wasn't capable.

Michael supposed his brother's wife would give him advice. They'd never been close, partly because she and Sheila hadn't hit it off, but Jennifer was a nice enough woman, with two kids of her own. But she wouldn't drop everything to come running over, either.

His hand stopped altogether. He grimaced, looking down at the plank without really seeing it. Once in a while he wondered if he was crazy, thinking he could raise a child by himself, thinking he could do anywhere near as good a job as Colleen. He'd seen the way she hugged her children and smiled at them and gave them quick kisses in passing, all so naturally. He pictured himself trying to do the same, as awkward as she was comfortable with physical affection.

Was he going to let his dream go that easily? he wondered. If he compromised now, he might as well say goodbye to it. On his own, he would *have* to learn how to parent. As a weekend father, he'd never get over being awkward. He would never know what it felt like to come first in a little boy's eyes.

Hell. Michael tossed down the sandpaper. There he went again, adding up reasons to justify what he was doing to Colleen. How many times had he gone over the same basic facts, counting them off like a clerk taking inventory?

Michael knew instinctively that nothing cut deeper to the bone than the loss of a child. If he hurt at the idea, what must Colleen feel? Bringing a baby home from the hospital was a pipe dream for him; for her, it was real. To go through labor and then walk out of the hospital with empty arms would tear her apart.

He rose to his feet with sudden violence and threw the first thing that came to hand—a rasp. It clattered off the potbellied wood stove at the other side of the room and fell to the floor. "Damn it," he said explosively, "she should have thought of that before she agreed to have my baby!"

Why in God's name hadn't he stayed away from her? But no, he'd had to go knocking on her door, driven by some bizarre need to know her better, this woman who was the mother of his baby. Well, look where it had gotten him. He'd discovered his wife's sister was everything Sheila hadn't been. He'd discovered that his body responded sexually to Colleen in a way it hadn't to Sheila in a long time.

He'd discovered that he didn't want to hurt this woman who should have stayed a stranger.

But that was exactly what he was doing. Every day that passed, he was hurting her. And her kids.

For starters, she couldn't afford that lawyer she'd had to hire to fight him. Thanks to Sheila, he knew damn near to the penny what Colleen had sunk into the shop and what she was living on. One of the things that was keeping Michael awake nights was wondering what she'd cut back on to pay Joseph Warren's ninety bucks an hour. How many nights lately had Colleen served her kids macaroni and cheese or canned chili for dinner because she couldn't afford anything else?

"Hell," he said again, and gave the rasp a frustrated kick before he picked it up and put it in its place.

He might as well face it, Michael thought in anguish. He wasn't going to be able to seize his own happiness at Colleen's expense.

So what was the answer?

CHAPTER EIGHT

"AH, YES. MR. DELANEY." The hostess picked up two menus from a rack. "This way, please."

Michael stood back courteously for Colleen to go ahead of him. She would just as soon have trailed behind. She'd reached the point in her pregnancy where she felt herself waddle. It didn't help that her maternity wardrobe hadn't included a dress even remotely suitable for a restaurant this elegant. But then, in silk she would only have looked like a Maharajah's elephant instead of a working one.

Some consolation.

The hostess seated them in a private alcove. The table was covered with a heavy white cloth; twin flames flickered atop tall white tapers set in silver candlesticks. Colleen accepted a leather-covered menu and opened it, making a pretense of scrutinizing the choices. But the truth was that she was too nervous to care what she ate.

What did Michael want to talk to her about? What was it that couldn't be discussed on the phone, or in her living room during one of his occasional visits?

"The London broil is good," Michael said suddenly. "Or the filet mignon."

"London broil sounds fine." Colleen closed the menu. The moment she set it down on the table, she was sorry. She could have hidden behind it for several more minutes.

"Wine?" he asked with lifted brow.

"I'd better stick to milk," she said.

"Milk?" His gaze dropped from her face to her stomach. "Oh. I'm sorry."

"That's okay."

Silence. The candlelight, intended to be romantic, cast shadows on his face, emphasizing the starkness of his cheekbones and his deep-set eyes. He'd lost weight, Colleen thought. She wished she could see him better, guess what he was thinking.

The waiter appeared just when the silence was becoming unbearably thick. "May I take your orders?"

But he left too soon, leaving them in their small circle of golden candlelight, alone as they had never been before.

Well, she'd been a coward long enough. Whatever he had to say couldn't be worse than worrying about it.

"Why are we here, Michael?"

She could feel the increased tension, though he didn't move a muscle. "You wouldn't rather wait until we've eaten?"

Colleen shook her head.

"All right." In a dark suit and white shirt, he was a stranger again, handsome, remote. "I've been thinking. You suggested once that we share custody. I'm prepared to consider the idea now."

On some level, she had guessed this was coming. "Why?" she asked.

"Because I made the mistake of getting to know you. You were...an abstraction originally. Selfish as it sounds, I didn't take your feelings into account. Once I add them to the equation, I have to admit it makes more sense for us to work something out."

His speech was smooth, businesslike. *The equation?* How many points had represented her emotions, how many his? Colleen didn't make the mistake of thinking him unemotional; she had seen too much pain in his eyes, seen his desperate need for his child. But even now he couldn't admit what he felt.

Carefully Colleen asked, "What did you have in mind?

His impassivity cracked. "I don't know. Alternate weeks. Or you have him Monday through Thursday, me Friday through Sunday. Something like that."

Tears stung at her eyes and she bowed her head, blinking hard. Ridiculous to cry, but she couldn't seem to stop herself. She felt as if somebody were wringing out her heart, twisting it to squeeze out every last drop of hurt and pity.

His chair scraped as he leaned forward. "Did I say something wrong?"

"No." Colleen shook her head blindly. "No, it's nothing. Pregnant women get emotional."

He didn't buy it, but he sat back. Out of the corner of her eye, she saw the waiter approaching. Grabbing the stiff, elaborately folded napkin, Colleen surreptitiously mopped her tears.

The salads and drinks placed in front of them interested Michael no more than they did her. Even after the waiter left, he made no move to pick up his fork.

As though they hadn't been interrupted, he challenged, "Can you think of a better alternative?"

"For us?" she said bitterly. "No. For the baby, almost anything would be better."

His shoulders had a rigid set. "What the hell does that mean?"

She knew how hard it must have been for him to reach a point where he was willing to compromise. He'd probably expected gratitude from her. She couldn't blame him if he was angry.

"Can you imagine what it would be like?" Colleen begged for his understanding. "To go home from school three days a week to one place, and then have to go somewhere else the other days? To want to tell Mom something, but today 'home' is with Dad? To wake up nights and not remember where you are?''

"Yes, I can imagine!" The suppressed violence in Michael's voice shocked her more than his offer had. "But what the hell do you suggest? That we slice the kid down the middle so we can each keep half?''

"No. I think maybe…'' This was hard to say. In a rush, to get it over with, she said, "Maybe there's no way all three of us *can* be happy. And I don't want a defenseless child to be the unhappy one just so you and I can get what we want.''

"Damn it!" He pushed back from the table and half stood, then forced himself to sit again, his entire body radiating tension. "You're the one who suggested this in the first place. Now you throw it back in my face!"

Colleen spoke past the lump in her throat. "I'm sorry. I hadn't thought then. But I have now. Endlessly. And I don't want to raise our little boy or girl that way. I'd almost rather give him up.''

A caustic laugh escaped him. "But you're not willing to give him up, are you?''

Wordlessly Colleen shook her head. She felt him glaring at her, but she didn't look up. Meeting his gaze now would be a form of challenge; it would acknowledge that they were enemies. And perhaps she was a coward, too; she didn't want to see the contempt that must be in his eyes, the dislike.

"Then I guess we'll be seeing each other four weeks from now in court." His voice was flat; he reached for his silverware. "Let's have dinner.''

Colleen had never sat through a longer meal. The food was tasteless, the candlelight and china and fine linen a mockery. She and Michael were trapped in a bubble of silence, isolated from the murmur of voices around them, the click of silverware on china, a throaty laugh, the efficient waiters. She tried not to look at him; the few times their gazes glanced off each other, he was as quick to return his attention to his food as she was.

She wondered how they appeared to the other diners, the waiter. A handsome man, a pregnant woman, candlelight… Would anybody else notice that they weren't speaking, didn't meet each other's eyes?

Afterward Michael took care of the bill and escorted her out, careful not to touch her. Outside, the warmth of the day still lingered though the sun had long since set. A canopy of stars glittered in the velvet darkness of the sky.

And still that terrible silence held. Michael opened the car door for her, circled around the front and got in himself. Colleen fastened her seat belt, then knotted her hands together on her lap and stole a glance at him. In the indirect light from the dashboard, his face was harsh, frowning, wiped clean of any soft emotions. Though the engine purred, he shoved the gearshift roughly into first, accelerating hard enough that the car leapt forward.

Colleen stared sightlessly out the window. Inside she was a mass of anguish and guilt and searing regret. She wanted to reach out and touch Michael, not drive him away! In her mind's eye she saw him the last time she had laid his hand on her belly. In that touch she had felt warmth and strength and yearning. She had wanted to sway toward him, to lay her head on his shoulder, to feel his arms around her. All impossible now.

Was she wrong, horribly wrong, to go back on her word?

The five-minute trip across town took an eternity, but at last the BMW swung into her driveway. Michael turned off the ignition and reached for his door handle.

"No!" In the well of silence, the one word was shockingly loud. Colleen struggled to moderate her voice. "Please. You don't need to walk me in."

Michael went still for a moment, then sat back, wrapping both hands around the steering wheel. Without looking at her he said, "You won't change your mind?"

"If I knew what was right—"

He interrupted her coldly. "I didn't ask you what was right. I asked if you've made up your mind once and for all."

Colleen desperately fumbled for the door handle. "I don't know!"

For an instant his control disintegrated. His voice was a painful rasp. "Good God, how did we get into this?"

Colleen succeeded in opening her side door. "Sheila," she said, scarcely recognizing her own voice. "We both loved Sheila."

For the first time Michael turned to look fully at her. Voice raw, he asked, "What do you think she'd tell us to do?"

Colleen had no answer. If Michael was right about their marriage, perhaps Sheila would prefer Colleen to raise the child who had been a gift between sisters. But Colleen couldn't help remembering how eager Sheila had been to tell Michael about the pregnancy. She'd held nothing back then; there'd been no suggestion that the baby was only for her, that she thought he didn't want it or wouldn't love it. No, she'd expected him to share her joy, and he had.

And so Colleen cried, "I don't know, damn you!" Her voice cracked. "If I knew, I'd do it!"

That night as she lay in bed, her window open so that moonlight and the scent of the roses she'd planted drifted in, she relived that last brief conversation.

What do you think she'd tell us to do?

Why hadn't she lied and said, ''I think Sheila would want me to raise her baby''?

Colleen knew the answer. Because whatever else she had done to Michael, she'd never lied to him. And although she'd known her sister better than anybody else in the world, Colleen hadn't the slightest idea what Sheila would have wanted for this baby.

Now, in the night when ghosts were supposed to walk, Colleen begged, *Sheila! Come back! Tell me what you want!*

But she felt nothing; no comforting presence, no sisterly touch. She tried to picture Sheila and saw only the teenager, laughing, twirling, dancing away from some responsibility or another. For the life of her, Colleen couldn't seem to dredge up the woman her sister had become, the woman who yearned so for a child of her own.

That woman, Colleen remembered bleakly, had died because she was careless, certain despite everything of her own invulnerability. And if the baby had been of her body, it would have died, too, that day.

No, there would be no help from Sheila. She lay silent now, her restlessness forever quieted. And Colleen was alone, as she had never been before.

COLLEEN HADN'T BEEN this scared since the dreadful day word came that her mother had had a heart attack. The flight to Seattle and taxi trip to the hospital had passed in a blur, but her wait for the doctor was all too clear in Colleen's memory. The hard, plastic seats, the coffee machine and paper cups, the magazines she picked up and put down when she couldn't seem to make sense of the words. And then the footsteps in the hall, the door opening. She had slowly risen to her feet, her heart hammering, her throat thick with unshed tears, knowing when she saw the doctor's face, before he spoke a word, that she had come too late. That the loving circle had been broken.

This waiting room wasn't so different, though the seats were upholstered. She'd opened a *People* magazine to an article on the latest sensational murder, but even the lurid details couldn't draw her out of her cycle of worries.

Where was her lawyer? What if he didn't show up? Would they postpone? What if this particular judge regarded the role of surrogacy with such distaste that he was biased from the start? Would having turned down Michael's offer of joint custody go against Colleen?

A footstep outside brought her head up. Joe Warren appeared in the doorway of the small waiting room, and Colleen's heart jumped, then resumed a hasty rhythm that made her dizzy. She felt a dreadful mix of terror and relief.

"It's time," he said, then raised a brow when he saw her face. "Hey, don't worry. Piece of cake."

Of course *he* looked completely relaxed; his hair was damp, as though he'd come straight from the health club. She could picture him playing a hard game of racquetball, maybe lying afterward in the sauna, dressing leisurely, taking his time getting to the courthouse. Half of her fiercely resented his casual attitude; the rest of her was comforted that he apparently regarded this as routine.

She struggled to her feet, feeling the baby lurch as her motion startled it, then followed Joe Warren past the reception area in the small courthouse to an unmarked door. To her surprise, inside was a conference room, not the anticipated courtroom. Her heart skipped another beat when she saw that Michael was already there, seated on the far side of the long table beside another man. His dark head was bent as he listened to something his lawyer was saying, but he looked up when she entered.

For just an instant their eyes met, Michael's bloodshot,

some flicker of emotion showing in them before a betraying muscle in his cheek jerked and he turned away.

Colleen wanted to cry out. But, painfully conscious of his lawyer watching her, she kept her head bent as she sat. If only her pregnancy weren't so conspicuous! She could no longer secretly touch her stomach under the table and tell herself her baby was safe. The birth was so close, and yet her child's fate was out of her hands. All she could do was plead her case today. But a complete stranger, the judge who would walk through the door, could condemn her with a few strokes of his pen.

Joe Warren had described Judge Garner as innovative but unpredictable with custody cases. What if he decided that, in agreeing to the contract with Michael and Sheila, Colleen had given up all parental rights? What if she couldn't even visit?

By now her heart was slamming against the wall of her chest; she was sweating, and the hands she pressed against her stomach were shaking. *Calm down,* she told herself. *Breathe slowly.*

Joe Warren didn't seem to notice her panic. He exchanged a few friendly remarks with Michael's attorney, then opened his briefcase and pulled out legal forms and a yellow lined pad covered with notes, arranging them neatly before him.

Almost immediately the bailiff appeared and they stood for the judge's entrance. Colleen had imagined a dignified, white-haired gentleman, but it was a woman who swept in, her black robe settling around her when she stopped abruptly at the head of the table. Middle-aged, with graying dark hair fastened in a bun, she had shrewd brown eyes and a pursed mouth. She seemed to assess Michael and Colleen as she sat down, arranging her robes around her.

She laid her gavel on the table, produced a pair of half

glasses and perched them on her nose, then peered at the paperwork in front of her. After a moment she looked up over the rims of her glasses. "Well, gentlemen, Mrs. Deering, shall we get started? As you can see, I prefer an informal atmosphere. I find it helps prevent an adversarial approach. Mr. Warren, why don't you explain the situation."

Colleen's lawyer smiled persuasively. "Thank you, Your Honor. As you can see, Mrs. Deering is expecting a baby in just a few weeks...."

Colleen listened in silence as he described her move to Clayton, her contract with her sister and her sister's death.

So much emotion, such drastic decisions, reduced to so little!

The judge leaned back in her chair, folded her hands and steepled her fingers under her chin. "So," she said after a moment. "I gather Mrs. Deering is less inclined to give her baby up to her sister's husband."

Her baby. With painful hope, Colleen wondered if the pronoun indicated that the judge sympathized. Or was it a casual reference?

"Exactly," Joe Warren said. "She was willing to go to extraordinary lengths for her beloved sister, but her acquaintance with Mr. Delaney isn't close. What Mrs. Deering could do for her sister, she doesn't feel able to do for a near stranger who was related to her only by marriage. A mother already, she can't face the agony of giving up her baby under these drastically changed circumstances."

Judge Garner's incisive gaze cut through Colleen's veneer of calm before being leveled at Michael's side of the table. "Mr. McDermott, have you any argument with the facts as Mr. Warren has presented them?"

Michael's lawyer, an older man, shook his head. "I don't believe Mr. Delaney and Mrs. Deering have any dispute over past history. The question is who will have custody. Mr. Delaney understands Mrs. Deering's qualms. He sympathizes with her pain at losing her sister, and shares it. But the fact remains that he and his wife had a verbal agreement with Mrs. Deering—she was to carry his child to term, then hand it over. I feel sure that even Mrs. Deering is aware that a contract doesn't have to be written to be binding. Mr. Delaney lost his wife. He does not want to lose his son or daughter, too.''

Throughout the attorney's plea, the judge had scrutinized Michael. Despite herself, Colleen did the same. He held his head up and unflinchingly met the judge's gaze. His expression was almost detached, the emotion beneath betrayed only by clenched jaw muscles and his very stillness.

Colleen wondered what that rigid control cost him. Did he ever go home and slam his fists into the wall, scream at the fates? Or was he never able to let go?

The judge pursed her lips. ''Mr. Delaney, Mrs. Deering, have you two attempted to reach a resolution on your own, or is compromise out of the question?''

For the first time since they'd begun, Michael looked directly at Colleen. His expression was implacable; he was passing the buck to her and daring her to lie.

Her attorney said smoothly, ''Custody is difficult to compromise over. I believe Mrs. Deering is reasonable—''

''Yes,'' Colleen interrupted. ''Yes. We have discussed it, without coming to a conclusion. Michael—Mr. Delaney—feels it's his right to raise his child. But this is my baby.'' She knew she was begging and didn't care. ''I know I can provide a loving home. We discussed—he suggested—joint custody, with alternate weeks or something like that. I refused. I believe with all my heart that children need routine and security and stability. I don't think those can be provided with alternating homes. We reached a stalemate."

Judge Garner directed a look of inquiry at Michael. "Mr. Delaney, is that a fair description of your negotiations?"

"Yes. I, uh…" His face twisted, and Michael shoved his fingers through his hair. "Yes," he repeated, his voice hoarse.

"Hm." The judge leaned back in her chair and appeared to contemplate them for what must have been a full minute. She drummed her fingers on the table, and Colleen was riveted to them. The tap-tap-tap might have been her heart, drumming in her ears. She sat frozen, enduring the wait, terrified of its end. She didn't look at Michael, couldn't bear to see his expression in case the decision went for her.

Finally the fingers stopped drumming and the judge said abruptly, "Mr. Delaney, Mrs. Deering, I have the impression that you're both well-meaning people, that you want the best for your baby. Now, I can make a decision. That's my job. But wouldn't you really rather make your own?"

Colleen's attorney leaned forward. "Your Honor…"

Judge Garner's glance silenced him. "Let's set a new date two weeks from now. In the meantime, I recommend that you attempt again to arrive yourselves at a parenting plan. Should you fail to, I'll do it for you." She picked up the gavel, whacked it on the table, then tucked her glasses into a pocket of her robe and swept out of the room, the court clerk and bailiff behind her.

In her wake, Colleen felt numb. She looked across the table at Michael and his attorney, but they appeared peculiarly far away and slightly distorted, as though thick glass separated her from them. Even Mr. Warren's voice sounded distant.

"…set up a meeting. Would Thursday…?"

Apparently they set a time and place; she nodded, though

she didn't really hear. Her attorney solicitously helped her
to her feet and escorted her out of the conference room.
Colleen didn't look back to see if Michael was following.
She tried to concentrate on what Joe Warren was telling
her. He talked all the way out to her car, assuring her that
the postponed hearing was a good sign, indicating that the
judge was sympathetic.

"If she was hostile to the idea of surrogacy, we wouldn't
have gotten this response. I'm confident that, at worst,
she'll settle on joint custody, and she may go all the way
for us. Now, we can meet with Mr. Delaney and Mc-
Dermott, but if you'd rather hold firm..."

"No." Colleen stopped at her car. She tried to smile.
"The judge is right. We should decide ourselves. Will you
call me with the time?"

"Hey." He lightly cuffed her on the arm. "Cheer up.
Things will work out."

"Thank you," she said tearfully, and hurried to get in,
hoping he hadn't seen that she was crying.

Afterward, she didn't even remember the drive home.
Thank God, she hadn't had to go back to work. Melissa
Anderson, a woman of about Colleen's age who'd taught
several classes in machine quilting at her shop, had offered
to fill in anytime. Colleen had an hour before the kids got
home from school.

She lay down on her bed and fell asleep almost instantly.
She woke up, disoriented, when the front door burst open
and Drew bellowed, "Hi, Mom! How come you're home?"

She got up and wandered to the top of the stairs. "Hi,
guys. I had a headache and came home to lie down. But
I'm feeling a little better. How was your day?"

Drew dropped his pack on the hall floor. "Soccer sign-
ups end this week. Can we go to the library and sign up
tonight?"

Right this second, Colleen didn't care if the check bounced. "I suppose," she said. "How was your day, Kim?"

She shrugged. "We got moved again in class. Now I'm sitting next to a *boy*. He's a jerk."

Drew had already disappeared into the kitchen. Colleen heard the refrigerator door open.

"Is he really a jerk," she asked as she came down the stairs, "or just your average eleven-year-old boy?"

Kim shrugged. "I don't know, they're all jerks. How do you tell the difference?"

"Good question."

Colleen had the weird feeling that she was outside herself watching as she maintained a perfectly normal conversation with her daughter. She was tired, bone deep, but Kim didn't seem to notice that anything was wrong.

As Colleen made dinner and then took Drew to the library to sign him up for soccer, she kept blocking any thoughts at all about the hearing. *Later,* she told herself. *Tomorrow. Just don't think about it right now.*

She tucked the kids in bed at their normal nine o'clock, then went into the living room, turned on the lamp beside the quilting frame and sat down. Her thimble protecting the finger that pushed the needle through the layers of quilt, she popped the knot at the end of the thread through the top. From long practice, Colleen began a line of tiny, even stitches.

She saw Judge Garner's face, but shoved the image back into hiding. *Not now.* Michael's face twisting. *Tomorrow,* she told herself. Heard the judge saying, "I can make a decision. But wouldn't you really rather make your own?" *I won't think about it.*

Colleen's hand rocked faster and faster, until she blinked and saw that the stitches were getting bigger, uneven.

"Damn," she whispered, and stopped, closing her eyes.

A knock on the front door brought her head up. Who would come by at nine-thirty? Colleen dropped her thimble onto the stretched quilt and hurried to answer.

She flicked on the porch light and opened the door a crack with the chain on. Michael stood on the front step.

Her heart lurched uncomfortably. He was large and solid, the kind of man who could make a woman feel safe for the rest of her life.

My enemy, she thought, but the part of her that so inexplicably responded to him didn't believe it.

"Can I come in?"

Colleen gave herself a shake. "Yes, of course. I'm sorry." She unhooked the chain and opened the door. "Come on into the living room."

He followed her. "Are the kids in bed?"

She turned to face him. "Yes."

"Good. I, uh, waited in hopes we could talk alone."

Michael wasn't doing anything to change her sense of unreality. Was she supposed to offer him coffee? Discuss whether their attorneys had earned their fees?

"I don't mean to be unfriendly, but what do you want to talk about?" Colleen asked.

He just stood there, hands at his sides, somehow filling the room with his presence. Perhaps it was the dark house or the silence from upstairs that made her so painfully aware of the hour and the fact that he was a man and she was a woman. Or perhaps she had the power of prescience.

For what he said was, "Will you marry me, Colleen?"

...held... open and... closer her eyes.
...there on the... door brought her back to... What
would come by... maybe...... Colleen dropped her chin into
...her... and turned to answer.

...She looked in the... and opened the door to
reveal... She... looked... for a... first two
it... look back it... readily, he was large and solid
...kind of man who... resembles a woman... just for her...

CHAPTER NINE

STUNNED, COLLEEN STARED at Michael. Without taking her
eyes off him, she backed up until her legs bumped the sofa,
then sank onto it. *Marry him?*

"Don't say anything yet," he urged swiftly. "Will you
just listen for a minute?"

She bobbed her head, still too shocked to speak or even
know what she felt.

Now he pushed his hands into his pockets and began to
pace. "I've been thinking. It's not like this baby—our
baby—was an accident. He was created out of love. Maybe
not in the usual way, but that doesn't matter now. What
does is that he deserves two parents." He paused and
looked at her.

Colleen nodded again, automatically.

Michael took a deep breath. "I was remembering what
you said about how all three of us couldn't be happy. And
then it occurred to me that there's one way we could be.
There are other advantages to marriage for both of us. I
know you're struggling financially. I can change that. I
know you worry about your kids not seeing their father
very often. I... They might not accept me, but if they
did..." His shoulders hunched. "I'm willing to try."

"But—" her voice was a croak "—what about you?"

For the first time Michael looked away from her.
Roughly he said, "I hate going home. It's so damned
empty. I've thought about selling the house, but a condo

doesn't hold a lot of appeal. When I'm over here, I see what I'm missing. That makes it even harder to go home.''

"But…marriage?"

He stopped his pacing right in front of her. Michael's eyes, never bluer, met hers. His expression was unguarded, leaving him vulnerable. "I won't say I'm in love with you," he said very directly, "but I'll do my damnedest to make ours a decent marriage. I think we have that potential. Unless the whole idea is repugnant to you."

Colleen's heart squeezed. "No, I…no. I'm just…you took me by surprise." A half-hysterical giggle escaped her. "Oh, Lord. I sound like some Victorian young lady. Except I'm not young. Michael, are you *sure?*"

"Yeah. I'm sure."

Colleen sat, staring up at him, this man she had trouble remembering had ever been her sister's husband. She studied him as though she had never seen his face before. He had movie-star looks: a high forehead and Slavic cheekbones, a straight, patrician nose and a mouth that gave little away. Only the lines from nose to mouth and beside his eyes showed his age and kept him from being too handsome. And those eyes of his, clear and blue as a high mountain lake, unexpected with his tan and his straight, dark hair.

Repugnant? Hardly, Colleen thought, a little stunned at what she'd just discovered about herself. Why had she never acknowledged how attracted she was to this man? Why had she told herself so many lies to explain her physical reaction to him?

Dumb question—there was something almost biblical in the prohibition: *Thou shalt not covet thy sister's husband.* It was natural that she had walled away the knowledge, hiding it even from herself. But Sheila was gone now, and it was Michael's baby Colleen carried. Nothing had to stop them now.

But…did she *like* him? Colleen wondered a little wildly. She supposed she must, she realized with near surprise, or she would have succeeded in hating him, as hard as she'd tried. Michael wasn't an easy man to know, but what woman really did know the man she was going to marry? Some things had to be taken on faith. Instinct was all she could trust.

Michael shifted uneasily, and she realized how long she'd been staring at him. She gave her head a shake to clear it and looked down at her hands, which rested protectively over the mound of her stomach and the child within.

"Is that a no?" Michael asked, sounding strained.

"No," Colleen said, in a sort of wonder. "It's a yes."

He crouched in front of her, and a part of her noticed how the denim strained over the muscles of his thighs. Urgently he asked, "Do you mean that? You'll marry me?"

It was the best she could do for her baby, Colleen told herself. And Michael would be a good father to her children if they let him.

"Yes." She felt very peculiar, light-headed, like a helium balloon. It was unsettling, this feeling, but exhilarating, too. "Yes," she repeated. "I'll marry you."

His expression didn't change, he didn't smile, but the invisible tension charging the air vanished. Michael's shoulders relaxed, his voice was still deep, but less gruff. "Good."

"How do we…well, go about it?" Colleen had a sense of déjà vu. She'd said that once before, to her sister.

The reminder was jolting. Colleen sent out a silent plea, as she had the other night. *Sheila? Are you there? Do you mind?*

She expected silence, the vacuum she'd felt that other night, but this time her call was answered differently. A sensation of warmth enfolded her, of comfort and close-ness, as though somebody had just hugged her.

But not Michael. He had stood up and retreated a few steps, as if the practicalities allowed him to restore his guard. "I thought—" he cleared his throat "—we'd talk to the pastor of the church Sheila and I attended."

Sheila. Feeling grief and joy in equal parts, Colleen mused about connections. The same minister who had bur-ied her sister would marry Colleen and baptize her child when the time came. The choice seemed right, if also pain-ful.

"Okay," she said steadily. "I suppose we'd better make it soon."

His gaze flicked to her stomach, then met hers again. "I'll call him tomorrow and let you know what he says."

"All right." That familiar sense of unreality was over-taking her. Had she really just agreed to marry a man about whom she had never consciously thought in romantic terms? A man who had never kissed her?

"Well," Michael said, sounding as awkward as she sud-denly felt, "I'll get out of here and let you go to bed. I'm, uh, sorry I didn't buy a ring."

"That's okay." Colleen struggled up from the soft cush-ions. "I'm not a diamond-solitaire kind of woman."

"I wouldn't have chosen diamonds for you," he said surprisingly. "An emerald would suit you better."

You were the deep pool below. The one with the trout and all the shades of green. Cold and clear, but somehow shadowy, too.

He had a talent for saying the unexpected, for leaving her at a loss as to how to respond. Well, she'd have to learn how, Colleen thought tartly, or this marriage would be very short.

"Thank you," she said, trying for dignity, "but don't

feel you have to buy a ring. It's not like ours will be that kind of marriage.''

Michael's brows had drawn together during her stiff little speech, but his voice was mild. ''I take the 'until death do us part' stuff seriously. I wouldn't have asked you to marry me otherwise.''

She flushed. ''Well, of course not, but we shouldn't pretend... I mean, I should be honest with the kids, don't you think?''

He was suddenly remote. ''That's up to you of course. They're your children.''

Colleen could only nod.

Michael took a step toward her. With one hand, he raised her chin. Before she could do more than feel a shiver deep inside, he bent his head and kissed her. His mouth was warm, but the kiss was frustratingly brief. As he lifted his head, she tried to read his expression, but without success.

''Good night,'' he said, and turned away.

By the time she reached the door, Michael was halfway down the walk. ''Good night,'' she called, but he apparently didn't hear her. He got into his pickup without looking back.

Slowly, Colleen shut the door and turned the dead bolt. Then she closed her eyes and rested her forehead against the doorframe.

What on earth had she agreed to?

COLLEEN AT HIS SIDE, Michael stood stiffly before the altar, facing the minister. Michael's brother, Stephen, waited a few steps away, as did a friend of Colleen's from the quilt shop. Behind them only the first pews were occupied, on one side with Drew and Kim, and on the other with Stephen's wife and two children.

Every cough, every shuffle of feet, was magnified in the

almost empty church, with its polished, wood floor and high, arched ceiling. Late-afternoon sunlight poured in brilliant, jeweled colors through the stained-glass window.

He should be listening to Pastor Norman, who was lecturing them about the duties and joys of the marital state, perhaps in lieu of the counseling he normally would have required but had forgiven this time for the sake of the baby. But his words, however wise, didn't seem to be penetrating. Other occasions were overlaid on this one, like a double-exposed photograph. Michael's first wedding. Sheila in traditional white satin and lace, radiantly beautiful, her face perfectly made-up, a star attracting all eyes in the midst of solemnity. He remembered the funeral, this same man talking about death and rebirth and eternity. And now Colleen, quietly dignified in the soft drape of a peach-colored dress that let her pregnancy be what it was: the supremely feminine moment.

"Marriage is a promise," Pastor Norman declared, "a sacred trust. You must have trust that this man, of all others, that this woman, of all others, will hold in cupped hands your pain, your fears, your dreams, and never let them slip away."

Why did he believe in this ceremony, in binding a woman to him, Michael wondered, when he knew perfectly well how often cupped hands could open and let pain and fears and dreams slip away? Why did he feel so sure that he was safe in Colleen's hands, that she gave only promises she would keep?

As though in logical succession, he wondered how her children felt about his marrying their mother. They had arrived with her, Kim in a green dress with ruffles, her brown hair French braided, Drew tugging at his necktie; both were unnaturally solemn and still. Even without looking at them, Michael could feel the intensity of their gazes.

His attention snapped back to the ceremony when at last the white-haired minister turned to Colleen, the open Bible in his hands.

"Do you, Colleen, take this man, Michael, to have and to hold from this day forward, for better or for worse, for richer or for poorer, in sickness and in health, to love and to cherish, till death do you part?"

She was pale, her skin almost translucent against the rich fire of auburn hair drawn back into a loose French roll. Her voice was a thin thread. "I do."

The minister's earnest gaze turned to Michael and he repeated his question. "I do," Michael responded, without hesitation, without glancing at Colleen. He would rather have walked barefoot up a rattlesnake-infested gully than show any of the emotions that twisted his gut.

"The ring?"

Michael reached into his pocket and produced the antique gold band encrusted with tiny emeralds that he had known was meant for Colleen the moment he saw it. The emeralds were leaves on a wandering vine etched in the gold. The ring was quietly pretty, as she was, and had the old-fashioned air of dignity that was so much a part of her.

Michael turned to her and held out the ring. Her lips parted when she saw it, but whatever protest she had meant to make, she swallowed. She must have realized, just as he had, that it was too late now for any kind of argument, too late for regrets. Touching her hand as little as possible, he slipped the ring onto her slender finger. It fit perfectly and looked right there, as he'd known it would.

In sonorous tones the minister proclaimed, "I now pronounce you husband and wife. Those whom God hath joined together, let no man put asunder." He paused for effect, then smiled faintly. "You may kiss the bride."

For the first time, a little color showed on Colleen's

cheeks. Her lashes fluttered, and then she looked up at Michael with wide eyes in which he read apprehension.

She was more than pretty, he thought, his heart squeezing. Even pale, even with shadows beneath her eyes, Colleen had the gentle beauty of a tiny, fragrant violet, the subtle grace of fine-grained wood, the warmth of a crackling fire. In the instant before he bent his head, Michael imagined her as an old woman and knew she would still be pretty, her fine bones more prominent, her skin crinkly and soft, her smile as warm.

She lifted a hand and rested it tentatively on his shoulder as their lips touched, lingered. He had to force himself to lift his head.

God, forgive me, Michael begged, *for wanting this woman. Sheila, forgive me.*

Their gazes met and held for a second too long, his gaze betraying all his torment. The emotions he saw in hers were just as complicated, defying him to understand them. He seldom prayed, but now he did: *Dear God, let us have done the right thing.*

If it was the wrong thing, they would suffer; they would punish themselves for the rest of their lives. This minute he felt enormous guilt. He had selfishly seized what he wanted when he saw the chance, even though he didn't deserve it—he didn't deserve *her;* even though Sheila, whom he had also promised to love and cherish, was only a few months cold.

He automatically went through the motions, turning Colleen to face their families. He saw her teeth close on her full lower lip as Drew and Kim rose to their feet but waited, instead of coming forward, too grave and self-contained for their ages. Michael's sister-in-law, Jennifer, hurried to hug each in turn, smiling with the forced gaiety of a good hostess.

"What a lovely ceremony! You look beautiful, Colleen."

Colleen gave a soft sigh and glanced down at her stomach. "How nice of you to say so. This isn't exactly how a woman imagines looking on her wedding day."

"You're beautiful," Michael said roughly. "Pregnancy suits you."

Jennifer glanced at him with surprise and faint speculation, which he ignored. Behind him, Stephen said, "Well, do I get to kiss the bride?"

Michael's brother, although about the same height, looked almost nothing like him. Stephen had sandy, sunstreaked hair and a grin that still reminded Michael of Dennis the Menace. Their personalities were different, too; instead of retreating in the face of their parents' remoteness, as Michael had, Stephen had sought affection and approval elsewhere. They were closer as adults than they'd been as children, though that still meant no more than a phone call every week or so.

Colleen smiled and tilted her face up for the obligatory kiss on her cheek, then said, "Drew, Kim, come here. Have you met Michael's brother and sister-in-law? Mr. and Mrs. Delaney…"

"Actually, it's Uncle Stephen and Aunt Jennifer now," Stephen pointed out.

Again Michael noticed the betraying flutter of lashes. It was probably no surprise that Colleen hadn't considered all the consequences of marriage, given the hurried arrangements they'd made. But seeing the emotions flit across her face, he wondered, Did she not like the idea of her children acquiring new relatives?

Jennifer said brightly, "And here are Stacey and Crystal." Michael's nieces stepped forward with a reluctance to match Drew and Kim's. Jennifer went on, "Stacey is eleven, Crystal fourteen. I hope you'll all be friends."

The younger kids gave each other sidelong glances and mumbled greetings. Only Crystal had the poise to smile and say, "Hi."

Colleen introduced her matron of honor. "Melissa teaches machine-quilting classes at my shop. She's been nice enough to offer to take over temporarily when the baby comes."

Melissa Anderson was petite and dark-haired, the possessor of a quick smile and a tendency to chatter. Michael didn't have the impression that she and Colleen were especially close. He was bothered that Colleen hadn't invited any old friends. Maybe she had, and they hadn't been able to make it. But maybe not; maybe she hadn't wanted any of them here because she didn't regard this marriage as meaningful or permanent. She had claimed not to find him repugnant, but that didn't mean she felt any attraction. If that was so, he couldn't blame her if she didn't want to make much of the ceremony.

His brooding was interrupted by Jennifer, who looked around expectantly. "Shall we go on to the restaurant?"

A poor excuse for a wedding reception, the dinner couldn't be called a success. The kids sat at one table, and despite Jennifer's effort to get them talking, Michael heard little but whispers between siblings.

Stephen offered an obligatory toast. After it was drunk, an awkward pause followed. Then Colleen said stiffly, "I want to thank all of you for coming. Our marriage is a little unconventional, and you've been nice about it."

"Don't be silly!" Jennifer said after a silent moment of communication with her husband. "We're all for it. I don't see how you two could have come up with a better solution."

Michael thought she was even telling the truth. Jennifer was a nice woman who, like Colleen, believed family came first.

Stephen and Melissa tripped over each other hastening to agree.

Colleen gave a wobbly smile. "Thank you. I only hope Michael's parents don't mind."

"They sent their best wishes," Michael said, hearing the flatness in his own voice.

Little crinkles appeared on Colleen's smooth brow. "You said they retired to Florida?"

Stephen said, "Yeah, on a nice little lake. I imagine they figured they could only make one trip, and they'd save it to see their new grandchild."

"I suppose that makes sense."

But Michael could tell that it didn't really, not to her. When Kim got married someday, Colleen would be there no matter.

"We're not close," he said brusquely, and was sorry when she gave a tiny nod and looked away.

Eventually Melissa asked about their plans.

"To tell you the truth," Colleen admitted, "we haven't gotten very far in discussing the future. It's not as though we've planned a honeymoon or anything like that. This was all kind of sudden."

Her friend sounded surprised. "But what are you going to do for the immediate future?" She stopped, looking flustered. "Not that it's any of my business."

Colleen's cheeks flushed, and she studiously avoided meeting Michael's eyes. She gave a laugh that didn't sound natural. "We did get that far. Michael's coming home with me. That way...well, we don't have to uproot the kids while we consider our next step."

"I'll sell my house." He hadn't consciously decided; the

words just seemed to come of their own volition, but they sounded right. "I don't see how we could live in it."

She looked at him as though no one else was in the room. He wished it were true, that his sister-in-law hadn't steam-rolled him into this dinner. Colleen sounded tentative. "I've been thinking about it since we talked. If you're just worried that I'd be uncomfortable..."

"It's Sheila's house," he said gruffly. "Let's make a new start."

She searched his face. "Michael, if this is for me..."

"For both of us. Let's buy a big house, one where all the kids can have their own rooms. And I need an office, and you a sewing room." His voice had quickened. Funny he could see it so clearly. An old house, with a huge kitchen and a wide front porch and gnarled apple trees. And lilacs, and maybe an acre or two with a barn. And a rope swing. He'd always wanted one himself.

But he abruptly remembered the other people around the table. "We can talk about it," he said neutrally. "See what Drew and Kim think."

The party broke up shortly thereafter, probably to the relief of everyone. Unfortunately that left Michael to trail Colleen up to her front porch, toothbrush and pajamas in hand. He had followed her home in his own car, wishing he could hear the conversation taking place ahead of him in her old Honda. After parking behind her in the driveway, he was now waiting patiently for her to unlock her front door. Beside him her two kids were shifting from foot to foot.

"Jeez, Mom," the eight-year old finally whined.

"It's just stuck." She blew out a puff of air, and her voice vibrated with tension. "Michael...?"

It seemed symbolic that he had to let himself into her house, rather than sweeping her across his own threshold.

The lock gave immediately, and Michael thought he heard her mutter something about hating helpless women.

Brushing past Michael, Drew thundered up the stairs, flinging his tie over the banister as he went. Kim wasn't far behind.

"Can I change, Mom?" she called as she went.

"I suppose..." Colleen's voice trailed off at the slam of a bedroom door. She offered Michael an apologetic grimace. "I'm sorry. Drew hates what he calls 'stiff' clothes, and Kim was sure she looked like a five year old in that dress. Of course she loved it back when I bought it last fall."

"That's okay. This is their house."

They were still standing in the front hall. Colleen bit her lip and looked around. "I guess it's yours now, too."

Was she trying to see it through his eyes? If so, she didn't need to worry. Maybe this house was just a rental, but she had made it a home. A quilt in shades of blue and green in a kaleidoscopic pattern hung on the wall. Below it, on an antique cherry side table with turned legs, was a stoneware pitcher filled with bright yellow roses. The table needed refinishing, the pitcher had probably cost a dime at a garage sale, but the effect was charming and cozy. It reminded him of Colleen and why he was so drawn to her.

He had to clear his throat. "I'll try not to get in your way. You don't have to change anything because of me."

"Don't be silly!" She frowned, but she also crossed her arms over her swollen belly, as though to hunch in on herself. "I don't want you feeling like a guest."

Which was exactly what he did feel like—an unwelcome guest, at that. Colleen would probably give anything right this minute for him to disappear, go home to his own house. He'd even thought of suggesting he do just that, but, damn it, he should start as he meant to go on! And he meant this to be a real marriage.

"We, um, haven't talked about sleeping arrangements," she began, her cheeks pinkening, and he interrupted.

"I'd figured on the couch for now."

"Oh, dear." She nibbled on her lower lip. "That's not fair to you. But I...I don't know what else to suggest..."

"It'll be fine," he said quietly. He wanted badly to touch her, if only in reassurance, but instinct told him he would alarm her if he did. Maybe he was wrong—she was comfortable with physical affection in a way he'd never been—but he didn't want to take the chance. "Why don't you just do whatever you normally would? Unless you want to talk."

"I suppose we should." She gave an unconvincing laugh. "But if you don't mind, I think I'd rather wait. I guess getting married is enough for one day."

On the surface, the evening was pleasantly domestic. Colleen quilted, Michael pretended to read first the newspaper, then a book. The kids appeared on and off, mostly to request snacks. About the third time, Colleen sighed. "I suppose this means neither of you ate your dinner."

Underneath the surface flowed powerful undercurrents. Except for stolen glances, Drew and Kim ignored Michael. He himself read sentences over and over, and still they made no sense. His nerves prickled with his awareness of Colleen. He felt every breath she took, every time she looked at him. The silence was worse than the conversation they weren't having.

He couldn't relax, couldn't think of any excuse to get out of the room for more than a minute. Gritting his teeth, Michael wondered what had made him think he had a place here. This marriage had about as much chance of succeeding as a chronic check bouncer did of getting a loan.

The only reason Colleen had married him was to hold on to her child. Maybe the thought of financial security had influenced her, too, he didn't know. But she didn't want him, she didn't love him, and chances were she didn't even like him. Things hadn't changed much; what still counted was his ability to father a child.

Without thinking, he swore under his breath, which earned him an anxious glance. Unable to stand the tension for another minute, Michael shot to his feet.

He said the first thing that came into his head. "I'm going to go shave."

"Shave?" She looked alarmed.

Hell. A normal groom probably did shave before his wedding night so his whiskers wouldn't scrape his bride's face. Michael seemed to remember doing so on his honeymoon with Sheila. He couldn't think of any subtle way now of denying that he had designs on Colleen, so all he did was add, "And brush my teeth."

"Oh." Blushing, she jumped up with unflattering alacrity. "I'd better get the kids tucked into bed. Then I'll find you some blankets."

"No hurry," he said.

Whisking out of the room, she said hastily, "No, no, I'm tired, too. It's been a long day."

His sardonic eye took in the clock on the end table. Eight forty-five, and they were going to bed. Separately.

What a wedding night.

WOULD SHE and Michael laugh someday, looking back at their wedding night? Colleen punched her pillow and turned again, trying to find a comfortable position. The baby kicked her right in the pelvic bone, as though to remind her of his presence. Colleen made a face into the darkness. Why kid herself about Michael's reasons for marrying her? He was a decent man who would do his best, but it wasn't her he wanted. It was his son or daughter. Theirs was a marriage of convenience, plain and simple.

Surely it would get easier, Colleen thought plaintively. Of course tonight had been awkward! Even her wedding night with Ben had been. Marriage was a big step. Who knew what to expect? The thing to do, she decided, was to be practical about this, try not to read all sorts of emotion into it. In just a few days, she and Drew and Kim would become used to having Michael here; they would settle on a routine, and tonight's awkwardness would be forgotten.

Although maybe he was right that they should look for a new house. Originally Colleen had been surprised when he suggested moving in with her, instead of her and the kids moving in with him.

"Just temporarily," he'd said, in that calm voice she sensed he was using to lull her fears. "That way you don't have to worry about packing yet, and things won't change too suddenly for Drew and Kim."

Now, Colleen could admit to how relieved she had been. Part of her was convinced that her sister would have approved her decision to marry Michael. But telling herself that was one thing; moving into Sheila's house, hanging her clothes in Sheila's closet, eventually sleeping in Sheila's bed, was another. If their marriage was to have any chance at all, they couldn't live with Sheila's ghost.

Colleen laboriously shifted again, feeling as if she had a bowling ball plopped on her bladder. "Kiddo," she said under her breath, "you're a load."

Michael had been nice about sleeping on the couch. She'd just *assumed* they wouldn't sleep together, at least until after the baby was born. Not until they'd walked in the door tonight did she realized they hadn't talked about it. Of course he couldn't possibly *want* a woman who was eight months pregnant, but probably they should have discussed it. There were lots of things they should have talked about, but especially that one. Sex.

Did he want her at all? Did he assume they would make love as soon as it was practical, or was it something that would come when—if—they were both ready? When Michael kissed and touched her, would he be thinking about Sheila?

This was the first time Colleen could remember wishing she and Sheila hadn't so resembled each other. Every time Michael looked at her, he must be reminded of Sheila. Would he ever quit seeing Sheila and see *her*?

Sighing, she rolled over for the tenth time or so. *Her wedding night.* It was almost funny.

Colleen found herself remembering Ben, the way he touched her, the feel of his body fitting to hers. Mostly their sex life had been comfortable, familiar. Any magic had faded away long before Kim was born. She couldn't remember caring very much. She'd vaguely thought that sex was a small part of marriage, and she was otherwise content. Obviously, Ben hadn't been. She didn't even blame him.

Contentment didn't seem like the kind of emotion a woman would feel with Michael. From things Sheila and he had said, Colleen guessed that all had not been well with their marriage. But Sheila hadn't descended to feeling anything as dull as contentment or irritation. She'd sometimes been angry, perhaps lonely or hurt. But Colleen had never doubted that Sheila still longed for her husband—for the man Colleen had just married—with all her being.

But she was gone, and Colleen now had everything that had been hers. Except Michael's love.

Did she even want it? Colleen was far from sure. Marriage was one thing; it meant an extra paycheck, somebody to talk over problems with, run Drew to soccer on occasion, mow the lawn, check the oil in her car.

But love—that was something else. Michael Delaney was an intense man. He wouldn't give his love lightly, and he would expect as much in return. Thanks to her upbringing, the only real relationship she'd ever had with a man was her marriage to Ben, and with him she'd been able to hold something back. That reserve had prevented her from being devastated by the divorce. It had allowed her to make her children the center of her life.

Colleen didn't know that she wanted to change that. Of course, Michael hadn't asked her to—might never ask her to. So why worry?

No, what they needed to do was have a nice, sensible discussion and lay everything out on the table. She would tell him that sex would be fine eventually—when they knew each other well enough. Which they didn't yet.

A children's ditty floated through her mind. *First comes love, then comes marriage, then comes the baby in the baby carriage.*

Talk about backward, she thought sleepily. In their case, first came the baby, then the marriage. Love was optional.

CHAPTER TEN

"THIS PLACE HAS 3500 square feet, and it's loaded with amenities. You'll love the kitchen," the Realtor enthused, as she climbed out of the car.

Colleen accepted Michael's hand and eased herself out of the back seat. "How do you feel?" he murmured.

"I'm fine," she said, although she pressed a hand to her lower back, which seemed to have a perpetual ache these days.

The Realtor, a pleasant woman named Evelyn Coats, was talking about the landscaping, the three-car garage and the rec room *plus* a family room. Colleen scarcely listened. Instead, she gazed up at the pretentious English Tudor facade. She couldn't imagine living in a place like this. Maybe in the normal course of events, a person would gradually get used to wealth. She, on the other hand, had been struggling to pay for groceries just a few weeks ago.

Reluctantly Colleen followed the Realtor and her husband inside. How odd it still felt to think of him that way!

Inside, the coolness was a relief after the June heat of eastern Washington, but she hated on sight the black-and-white marble foyer and the cream carpet in the living room off to one side.

She hadn't liked any of the houses they'd seen today. The price range Michael had given Evelyn still staggered Colleen. She kept feeling as if somebody would slap her hand and tell her she didn't belong here.

"Michael..." she said tentatively.

But he was disappearing after Evelyn toward the kitchen and didn't hear her. Instead of following them, Colleen drifted into the living room and looked out the bay window. The house stood halfway up a dry hillside, the winding road lined with equally ostentatious houses in this new, upscale development. Below, Clayton was a green oasis; mature elms and maples lined the streets of pleasant old houses. In the apple orchards on the outskirts, trees marched in disciplined lines, heavy branches propped up with sticks. Beyond town were the hills, gold-green waves of wheat fields beside purple stripes of fallow earth that swept in curves over the crests.

"You don't like it."

The carpet was so thick she hadn't heard him coming. She tried to hide her start. She didn't want Michael to know how unsettlingly aware she was of him when he stood this close. Her nerves prickled, and even without turning she knew how lean and broad-shouldered he was in his dark business suit, how silent and contained the way he moved. She even knew that his face would be impassive, that he would be taking care not to give away his own feelings.

"Do you?" she asked.

The pause probably only lasted a few seconds, but to her it stretched out painfully. Still gazing out the window, she noticed Evelyn hurrying down the driveway to the car and leaning in as she hunted for something.

"No."

Damn him for being so uncommunicative, Colleen thought in frustration. It wasn't as though she hadn't tried; several times they had sat down to talk. Michael had suggested again that they put his house on the market and look for a new one. Colleen had agreed. If it was all right with her, he would call the Realtor. Fine. She had groped to remember all the other things she'd meant to discuss with him and could think of only one. Sex. As distant, as coolly polite as the conversation had been, there was no way on God's green earth she could ask, "Do you want to have sex with me? Or do you not care?"

And somehow, with that one subject lingering unresolved, with the constant wondering on her part, if not his, any openness between them had been barred. They had stayed strangers coexisting in the same house. When he cleaned up the kitchen after dinner, Colleen thanked him. When she cooked breakfast, he thanked her. They conducted polite conversations. Instead of getting used to his presence, she was more aware of it by the day. More aware of *him*.

But some things had to be said.

Colleen took a deep breath. "Michael, I don't know if this is such a good idea. Somehow when we talked about it, I wasn't picturing houses on this scale. Buying a place like this would be such an expensive commitment. And under the circumstances..."

She felt his sudden tension. "The circumstances?"

Why pretend? Colleen lifted her chin. "What if our marriage doesn't last?"

A flash of raw emotion crossed his face before he snapped, "Is that the attitude you went into this with?"

Colleen pressed a hand to her throat. "I didn't say—"

"Is our marriage so bad?"

She had a sudden memory of two days before, when she'd come home from work exhausted to find that Michael had already started dinner. He'd sat her down, made her a cup of herb tea and helped Kim with her math homework. Right this minute, it wasn't what Michael had done that she remembered; it was the tenderness she'd imagined she saw in his eyes.

"No," she said huskily, shaking her head. "No, it's not bad."

As simply as that, the atmosphere changed. He was still looking at her, but his eyes held a light that quickened her pulse, made her swallow hard. The air shimmered with unspoken emotions—all those things they should have said and hadn't. She was suddenly quite sure that he wanted to kiss her, that he was going to kiss her, and she forgot everything else in a rush of yearning for something she hadn't even known she wanted.

But they both heard the front door slam, and as quickly as a slide projector clicks to the next frame, Michael was stepping back.

His voice was hoarse, however, letting her know she hadn't imagined the stark hunger in his eyes. "We've made the commitment. Let's not worry about the money side of it. I think we'll be happier when we move."

Before she could respond, Evelyn appeared in the arched entry to the living room. She carried the multiple-listing book.

"Why don't we sit down and take a look. Obviously I'm not clear on what you want."

In the kitchen they all sat at the built-in booth and thumbed through the dog-eared pages showing houses for sale. Colleen was surprised when Michael zeroed in on a couple of old houses, both of which had acreage. Daily, it seemed, she had to readjust her image of him. Sheila's taste had apparently predominated more in her marriage than Colleen had realized.

"We'd better save looking at them for another day," he said at last, glancing at his watch.

Evelyn promised to make appointments with the owners for Saturday morning, and they headed back to the realty office.

Over dinner that evening, Michael suggested that Drew and Kim come with them on Saturday. So far, they still seemed to think of him as Uncle Michael, a favored visitor. His approach to them was diffident. On the couple of occasions he'd asked for help, there had been no suggestion he was issuing an order. Colleen wasn't quite sure what would happen when that changed.

She'd told them about her decision to marry him in the same, upbeat way she'd presented her foray into surrogacy. They had asked a few questions. Would Uncle Michael live with them? Would their last name change? Had he kissed her? She had been left uneasily wondering how they really felt about it, but knowing she couldn't change her mind. Drew and Kim would adjust. They *had* to.

Now, he reminded the kids, "It'll be your house, too."

"Sure, I don't mind going," Kim said, shrugging.

"What kind of house do you wish we'd buy?" Michael asked. He nodded at Drew. "Would you pass the broccoli, please?"

"I want my own bedroom," Kim said.

"You have your own bedroom now," Colleen said pointedly.

"Yeah, but if the baby's a girl, I'll bet you'd stick her in with me."

Drew scrunched up his face. "Or with me if he's a boy."

"Uh..." Colleen met Michael's amused eyes. "Probably," she admitted.

"And a family room would be cool, so we could have two TVs. Then we wouldn't have to fight about what to watch."

"Yeah!" Drew agreed. "And a hill for sledding."

Michael grinned, more relaxed than Colleen remembered seeing him with the kids. "I won't promise that. But we'll take it into consideration."

"I want a sunken bathtub," Kim chimed in. "Remember how Lorelei had one, Mom?"

"Uh-huh. It always sounded like the height of decadence," Colleen said.

"What's decadence?" Drew asked.

"Luxury," Michael said. When Drew still looked puzzled, he added, "Steak, instead of hamburger."

Kim, who had just taken a bite of her hamburger, said around the full mouthful, "Now that we have all of Uncle Michael's money, can we be decadent and eat steak, instead of hamburger?"

Colleen winced. Maybe, in her explanations, she had leaned a little too heavily on the practical reasons for her marriage to Michael. As sharply as she ever spoke to the kids, she said, "That was rude. Please apologize to your uncle..." She stopped, realizing she hadn't improved matters.

"Why don't we just make it Michael," he suggested, sounding unperturbed, not looking at her. "If you two are comfortable with that."

Drew frowned. "Aren't you our uncle anymore?"

"I don't think so. Here, do you want the catsup?"

Her son ignored the distraction. "What are you, then?"

Colleen touched his hand, half in warning. "Your stepfather. Do you remember our talking about it?"

Loudly Kim said, "I won't call him Dad."

Colleen glanced quickly at Michael, but if he was hurt by this first, small rebellion, he didn't show it.

"You have a father," he said, his tone mild. "That's why I suggested you just use my name. Unless you have a better idea."

Kim bent her head so that a curtain of brown hair hid her face. She pushed her baked beans around with her fork. "No, I guess that's all right."

"Sure," Drew said.

Colleen used the lull in the conversation to change the subject. "Drew, after dinner I want you to clear the table. Kim, you load the dishwasher, please. Then both of you be sure to finish your homework."

"Are you going somewhere?"

"A Lamaze class." Colleen picked up her dishes and took them to the sink. "You learn about childbirth in them. Your...Michael is going with me. The sitter should be here any minute."

"You already had *us*," Kim said. "How come you're taking a class?"

When Colleen came back to the table, she planted a kiss on the top of her daughter's head. "You know what, kiddo? I haven't had a baby in nine years. Just like I have to read your math book sometimes before I can help you, I figured it wouldn't hurt to brush up on the breathing techniques."

Michael stood, too, and smiled at Colleen over Kim's head. The rare smile transformed his lean face and reminded her of the simple joy and wonder there the day she'd announced her pregnancy. She felt an uncomfortable tug in her chest when he said, "Your mom may know everything, but I don't. I need a class. Otherwise, while your mom's in labor I'll be standing around wringing my hands."

Colleen's sense of humor had deserted her these past weeks, but now she felt a bubble of amusement at the picture. "Maybe you should pace and tear at your hair, instead," she suggested.

His smile widened into a grin, crooked and sexy. "You never know, I might even faint."

But at the class that evening, Colleen could see that he was taking his part in the business of childbirth far too seriously to opt out by keeling over. It was a very strange hour. There they were, the two of them, a couple just like all the others. The participants ranged from the absurdly young, a frightened-looking girl who couldn't have been more than eighteen with a long-haired boy no older, to several couples in their thirties. Most held hands as the instructor talked about the stages of labor.

Colleen looked down at her own enormous belly a little ruefully. She was obviously the closest to the end; under other circumstances, she would have started the four-week course at least a month ago. But Sheila was to have been her partner in labor, the one who sat beside her tonight, and since her sister's death, Colleen had blocked out thoughts of everything they'd intended to do together.

Asking Michael had been an impulse. Even as the words came out of her mouth the previous week, she'd half-hoped he'd make an excuse. But in her heart she'd known he wouldn't. He'd glanced up from the newspaper and said with what sounded like deliberate casualness, "Sure, if you'll be comfortable having me there." But his expression had told her more. For that moment, Michael wasn't a stranger staying with her; he was her husband.

In the classroom, the lights went out and a film began to roll. Colleen sneaked a glance at Michael and saw that he was watching with obvious fascination. She made herself look back at the screen, where a woman, cheerfully smiling through the early stages of labor, was having a fetal monitor hooked up.

Ben had attended Lamaze classes with her, though reluctantly. He'd felt like an idiot puffing and panting, he said, and made her feel foolish, too. But during labor itself, he was a rock, encouraging, supportive, occasionally funny. It had been one of his better moments, Colleen reflected.

She had a flash of remembering herself alternately whimpering and swearing, and Ben holding her hands throughout. "You tell 'em!" he'd said, his face inches from hers. Then, "Breathe, damn it!"

As she remembered it, her nightgown had been hiked up around her waist, her feet were in the stirrups, and she'd been sweating and gasping and pushing. Not a pretty sight.

What a horrifying thought. Did she really want *Michael* to see her like that? Worse yet, for that to be his first sight of her naked?

Some introduction to marriage.

The woman on the screen wasn't smiling anymore, but she wasn't screaming or swearing, either. No, she was dutifully doing her breathing while her unruffled husband rubbed her back. No sweat there.

Colleen sneaked another look at Michael, only to find that now he was watching her. She gave a weak smile and firmly fixed her eyes on the screen, though she remained so conscious of him beside her that she didn't even notice the triumphant conclusion to the film. Before she knew it, the lights were back on.

The instructor beamed at them. "Now, husbands, help your wives get comfortable on these mats. On your side, ladies."

Husbands got a lesson in giving back rubs, which had the saving grace that Michael was behind Colleen when he lifted her shirt and laid his large, warm hands on her back. Her reaction was shockingly intense, considering how essentially impersonal the contact was. Heat rushed over her in a tide, leaving goose bumps in its wake. He could hardly fail to notice them, but she was grateful that at least he couldn't see her expression.

Colleen closed her eyes when Michael began to gently knead her shoulders, then the long muscles on each side of her spine. It was natural for her to be starved for physical affection, she told herself briskly—except, she couldn't help remembering, that the couple of times she'd dated since her divorce, she hadn't felt any desire at all to get physical, much less be affectionate.

Never mind, she told herself. *Quit analyzing everything. Just enjoy.*

Michael seemed to know all the places that ached, and his deft touch untied knots that fussing about him had probably tied in the first place. But he also seemed to have a second sense about all the spots where she was most responsive. His fingers lingered on her neck and then traveled slowly, sensuously, down her spine to the small of her back. She imagined his hand traveling lower yet and gave a small groan, arching her back before she snapped her eyes open.

Good Lord, she was about to start rubbing against him like a cat in heat!

"Excellent!" the instructor proclaimed, standing just above Colleen. "See how you've relaxed her? A good massage is invaluable during labor." She proceeded to the front of the room and clapped her hands. "All right, class, let's work on the first stage of breathing now."

Colleen felt like an idiot all over again as she panted rhythmically to Michael's coaching. She could feel the heat in her cheeks, and her skin still tingled everywhere he'd touched. His deep voice was calm as he counted for her and then said, "Now, a deep breath. That's right," but she couldn't help noticing he was looking at her mouth and not meeting her eyes.

No wonder. She had forgotten how, well, *intimate* this was. What on earth had possessed her to ask him to come? He'd probably imagined the joys of seeing his son born without realizing he was going to have to hold her hand for hours first. But unless he chickened out, there was no way she could uninvite him.

In the BMW on the way home she asked, "Well, what did you think?"

"Does that breathing stuff really do any good?"

"Believe it or not, it does. Probably anything that distracted a person would work."

They traveled several blocks in silence, the interior of the car dark. Abruptly Michael asked, "Are you scared?"

"*Scared?*" She glanced at him in surprise. "Heavens, no! To tell you the truth, I'm looking forward to getting it over with. It'll be nice to be able to get out of bed again without it being a major production. I must look like a beached whale."

"You don't."

"Really?" she said hopefully.

"No. You look—" He stopped.

"I look?" Colleen prompted, in a near whisper.

"I told you." Michael spoke gruffly. "Beautiful."

"Thank you." What else could the poor man have said? Colleen studied his profile. "Michael, you don't have to do this if you don't want to."

"Do this—?" Frowning, he glanced at her. "What do you mean?"

The edge to his question made her feel defensive. "Stay with me when I'm in labor. If you'd rather not..."

"Don't be ridiculous," he said dauntingly, ending the discussion.

As soon as they got home, while he was still closing the garage door, Colleen paid the baby-sitter, a teenager who lived down the street. The head start gave her a chance to escape upstairs to kiss the kids good night and go straight to bed herself, even if it was absurdly early. She had done that a lot lately, sometimes quilting on the baby's Carousel Horses, using her hoop, but also discovering somewhat to her surprise that she could fall asleep at eight-thirty. She only hoped that Michael attributed her early bedtimes to pregnancy, not cowardice.

The next three days were long. Colleen sat as much as possible at work, but even so, by closing time her ankles were swollen and she was exhausted. Melissa had started out by taking over for an hour or so, when Colleen was desperate, but now she was working Saturdays and Sundays, and she'd insisted she could manage by herself for three or four weeks after the baby was born.

"I'll turn all your hand quilters into machine quilters," she'd promised impishly. "Just think how much faster they'll be able to churn out quilts, and how much more fabric they'll need!"

Business was steadily increasing, thank goodness, enough to pay Melissa's salary. Colleen kept reminding herself that she didn't have to worry so much about money anymore, but deep inside she didn't quite believe it—or wouldn't let herself believe it. Anyway, she had no intention of becoming dependent on Michael. Her shop was more than her joy; it was her safety net.

Saturday morning Michael insisted on taking the whole family out for breakfast before they met the Realtor at the first house. The kids were so excited about the prospect of having waffles at a restaurant, it made Colleen realize how few treats they'd had this past year.

"Can we order *anything?*" Drew asked, wide-eyed as he looked at the glossy menu.

"Why not?" Michael said, with a grin that made him look almost as young as her son.

Kim asked daringly, "Can I have a side of smoked ham *and* waffles?"

"You bet."

Colleen opened her mouth to ask if Kim really thought she could eat that much, then closed it. Michael was having fun indulging them. Did it matter if they didn't eat every bite? Thrift had become so ingrained in her she had trouble accepting that she didn't have to be so careful anymore. Maybe that was typical of someone in her circumstances who was newly married. Or maybe it was because she didn't *feel* married.

Evelyn Coats was waiting for them at the first house, a Victorian that would have had more charm if housing developments hadn't sprung up all around it. When Evelyn asked if they wanted to see inside, Michael glanced at Colleen with a lifted brow.

"It's up to you," she said, and wondered at his frown.

"Let's go on to the next place," he said.

On the way, they briefly discussed whether they ought to lower the asking price on his house. At the moment, his cleaner was coming in twice a week, but otherwise the house sat empty.

Colleen wondered how Michael felt about the prospect of going through Sheila's things and deciding what to save and what to get rid of. Everything that Sheila had touched or used or worn would hold memories. Even with everyday stuff—kitchen utensils or linen—some had been wedding presents, or the object of one of Sheila's passing obsessions. How many times had Colleen heard her sister say, "Col, you should see it! I've absolutely got to have one."

Perhaps cleaning out his house would be cathartic for Michael. Obviously he didn't want to live with those memories, but closing the door and walking away hadn't resolved anything. The memories were waiting, preserved, as though the house he'd shared with Sheila had been frozen in time.

Colleen shook herself out of her brooding when the car slowed to turn into a driveway. This place looked more promising even from the quiet road. The turn-of-the-century house was on the outskirts of the old part of town within bike-riding distance of the elementary school. The houses here were all well cared for in a comfortable way. Many still had an acre or more, and behind them stretched a young orchard of apple trees knee-deep in grass.

"Looks like it might be possible to keep a horse here," Michael said casually.

Colleen would have liked to clap her hand over his mouth. It wasn't fair to raise Kim's hopes like that when so much was up in the air.

But it was too late.

"Cool," Kim breathed as Michael drew the car to a stop behind Evelyn's. Both kids were out in a flash, heading for a small barn, painted gray-blue to match the house, with double doors standing open.

Despite her disquiet about their expectations, Colleen didn't even watch them go. She was pierced by an achingly sweet feeling of homecoming. The tall, straight house with gingerbread trim, a wide porch and a bay window reminded her of the one she'd grown up in, though it had been on a smaller scale. Perhaps it was the smells of freshly mown grass, the heady scent of the white, old-fashioned roses climbing the porch, that brought a sudden rush of memories: herself playing dress-up on the porch in her mother's clothes, tucking a rose behind her ear; her mother twirling her until they were both so dizzy they fell down laughing on the grass; hiding under the porch, peering out through the latticework, determined to stay there despite the cobwebs and the damp earth, watching as Sheila—maybe five or six at the time—ran from shrub to shrub in the yard hunting for her with cries of, "I know you're there!" and getting increasingly anxious.

Colleen gave her head a shake. Evelyn was talking about the new roof and remodeled kitchen, but Michael, although seeming to listen attentively, was watching Colleen. She crossed her arms self-consciously and said, at the first pause, "Well, shall we go in?"

The kids, chattering about the two stalls and the pasture, joined them as they wandered through the ground floor of the old house. The small front parlor had a window seat, as she'd somehow known it would; when she'd been about Kim's age, Colleen had spent hours reading and dreaming on the window seat. The kitchen was huge, with a brick floor, glass-fronted maple cabinets and tile countertop, the modern appliances discreetly hidden behind false fronts. Ceilings were high, the twelve-inch molding refinished to a warm glow. After following Michael and Evelyn through the library, dining room and back parlor, Colleen emerged into the hall just in time to look up and see her son swinging his leg over the stair banister preparatory to sliding down.

One look from Colleen had him innocently waiting at the top of the staircase. From there he and Kim ran ahead, calling, "I claim this bedroom!"

"I understand a third bathroom has been added here in the master suite…" Evelyn pushed open a door. "Oh, look at the claw-footed tub!"

Colleen stood in the middle of the large bedroom with sash windows that overlooked the lawn and the orchard, and thought, *This house is perfect. If only…*

At last she identified the source of the ache that gripped her heart. *If only we really were a family.* Instead, she had to wonder, Would Michael take another of the bedrooms? How long could they live together as strangers?

Beside her, he said quietly, "The small room next door would make a good nursery."

"Yes."

He must have expected more, because his gaze stayed

on her face. At last he gestured around them. "What do you think?"

"Do *you* like it?"

"Why do you keep doing that?" The edge she seldom heard was in his voice.

"Doing what?"

"Deferring to me. As if you don't have an opinion."

"I..." If she'd had time to think, she would have been more careful, but as it was, the truth just slipped out. "It's your money."

"*Our* money." His voice was still quiet, but real anger glittered in his blue eyes. "I don't remember signing a prenuptial agreement that labeled yours and mine. This is a community-property state, you know."

Evelyn was down the hall somewhere now; Colleen heard her talking to one of the kids. She and Michael were alone in the bedroom that would be theirs if they bought the house, the room in which they might someday share a bed like the four-poster here now.

"Do you *feel* married?" Colleen asked, surprising herself.

He blinked, silent for a moment. "Yes," he said finally in an odd tone. "I took the vows seriously."

Even the promise to love and cherish? she wondered. "I'm sorry," she said, pushing her hair back from her forehead. "There have just been so many changes lately. I guess I'm overwhelmed. Sometimes I have this feeling of...unreality. Do you understand?"

"Yeah." Michael let out a long breath. "You're right. I've been pushing you. Shall we forget moving for now?"

She should have felt relieved. She realized she'd been disgruntled from the start of their house hunting. The rental was *hers,* and on some level she hadn't wanted to surrender it, even if it was too small, even if they could afford a nicer place. However irrational, she would have said, "Yes, let's forget it," had Michael asked her yesterday. Or even this morning. But now...

Colleen looked around at the bedroom, with its pale yellow wallpaper and lacy window valances, the gleaming oak floor and the black claw foot of the deep porcelain bathtub with shiny brass fittings she could just see through the open door. Over the windowsill peeked one of those roses, elegantly packed with white petals that swirled around a green button eye. She could hear Drew's excited voice as he discovered the entrance to an attic, and the tap-tap-tap that could only be Kim twirling in one of the spacious bedrooms down the long hall.

Feeling as though she were stepping out of an airplane, trusting the parachute someone else had packed, Colleen admitted in a rush, "To tell you the truth, I love this house."

It wasn't what he'd expected. Michael's face was blank for an instant as though he'd braced himself for disappointment. When her admission at last sank in, his grin dawned slowly. "Yeah? Me, too. Shall we buy it?"

She blinked. "Just like that?"

"Why not?"

"Can you...can we afford it?"

His smile took her breath away. "Hell, yes."

"All right." Colleen gave a little nod, then a firmer one. "Let's do it."

Michael grabbed her hands, swung her in a circle, then planted a kiss on her cheek before vanishing out the bedroom door. Astonished, she stared after him. Then she smiled, feeling a funny little fizz of excitement mixed with her terror.

"Well, baby," she said, patting her stomach. "Shall we go look at your room?"

THEY'D MADE one more childbirth class. It was a good thing she'd already been through this twice, Colleen reflected, sitting on the edge of the bed now and waiting for the contraction to pass. If she'd needed more than a refresher, she would have been out of luck. When her muscles relaxed their grip, she hurriedly slipped into her robe and opened the bedroom door.

"Michael?" she called. "Hey, kids!"

"Do I have to get up?" Kim groaned from her bedroom.

"Yes, and hurry," Colleen said. "Wake your brother."

Could Michael have left for work already? she worried. But she'd have sworn she'd heard the kettle whistling in the kitchen only a few minutes ago. Colleen raised her voice and tried again. "Michael?"

He came out of the kitchen to stand at the foot of the stairs, a cup of coffee in his hand, his white shirt unbuttoned and a tie dangling around his neck. Even with another contraction coming on, Colleen noticed the expanse of brown chest and lean stomach, with only a dusting of dark hair.

"Yeah?" His expression altered and he set his cup down on the hall table. "Are you all right?"

"Um." She tried to smile, closed her eyes and leaned against the doorframe. A small gasp escaped her. By the time the pain receded and she opened her eyes, Michael was at her side. She licked dry lips. "It's show time."

Michael's hands closed on her upper arms. "Now? Good God, I don't know if I'm ready. Are *you* ready?"

Colleen gave a weak laugh. "I don't think that matters."

He was suddenly all business. "Can you get dressed while I rouse the kids?"

"Sure."

His hands slid down her arms, lingering, caressing. "Then I'll get them in gear." She'd have sworn he released

her reluctantly. But the moment she turned away, he was
moving. His bellow would have roused the dead. "Kim!
Drew! Up and at 'em!"

Colleen eased herself back down on the bed to wait out
the next contraction. They were coming closer and closer
together. "Well, Sheila," she said softly, "our baby is impatient. I think that's a good sign. So wish me luck, okay?"

A moment later, smiling, she reached for her bra.

CHAPTER ELEVEN

COLLEEN CONCENTRATED with all her being on Michael as the wave of pain lifted her and flung her forward. She gripped his hand so hard it must have hurt, focused desperately on his face. His blue eyes glittered and he wiped sweat from his forehead with his forearm, bared below the rolled-up sleeves of his shirt.

"One, two, three," he said steadily, "push!"

Groaning, sweating, Colleen gritted her teeth and squeezed her muscles tight.

"I see the head," her doctor reported. "That's it, keep pushing!"

Gasping, Colleen complied, though she wanted to scream and quit. The world had narrowed to this room, to the graph that showed the rise and fall of her contractions, to Michael's calm voice and clever hands and vivid blue eyes.

When the contraction washed away, Colleen seized the brief respite to close her eyes. She felt Michael's hand smooth her hair away from her sweaty face, and she tilted her head to prolong the caress.

This labor was longer than her others, more intense. She'd been at the hospital seven hours now, most of it in the grip of powerful contractions. Her baby was big, the doctor thought, and none too eager to come out. Colleen didn't know what she would have done without Michael, who'd been at her side from the beginning, encouraging, nagging, comforting, letting her feed off his strength.

"Here we go again," he said, the tension in his voice telling her that he hurt and hoped with her. "Breathe. That's it. One, two, three, *push!*"

Through the haze of her narrowed focus, she was only dimly aware of Dr. Kjorsvik declaring, "The baby's head is out! Keep pushing, keep pushing."

With an exultant cry, Colleen felt the baby slip out. She fell back against the pillows, sobbing for breath.

Now Michael's hand was the one to squeeze hers almost painfully. "You did it!"

A thin cry brought Colleen back up on her elbows. Dr. Kjorsvik stood, holding up a kicking, squalling, red baby. "You have a son," she announced.

At the sight, Michael looked as stunned as if somebody had punched him. It was as though he hadn't believed in his heart that a real baby would come out of all this. Colleen remembered feeling a little like that herself the first time.

Michael's white shirt was wrinkled, his dark hair standing in tufts, his exhaustion showing in bloodshot eyes and the deepened grooves between nose and mouth. But apparently he at last believed, for he turned an unfettered grin on Colleen, his exhilaration and astonishment almost childlike.

"Incredible," he murmured.

She was vaguely aware that she was smiling as foolishly. "We did it."

"You did."

She swallowed hard and reached out to take his hand, which closed warmly around hers. Her emotions felt raw. She suddenly wanted even more from him; she wanted to burrow her face into his shoulder, maybe even shed a few tears in the strong circle of his arms. But her inhibitions were flooding back, and the strength of her own feelings confused her.

"Nine pounds, three ounces," the nurse told them from Colleen's other side. "Who wants this cutie?"

However anxious she was to hold her son, Colleen deliberately held back. Let Michael have this moment.

"I guess I do," he said, sounding less than sure. The nurse gently laid in his outstretched arms the now cleaned and bundled infant whose tiny face was screwed up in a look of utter misery. The uncertain but wondering expression on Michael's face as he gazed down at his son would have been comical, had it not unexpectedly brought tears to Colleen's eyes. "He's so…little," he said, looking at her. "He hardly weighs anything."

The nurse smiled. "Believe it or not, that's hefty for a newborn. Does he have a name yet?"

Obviously afraid he would drop his son, Michael passed him to Colleen. For the first time, she cuddled her new baby close. She gently stroked a finger down his wrinkled cheek.

At the same moment, she and Michael both spoke. "Well, I thought…"

"What do you think of…"

They stopped. "You first," she said.

"I thought, if you didn't object, that maybe we could name him Cameron."

"For Sheila," Colleen said softly, her smile tremulous. She remembered talking about names with her sister. Perhaps it wasn't surprising that Michael, too, wanted the son who would have been Sheila's to bear a name she had chosen. Sheila must be on both their minds at this moment, which would have meant so much to her.

Michael nodded, his eyes on his son.

"Cameron," she murmured, rubbing her cheek against

the dark fuzz on the baby's head. "Cameron Delaney. I like it."

In the unfathomable way of babies, Cameron had recognized the soft pillow of her breasts, because he turned his face against her and began rooting for a nipple. Colleen laughed and started to open her gown. Then on a sudden surge of shyness, she hesitated. Michael had seen just about everything else today, but not her breasts. On the other hand, if she was planning to nurse, she was going to have to get used to him watching.

Heavens, she was blushing! Well, no wonder. How many women had had a baby fathered by a man who had never seen her breasts?

Cameron was beginning to make unhappy squeaks. Colleen took a deep breath and parted her hospital gown, trying to leave the fold so that it partially shielded her from Michael's gaze. Gently she guided Cameron's seeking mouth to her nipple, where he immediately got the idea and latched on.

Only then, horribly conscious of her hot cheeks, did Colleen let herself look up. Michael still stood beside the bed, his fascinated gaze on his son. Or was it on her breast?

Blushing even more fiercely now, Colleen concentrated on her newborn son, whose tiny fingers were curled into fists as he suckled. Dark hair like his daddy's, she thought, and blue eyes—at least for now. His nose looked like Kim's, but then with baby noses it was hard to tell. He was long and skinnier than Drew or Kim at birth.

"Cameron," she whispered, savoring the feel of his name, the tug on her nipple, the incredible closeness. Would Michael feel that bond, too? she wondered. She had never thought Ben felt the same way about their children as she did. Was that true for all men, or would Michael be different?

He was still watching his son, she discovered, and seemed unaware that she was studying him. Lean, dark and sexy, this man was her husband, the father of her baby, and yet so many of his thoughts and dreams were still mysteries to her. Colleen had one of those moments of disorientation, even disbelief. Nearly a year ago, she had agreed to carry his child, a momentous enough decision, but since then her world had turned upside down, and sometimes she didn't recognize it.

My husband, she thought, disbelievingly. *Sheila, where are you?* But she couldn't seem to summon a memory of her sister at this moment. Colleen tried to imagine the day as it had been intended to be: herself cradling the baby, her son, kissing the silky top of his head, and with regret and love handing him to her sister.

The thought was unimaginable now, but then, Sheila was gone, and nothing could bring her back or change the way things had come to pass.

My husband.

Colleen blinked and realized he was gazing at her.

His voice was deep. "Well?"

Time for another blush. "Well, what?"

"Any conclusions?"

"I was trying to decide if he looks like you," she lied.

She'd said the right thing. He stared down at his son. "God, I hope not," he said fervently.

Colleen was surprised into a giggle. "Well, you don't have quite so many wrinkles."

"Yet."

"And, um, you have a little more hair."

Darkly, Michael said, "For a few more years. Did I tell you my father's losing his?"

This time when she laughed, her nipple slipped out of

Cameron's mouth. He had fallen sound asleep. Colleen hurriedly covered herself with her gown.

The nurse appeared as though summoned. "Let me take him off to the nursery so he can be checked over," she said briskly, "and you can get cleaned up and we'll find you a room."

"I'll go call the kids," Michael said. "Do you want to see them?"

His sister-in-law was to have picked them up from the day camp several hours ago. "Could I?" she asked hopefully.

His eyes were tender, his smile lopsided. "I'm on my way."

A moment later he was gone, and her son was whisked off to the nursery. Only then did her tiredness sink in. She felt teary, and had never been so grateful for anything as she was for the warmed blanket the nurse tucked around her.

Later she vaguely remembered being transferred to a room, but she must have slept, because suddenly she became aware of Drew bouncing on her bed and Kim hovering shyly in the doorway, Michael behind her with his hand on her shoulder.

Colleen reached out one arm to Drew to give him a hug, then her other to Kim. "Come here, sweetie."

"Are you okay, Mom?" Kim asked, circling the bed to perch on its edge.

"You bet." Colleen smiled at Michael. "Do you want to go get Cameron?"

"One Cam, coming up," he agreed, and disappeared.

"We saw him through the glass," Drew said.

"What did you think?"

"To tell you the truth—" he wrinkled his nose "—well, he was kind of ugly."

"That's not true! He's cute," Kim said indignantly.

"He'll be a lot cuter in a few days," Colleen told them. "It's been a rough day for him, you know. All babies look funny for a while. Even you two did."

"Yeah, well, Kim still looks funny," Drew said, laughing uproariously at his joke. He gave a few more bounces and dodged the arm she flung out.

They were distracted by Michael's arrival with a bassinet. Inside it, the bundled baby was astonishingly small, only his face showing below a knitted cap. The motion had awakened him and he was trying to lift his head.

The frustration of failing brought a few grunts and snorts that escalated into a cry. Michael gingerly picked up his son and handed him to Colleen. Drew and Kim watched unblinkingly as Colleen eased open her gown and helped Cam find her breast. She knew darn well she was blushing again. It was a long moment before she sneaked a peek at Michael, to find him staring at the precise place their son was latched on to her breast.

She felt a tingling, and then a warmth that settled between her legs. Mildly shocked, she tried to convince herself that her response wasn't sexual. Her uterus was supposed to contract when her newborn nursed. That was all she was feeling.

Except she couldn't quite bring herself to look at Michael again.

When Cam had given up struggling for the milk that hadn't come in yet, Colleen let the kids take turns holding him, instructing them in how to support his head and how to pat him gently on the back until he burped. Out of the corner of her eye, she was aware of Michael listening intently, and realized he probably knew no more about babies than they did. Cam gazed fuzzily at them and seemed to have no objection to their efforts. Eventually she let Kim change his damp diaper and then he snuggled sleepily into the curve of Colleen's body.

She'd half expected jealousy—surely that would come—but right now even Drew was more fascinated than resentful.

"His belly button's gross." Drew made the same face he did when she put corn chowder on the dinner table. "It's going to fall off?"

"Uh-huh."

"Can I keep it when it does?"

Michael covered his laugh with a cough.

"See how little his fingernails are," Kim whispered.

Over her head, Colleen looked at Michael, who had pulled a chair up to the bed. He smiled at her, and she found herself smiling back, as though there was no tension between them, no doubts or fears or hesitation.

She felt tired, contented, accepting. *My husband.* No, better yet, *my family.* She had made the right decision, she thought. There might be a few rough spots ahead, but it was all going to work out fine. She knew it.

THINGS WERE GOING well. Too well, Michael thought. Nothing worth having was as easy as these two weeks since Cam's birth had been.

He stopped in the living room doorway, taking in the cozy scene. Colleen was curled on a corner of the sofa, nursing Cam, who was patting her pale breast. Michael almost groaned at the sight. He could easily become jealous of his own son.

Drew was off at a friend's house, but Kim sat on the other end of the sofa working a crossword puzzle in a desultory way.

Michael leaned one shoulder against the doorframe. "Kim, any chance you'd empty the dishwasher?"

The eleven-year-old dropped her pencil and jumped up. "Sure," she said cheerfully.

Michael realized he wasn't the only one who was waiting for the other shoe to drop. Small creases furrowed Colleen's brow as she watched her daughter willingly depart for the kitchen.

"This is unnatural. I'm starting to get worried about her."

"It'll wear off," he said, wandering into the living room. Despite himself, his gaze locked on his wife's open shirt. At that precise moment, Cam pulled back, exposing a damp, pink nipple. *Hell*, Michael thought savagely, wrenching his gaze away. He dropped onto the sofa, aware out of the corner of his eye that Colleen had flushed and covered herself. He'd no idea how much of what he felt she was sensing, but clearly it was enough to make her uncomfortable.

"Evelyn called," he said, with no particular inflection. "We have an offer on my house. She thinks it'll be in the ball park."

Colleen lifted Cam to her shoulder and patted his back. "Oh, good."

He waited, sensing she wasn't done.

"Michael, have you thought about cleaning the house out?"

"God, yes." He leaned his head back against the couch. "Sometimes I'm tempted just to hire movers and have them throw everything in boxes and put 'em away in storage. But I suppose we'll want some of the furniture, at least."

"Will it be so painful?" Colleen asked softly.

"Not painful." He wondered if he was lying. "Overwhelming. One decision after another. I'm not sure I'm ready to be ruthless yet. Getting rid of her stuff seems..." Michael hesitated, tapping his fingers on his knee. What a bizarre conversation to have with a new wife. In with the new, out with the old. Even more bizarre, given the relationship of his two wives. And yet, he knew that historically it had been common for men to marry their dead wives' sisters. Maybe the reasons hadn't been that different than his and Colleen's.

Colleen finished his thought for him. "A betrayal." He heard her take a deep breath. "If you want help…"

"Thanks." His smile felt more like a grimace. "I haven't opened Sheila's closet since before the funeral. I had to pick something out…" Hell. He wouldn't think about that. "I didn't know she had so many clothes. Dresses, blouses, sweaters. She must have owned thirty pairs of shoes. We could just give it all away, I suppose. Or keep things you or Kim would use. I don't know. You can do whatever you think's best, if you're willing to deal with it."

She managed a nod before they were interrupted by Kim, who stood in the doorway.

"Can I call Dad?"

"Honey, you don't have to ask my permission."

When Kim made no move to leave, Michael glanced up to see a peculiar expression on her face, a mix of defiance and trepidation. Abruptly she asked, "You know how I'm supposed to go to Dad's in a few weeks?"

Colleen put a hand to her head. "Oh, Lord, I haven't gotten the airline reservation yet. I'm sorry, sweetie, I'll—"

"No. The thing is, I don't want to go."

"You don't want—" Colleen stopped, obviously flabbergasted. "But you were so anxious…"

"That was before." Kim shrugged with elaborate nonchalance. "I want to be here when we move and stuff. And Cam would probably forget me if I was gone even for a couple of weeks."

"But you've been complaining about being bored from the minute school let out!"

Michael rarely intervened. What did he know about kids? But Kim was flushing and he could tell that Colleen just didn't get it. Casually he asked, "Do you want to think about it for Christmas vacation?"

"Yeah, sure. Maybe. Anyway, I'll call Dad." She vanished from the doorway.

Colleen shook her head dazedly. "Maybe I should have stayed in the hospital."

"Or we could check Kim in for the next four or five years."

"Aargh!" She managed to scream in a whisper, if such a thing were possible. It didn't take much to wake Cam, asleep on her shoulder. "Do you know, not that long ago we had a crisis because Kim decided she was going to live with her dad. And now she doesn't even want to visit him?"

"Jealous?" Michael suggested.

"Of what? Who?"

"Cam, probably. Me, maybe."

One minute, they were talking. The next, Colleen gave an artificial-sounding laugh. "Oh, I can't imagine. I suppose she thinks Cam'll be crawling any minute and doesn't want to miss it. And Lord knows, her relationship with her father warms and cools on any given day depending on whether or not he's returned one of her phone calls."

Did she not want to admit Kim might be suffering from any real confusion? Or did she view his comment as criticism and didn't want to hear it from him?

"You know her best," he said mildly. "You've never said how the kids felt about our marrying."

She raised her eyebrows. "They took it fine. They haven't said anything to you about it, have they?"

"No."

"I'll talk to Kim. If she's jealous of anybody, it's probably Cam. Don't worry about it." Colleen carefully straightened and put her bare feet to the floor. "Do you suppose I can get Cam into the crib without waking him?"

"Why don't I try?" he offered, starting to stand.

But Colleen shook her head. "We'd probably wake him up handing him off. Wish me well. If I fail you'll hear an almighty scream."

Michael waited until after she'd left the room to snatch up the nearest object, a magazine, and slam it to the floor. Really mature, he thought in disgust, bending to pick it up and smooth the pages. But what the hell other outlet did he have for his frustration?

If he'd thought he was marrying Colleen for a home, he might as well admit now he'd been dreaming. They'd been married a month now, and he was still a guest. Maybe more than ever a guest. A couple of conversations like this one had left no question who the parent around here was. How many times had she told him not to worry about the kids? It was as if she held up a sign that said Not Your Problem.

Hell. He was probably overreacting, expecting too much too quickly. He wanted to be an instant father, but Colleen and the kids didn't see him that way. Maybe never would.

Patience, he told himself.

The front door slammed just as the phone rang. Feet thundered through the front hall to the kitchen at the same time Kim raced down the stairs yelling, "I'll get it! Drew! I'm expecting a call!"

The phone was cut off on the third ring and a moment later Drew bellowed, "Mom!"

Right behind him was Kim, yelling, "Mother, tell him it's rude to race somebody for the phone! What a jerk!"

Michael was mighty tempted just to put his feet up on

the coffee table and let Colleen handle all three kids and the telephone, too. But he knew exactly how many times she'd been up during the night. Surely even Superwoman occasionally admitted she could use a hand.

By the time he got out there, Colleen was storming down the stairs. Cam's wail from the open bedroom door trailed her. "How many times do I have to tell you to be quiet!" she snapped. "I was just getting Cam down for a nap, and now listen!"

"I can't help it," Kim said furiously. "He's such a brat! He just *had* to beat me to the phone."

Drew gave her a push. "I was there first!"

Kim lunged for her brother just as Michael collared both kids. "Let's have a little talk. Colleen—" he nodded toward the kitchen "—the phone is apparently for you."

Without waiting for her reaction, he steered Drew and Kim into the living room. "All right. Sit down."

They sat.

"Is it unreasonable for your mother to ask you to keep your voices down?"

Kim stuck out her tongue at her brother. "If he wasn't such a little jerk—"

"Was he the one who yelled in the hall right outside the bedroom?"

"I wouldn't have yelled if he—"

"I was the closest one to the phone," Drew said, smirking.

Michael held up a hand. "Enough. Your mom was up off and on all night with the baby, and she needs a nap she's not going to get now. She was intending to let you stay home tomorrow from the day camp, but you guys have blown it. We'd better have cooperation from you, or you won't be staying home Tuesday, either."

The boy jumped to his feet. "That's not fair! Just 'cuz *she's* got a big mouth—"

His sister's sullenness became outright anger. "I'm going to talk to Mom!"

"What about?" None of them had heard Colleen enter the room.

"You promised we could stay home tomorrow," the eleven-year-old said. "*He* says we have to go."

Colleen looked at him. "You told them they had to go to day camp?"

Michael crossed his arms. By God, she'd better back him up. "I told them," he said levelly, "that we'd agreed they could stay home these next couple of weeks only if they gave you a hand when you need it and didn't get in the way of your getting your rest. This is the third time they've woken up Cameron this weekend. I'd say they're not taking us very seriously."

Her hesitation was brief, but long enough to make him mad as hell. When she turned to the kids, Colleen shook her head. "Michael's right. Tomorrow will give you time to think about whether you can try a little harder."

"Mo-om!" Kim wailed.

"Sweetie, I know you hate it, and maybe making you go is a little harsh—"

Harsh! Gritting his teeth, Michael said, "Kim, why don't you go see if you can rock Cam back to sleep. Drew, you didn't take out the garbage this morning. Please do it."

"You're not my father!" Kim screeched, and ran from the room.

"I just came home to get a snack—" Drew stopped. "Gol, it wasn't even full." His gaze dropped from Michael's and he muttered, "Oh, all right."

The slam of a bedroom door upstairs raised the pitch of Cam's screams. Michael waited until Drew slouched out.

"I take it you don't like the way I handled this," he said.

"I didn't say that," Colleen protested. She tiredly pushed back the heavy mass of hair from her face. "It's just that Kim doesn't have any friends at all—"

"And therefore she should get away with anything at home?"

Colleen's chin came up. "I didn't say that, either! But maybe we should have talked about this—"

Michael swore and turned his back. "Hell, I knew I should have stayed out of it."

"Now wait a minute! I agreed with you, didn't I?"

"Reluctantly." He faced her again, distantly aware that he was overreacting, but too frustrated to shut up. "Sends quite a message to the kids, doesn't it?"

Colleen was so pale he reached out a hand to her, but she stepped aside. "Damn it, Michael, I'm doing my best. If it isn't good enough, you can...you can stuff it!" Back straight, she stalked out.

Michael swore again, feeling like a heel. He should be upstairs rocking their son, instead of sulking down here because Colleen hadn't provided a ready-made place for him in the household. What the hell had gotten into him?

He knew the answer, and he didn't like it.

ROCK-A-BYE, BABY, in the treetop. When the wind blows..."

Colleen faltered when she heard the front door close quietly and a moment later the sound of the pickup backing out of the driveway. But Cam stirred against her shoulder and she resumed the hypnotic rhythm of the lullaby.

"...the cradle will rock," she murmured. "When the bough breaks, the cradle will fall, and down will come baby, cradle and all."

She held her breath for a moment in hope, but Cam's wobbly head bobbed and he began to scream. On a sigh Colleen lifted her shirt and guided him to one breast, but he wouldn't nurse. She checked his diaper. Dry. And still his legs churned and he sobbed as though she was hanging him upside down by his heels.

"Cameron Delaney, what are we going to do with you?" Colleen asked. "Where do you suppose your daddy went?"

Cam didn't know and didn't care. He kept kicking and screaming and pummeling her with tiny fists. He quit crying only as long as she walked with him.

"Was your father as disagreeable at your age?" she asked the red-faced baby. "Probably."

Her every attempt to ease him into the crib failed. She desperately needed some sleep, but obviously she wasn't going to get it. Finding some slip-on tennis shoes, she carried Cam out to the hall. "Kim," she called, "I'm going to take Cam for a drive."

After the air-conditioned house, the garage was warm and the car even more so. She rolled down her window and buckled Cam in his seat, then put on her sunglasses. As usual, the baby liked riding in the car. Within a couple of blocks he'd settled down, shoving the two middle fingers of his left hand into his mouth.

Colleen drove with no particular destination in mind, hardly even noticing the summer heat, her thoughts completely given to this afternoon's scene. Was Michael justified in being angry with her? But what could she have done differently? Maybe she was too soft on the kids, but immediately following two major upsets in their lives—her marriage and Cam's birth, not to mention the earlier move—didn't seem like the moment to crack down. And she was used to being the only parent. If she didn't always know instantly how to react when Michael stepped in, why couldn't he understand that?

Her mind returned to the sound of his pickup backing out of the driveway. How upset was he? Where would he have gone? Surely not to his house; she knew he'd hardly set foot in it since their wedding day. Maybe the office, or maybe he was driving aimlessly around, too, wondering just as she was if they'd made a mistake.

But the alternatives were no more acceptable today than they'd been when she'd made her decision. Less acceptable, now that Cam was an individual, instead of an abstraction. No, marriage had been the only way. It was just requiring more adjustment than either she or Michael had anticipated. Surrendering her autonomy was hard for her, but trying to fit in when he didn't have a defined role must not be any picnic for Michael, either. And meantime they were trapped together in a small house, constantly playing on each other's nerves.

Trouble was, Colleen thought grumpily, she hadn't really *needed* a husband, and she didn't know what to do with one now that she had him. She'd done fine on her own. She wasn't even sure she wanted a man in her bed, though her body kept trying to tell her it did.

But that was just proximity, she told herself. Living with a man, it was hard *not* to start wondering what it would be like with him—not to catch herself studying his hands, long-fingered and strong, or remembering that glimpse of smoothly muscled chest and fine, curling, dark hair. Or reliving their two brief kisses, one accompanied by a proposal, one a wedding ring, and extrapolating therefrom—if she had lifted her hands and laid them on his shoulders, would he have taken her into his arms? Had she imagined the instant when his mouth firmed, before he stepped back?

Did he *feel* anything, or had his kisses been perfunctory, obligatory?

Frowning fiercely at the direction of her thoughts, Colleen looked around and discovered she'd had a destination, after all. She'd driven straight to the cemetery.

Deciding not to argue with her subconscious, she turned her small car into the lane that curved between the maples. To each side, sprinklers flung glistening arcs of water over the velvety grass between gravestones, keeping it green even in the midst of a dry, hot summer.

Another turn and she was in the new part of the cemetery. With a sense of inevitability, she saw Michael's pickup ahead, parked on the verge. Across the grass, he stood with his back to the road, looking very alone. At Sheila's grave.

Colleen pulled in behind his truck, set the emergency brake and turned off the ignition. Cam had finally, blessedly, fallen asleep, but she wasn't going to leave him in the car, even if taking him out woke him.

With no shade here, the heat struck her like a wall when she stepped out of her car. It must be ninety-five degrees today; the air was completely still. She could hear the shush, shush, shush of a sprinkler, the distant sound of cars. A backhoe stood deserted beside rawly turned earth. Colleen gently lifted Cam out of his seat and snuggled him, half-awake, against her shoulder as she started across the plush grass.

Michael had turned and was waiting for her. He still wore jeans and a chambray work shirt, the rolled-up sleeves and ratty canvas shoes with no socks his concession to the heat. Here away from the house, when she hadn't had a chance to brace herself to see him, the impact of his presence was even stronger. Living with him, she sometimes forgot how handsome he was—her feelings toward him were so complicated, so messy, they filtered the way she saw him.

But beyond broad shoulders and those startling blue eyes was something amorphous. She could feel tension radiating from him, yet it was always so contained she wondered if she was imagining things. He shuttered his thoughts easily, leaving her guessing what he felt by the slight huskiness in his deep voice, the unconscious hunching of his shoulders. His remoteness made her want to goad him, make him *feel* something. It made her want, with eternal female idiocy, to shatter his self-control.

Not smart, she told herself, stopping a few feet from him. His eyes were hidden by dark glasses, his expression was enigmatic. She was suddenly conscious of the patches of sweat between her shoulder blades and under her arms, that her hair clung to her neck, and that her face, untanned and incapable of tanning, was flushed from the heat.

Michael nodded and reached for Cam. Colleen gratefully surrendered their son.

Anxious that Michael not think she was following him, she said, "I didn't know you were here. I was just driving around."

"I've been meaning to come for a while."

"Me, too," she admitted.

Almost reluctantly Colleen looked down at the polished gravestone, flush with the grass. The inscription was bald: Sheila's name, the thiry-two year span of her life, *May she rest in peace.*

Are you? Colleen cried inside. Or was Sheila too restless a spirit to find peace?

"It sounds dumb," Colleen said aloud, "but I brought Cam to meet her." She hadn't even known that herself.

"It's not dumb." Michael spoke roughly. "I had thought...some Sunday, we could all come."

"We still could."

He didn't answer directly. Instead, his voice softened. "Are you hot, big boy? No? Just sleepy. Mom was such a brute she wouldn't let you nap, would she?" Michael's large hands dwarfed their son, but they were gentle, secure.

Colleen felt a peculiar pang she couldn't quite identify. It wasn't envy, but something close. If their marriage had been different, she would have heard that tone of voice from Michael before, known the security of being held by him. She might have been standing close enough to him now to be brushed by his shoulder, to reach out and tickle Cam, instead of stiffly keeping her distance.

Colleen stared down at the stone, at the lawn that grew over her sister's grave as though the ground had never been disturbed, and begged for an answer. Was it selfish to covet something that was never meant to be hers, something that death had snatched from her beloved sister? Even from the grave, would Sheila want to hold her husband?

Beside Colleen, Michael asked suddenly, "Could you really have given him—Cameron—to Sheila, if she'd lived?"

Colleen looked at her son, so small, so vulnerable, cradled in his father's strong arms, and felt a terrible constriction of her heart. Dear Lord, could she have? Or had she deceived herself all along?

But then she remembered Sheila looking up at her as she had that day in Colleen's kitchen, her eyes so desperate. She saw the little sister she'd fought with, comforted, encouraged and loved. She saw her best friend. And she nodded slowly.

"I think...I would have thought of him as hers from the beginning. She would have loved him."

"Yeah." He cleared his throat. "She would have."

Oh, Sheila, Colleen thought sadly, but she was past tears

now. Too much had been set in motion that day when one sister offered a gift to another. Whatever bitterness Sheila might have felt about all she'd lost, she wouldn't want her memory to take anything from Cameron. She'd want her husband and sister to do the best they could for the son she had named.

"Ah, well." Michael looked over Cam's head at her, regret in his voice, but not unbearable grief. "Cam's going to get sunburned. What do you say? Shall we go home?"

There was that pang again, that longing for something indefinable. *Home.*

And Colleen nodded.

CHAPTER TWELVE

"SMELLS GOOD."

Colleen jumped. The paring knife slipped and she came close to adding some blood to the strawberries she was slicing for dessert. Michael had a gift for appearing unheard; he was always just *there*, with no warning.

To hide her start, she offered a smile that was probably unconvincing. "Thanks. It'll be ready in a minute."

Instead of leaving, Michael leaned against the counter and crossed his arms. Apparently he was settling in comfortably to watch.

For no good reason, Colleen felt crowded. She realized ruefully that she felt that way most of the time these days. Cam was a month old now, and this house was too small for a family of five, especially when the two adults were trying very hard not to touch each other.

It had taken a while for her to realize that was what they were doing. She would rush to get through a doorway before he reached it; he would step well back to let her go by in the hall; at the dinner table she'd pass a serving dish to Drew at her right, rather than giving it directly to Michael. Ridiculous, but somehow necessary.

It was as though touching might actually be dangerous. What an absurd notion, she thought again, but uneasily. She wasn't afraid of Michael. And it wasn't as though they could barely keep their hands off each other. It was true that occasionally she surprised an expression on his face that was somehow raw, frustrated. Desperate. But of course she might be imagining things. She might be imagining even the tension, so thick it could be used as quilt batting.

A moment like this was more typical. Michael's eyes were cool, guarded.

"Did you want to talk about something?" she asked.

"Not really." He hunched his shoulders. "No, that's not true. I'm going to take Friday off work and tackle the house. Any chance you'd come? Or are you sick of packing?"

"Don't be silly. Of course I'll come." She hesitated. "Would you mind if Kim helps? She seems to be feeling left out these days."

Just yesterday, Kim had told Colleen glumly that this was the worst summer of her life. Colleen couldn't argue. Kim's twelfth birthday had come and gone with only a family party. She didn't have a single friend to invite even to go to a movie with her.

"Why not?" Michael sounded relieved. "Thanks. Which reminds me. Are you still planning to go back to work next week?"

"Yes, I think so." Colleen spooned strawberries onto the shortcake in each bowl, concentrating on the task, trying not to be so aware of his every breath, his every expression. "Why?"

"Have you thought of taking Kim with you? Couldn't she learn to help?"

Of course she could. So why, Colleen wondered, troubled, hadn't she thought of it herself? Kim's self-esteem was at an all-time low; it would be good for her to feel she was really helping out at the shop.

But Colleen also discovered how petty she was capable of being. She hated it that Michael had had to suggest something so obvious concerning *her* daughter.

"I'll think about it," she said. "Did Kim suggest it?"

"No. I noticed how disgruntled she looked when you said you were taking Cam with you. My first thought was that she could just hang out. Read or something. My niece—Stacey—is a heck of a good cook." He shrugged. "She's the same age. No reason Kim couldn't measure yardage and use scissors..."

"A rotary cutter. It's awfully sharp." So was her tone.

Despising herself, Colleen was careful not to look up, although she felt Michael's gaze on her.

After a moment he said flatly, "Okay, it's a lousy idea. Forget it."

"I didn't say that."

"No?"

"No, it's a good idea." Colleen closed her eyes for a heartbeat before she admitted, "I wish I'd thought of it myself."

"What the hell difference does it make?"

"I don't know!" she cried. "I just feel..." *Threatened.* But she didn't understand why and couldn't have begun to explain herself. She shook her head. "Nothing. Never mind. I'll ask Kim if she wants to go."

Michael chose to back off, for which Colleen was grateful. She knew she'd behaved badly. She seemed to be at her worst when he was being the nicest. Was she *trying* to drive him off?

The worrisome thought stayed with her over the next few days. She watched the way she had of insinuating herself in Michael's conversations with the kids, gradually taking over. She did it so subtly she wasn't sure anyone else noticed, but she began to remember times with Ben when she had done the same. Had she resented his letting the kids down one minute, then being best buddies with them the next? Or had she ever given him a chance in the first place?

She'd always known that her marriage to Ben had been fine until she had Kim. She'd blamed the failure on him; *he* didn't really want children; *he* didn't want to change their lives to accommodate Kim and later Drew; *he* resented her putting the kids first.

But it was becoming painfully obvious that *she* didn't want Michael to be a real, honest-to-God parent to Kim and Drew. Or even Cam? she wondered guiltily. She was breast-feeding, which meant that logically she took the lion's share of baby care, but it wouldn't hurt Cam to have a few more bottles. Maybe even a regular bottle or two a day that Michael gave him.

Colleen started listening to the voice in her head, the one that wasn't quite conscience but might as well have been. If she considered taking a nap, instead of picking up the living room, her inner voice would demand, *What if somebody dropped by and saw the house looking like this? What would they think of you?* Kim would beg to skip her bath one night and Colleen would hear a mental chide: *Kim can't possibly put off washing her hair until another night; the teacher might think you don't care if your children are clean!*

But there were other refrains, familiar from her childhood, that she hadn't even realized were still playing in her memory. *Women are perfectly capable,* the voice—her mother's voice, Colleen finally realized—said briskly. *We don't need your father. You've never missed your father, have you? We're just fine on our own.* How often had she heard her mother say with disdain, *Her* father *is bringing her? Where's her mother?*

Men were second-best. Possibly useful in their own way, but not as parents. Women were family, a loving circle.

Colleen remembered how Drew had sneered at the idea of a father meaning much of anything to his friend. Was he echoing her? Was she echoing her own mother, who'd tried to make up for a loss she'd never let Colleen and Sheila realize they had suffered?

Had Colleen made certain that Ben was kept outside the loving circle? Was she now pushing Michael out, too?

Would Sheila have done the same?

Colleen found it fatally easy to brood on such subjects the next day when she tackled Sheila's closets and drawers. Michael carried in Cam's bassinet and heaps of cardboard boxes, picked up at the grocery store. The room, carpeted in plush burgundy, was dominated by the king-size bed covered by the Rose of Sharon quilt that had been Colleen's wedding gift to her sister and Michael.

Sheila had loved the glorious "Song of Solomon" in the Bible: "Let him kiss me with the kisses of his mouth: for thy love is better than wine. / I am the Rose of Sharon, and the lily of the valleys." The appliqué pattern was an old one and had been Sheila's choice, rather than the traditional Wedding Ring.

Now Colleen went to the bed and touched the quilt, with its rose-colored flowers and green leaves and stems against a muslin background, quilted in a crosshatch with a feather border.

"I'd forgotten the quilt," she said, feeling a lump in her throat.

Behind her, Michael said quietly, "I thought, if you don't object, that we'd put it away for Cameron. When he marries."

"What a good idea." She blinked and gave herself a shake. "I'll fold it when we're done here."

"Then I'll get to work. Do whatever you want with her stuff."

He added something about his workshop, but Colleen scarcely heard him. She'd turned away from the bed and now stood frozen in front of her sister's dresser, caught by a silver-framed picture in the midst of the clutter. In the photograph, their mother sat in the middle, her arms around Colleen and Sheila. She and her sister had been perhaps thirteen and sixteen, Colleen guessed, pretty in the way of the young, but still gawky, unfinished. They looked happy, mother and daughters, their smiles and closeness genuine. As if she were that age again, Colleen could close her eyes and remember the warmth and security she'd thought was forever.

She had never really rebelled; she had always been good friends with her mother. Sadness brought an immediate lump to her throat, but she ignored it, studying the photograph with new eyes. How odd she'd never much thought about the fact that she and Sheila didn't look at all like their mother. Irene Muir had been dark-haired and dark-eyed, with white skin she took care to protect. Her cheekbones and nose were Slavic; there was pride in her carriage and the tilt of her chin. In contrast her daughters were softer, with auburn hair and freckles and faces that were rounder, less decided.

Their coloring and bone structure must have come from their father. But Colleen would never know for sure, because her mother hadn't kept a single picture of him. Colleen had half expected to discover some photos tucked away somewhere when she and Sheila cleaned out their mother's house after her death. But they hadn't found one. No letters, either, nothing personal. The day he left, he'd ceased to exist; their mother must have thrown away anything that would remind her of him.

Colleen had a few vague memories of her father, the kind that might have been real or made-up. If she'd asked questions, her mother had deflected them. He wasn't important; if his daughters had meant anything to him, he wouldn't have walked away. Colleen felt almost traitorous when she wondered if he might have tried to see them, to write or call. Could the woman who had thrown away every picture of him also have torn up letters?

Well, Colleen would never know. But she had an unsettling awareness that she would never think about her mother and her own childhood in quite the same way again.

She picked up the photograph and laid it carefully, face-down, in a box labeled To Keep.

"What do you want me to do, Mom?" Kim was patting her baby brother's back. "I think he's asleep."

"Oh, bless you! Let's try not to be too noisy." Colleen glanced around. "Why don't you tackle the drawers? It'll be easier to decide about that stuff than her nicer clothes in the closet."

In the end they put most of Sheila's clothes in the boxes that would go to a charity. Colleen could have worn some of the dresses, but didn't think she wanted to. And she was just enough taller so that nothing else fit—even Sheila's shoes were a hair too small for her. She packed a couple of boxes with things Kim thought she might wear—sweaters, jeans, jackets and sweatshirts. Colleen might be bothered the first time she saw Kim in them, but was too practical to get rid of everything.

At first Colleen was uncomfortable even at being in the bedroom Michael had shared with Sheila; when she laid the first few garments out on the huge bed, the Song of Solomon ran through her head: "His left hand is under my head, and his right hand doth embrace me." She imagined Michael in the bed. Michael and Sheila. "My beloved is mine and I am his: he feedeth among the lilies." The two of them laughing, him smiling down at her, bending his head to kiss her, his shoulders sleek and bare.... Flinching, Colleen drew a mental curtain. She felt as though she were violating his privacy. No, it was worse than that, more disturbing. She didn't *want* to think about him and her sister together. With determination she blocked out awareness of where she was; the room was a storehouse of Sheila's possessions. It had nothing to do with Michael.

Behind her, Kim said, "I wonder why Aunt Sheila kept this ratty old sweatshirt."

Colleen let the silk dress she was folding fall unheeded. She went over to plop down on the bed by her daughter. "Oh, I remember that. The Kittens were a high school sorority. How unfeminist!"

"Did you belong?"

Smiling reminiscently, Colleen shook her head. "They were the in-crowd, the cheerleaders, the girls who dated the jocks. I was too quiet and studious for them, though of course I envied them dreadfully. That's funny." She touched the shirt. "I'd forgotten she joined. I was off at college by then, but Sheila wrote me about some of the activities."

"Then you weren't superpopular?" Kim asked casually, as if her answer didn't really matter. Colleen wasn't deceived.

"Nope. If your aunt Sheila had been older, I probably would have been painfully jealous of her."

"And look. I found this ring in her underwear drawer." Kim dropped a chunky boy's ring with a high school emblem on it into Colleen's hand.

She held it up. "Why, this was our high school ring. We were the Tigers."

"Is that how come the sorority was the Kittens?"

"Uh-huh. I suppose Steve Galvin gave it to her. He was her boyfriend in high school. The quarterback, wouldn't you know." Her voice was dry. "Actually," she admitted, "along with being a hunk he was a pretty decent guy."

Kim listened raptly. "But they broke up."

"Yeah, but it wasn't anything dramatic. I think he went off to Cal State Davis and your aunt Sheila to the University of Washington. I didn't hear much about him after that." Colleen thoughtfully bounced the ring in her palm. "I suppose she couldn't bring herself to toss it. The dumbest things bring back memories."

"But what should we do with it?"

Colleen didn't even hesitate. "Keep it. I had a box here somewhere...." She looked helplessly around at the disorder.

"There's the one with the stuff for me," Kim said.

"Yeah, but I had one just for keepsakes."

"A remembering box." Kim stood up. "I know where it is."

A remembering box. Colleen felt a wrench of the sadness she hadn't been letting herself feel. Softly she said, "That's a nice way to put it."

As the morning wore on, they added a few other items to the box: some photographs, a packet of letters from Colleen when she was in college, a Breyer horse statue left from the herd Sheila had collected as a child. Any jewelry of obvious value Colleen set aside to ask Michael about; the clothes were all in labeled boxes by noon. Just when she was about to send Kim to look for him, Michael appeared in the bedroom doorway.

His gaze went straight to the empty closet, then back to Colleen, sitting on the stripped bed nursing Cam. As it always did, his gaze dropped briefly to his son—or to her open blouse. She felt a familiar stirring inside, a warmth unrelated to her joy at holding Cam.

"You're done already?" Michael sounded surprised, but a rough timbre in his voice made her think again about that fleeting glance at her breast.

"Thanks to Kim." Hoping her own voice didn't sound unnatural, Colleen smiled at her daughter. "She's been a big help."

He grinned at Kim. "I'll let her finish my workshop, then. The way I've been tossing stuff in boxes, I'm afraid I'll never be able to find anything again."

Kim was actually blushing, which made Colleen realize how hungry for compliments she was. "I don't mind," she said shyly.

"How about some lunch first?" Colleen suggested.

"I ordered a pizza. I hope that's all right. Should be here any minute."

"Cool," Kim pronounced.

Michael glanced around the bedroom, then looked directly at Colleen. "Thank you. I feel like a coward. This can't have been easy for you, either."

"You know," Colleen said, surprising even herself, "it really wasn't too bad. A lot of her clothes I'd never seen before. And some things triggered happy memories. Kim and I held a sort of wake. I think it was good for me."

His blue eyes searched hers with unsettling intensity, as though he sought some deeper meaning. "I'm glad," he said gruffly.

"Do you want us to tackle the kitchen this afternoon?" Colleen asked.

"You bet." The doorbell chimed and Michael said, "Ladies, I do believe lunch has arrived."

In the kitchen they all pulled up stools to the curved eating space at the end of the counter. "Drew'll be jealous," Kim said with satisfaction as she watched her stepfather dish up the pizza.

"Well, you worked for it," Colleen said. "He could've helped, too."

"He would've been in the way," Kim said with older

sibling superiority. "He would have asked you about every single thing."

"Don't you know that women are the ones who are naturally indecisive?" Michael said with a straight face. He handed over a plate of pizza with everything on it.

Kim sank her teeth into the first piece and protested around the bite, "Well, it's not true!"

"I'd be insulted," Colleen told him, "if I hadn't seen too many women staring at bolts and bolts of fabric, totally unable to make up their minds."

"That's because the fabrics are all so pretty," Kim said, chewing. "I bet men couldn't decide which one they liked the best, either."

"I can vouch for that," Michael agreed. "You ought to see men at the lumberyard. You ought to see *me* at the lumberyard."

"What's to like there?" Kim asked doubtfully.

"I'll show you." He stood up. "Come on. Bring your pizza."

Colleen didn't know if the invitation included her, but not even a door slammed in her face could have stopped her. Something in his expression told her that what he was going to show them was special to him, might even be a key to the puzzle of his personality. Holding Cam against her shoulder, she trailed her husband and daughter.

His workroom off the garage was in the same state as the bedroom; half of it was taken up by tall stacks of cardboard boxes, all labeled in black marker. She wished she'd seen it before he'd started packing. Sheila had offhandedly mentioned Michael's workshop, but Colleen realized she hadn't asked what he *did* in it. She had vaguely assumed it was the kind of place men had so that they could fix things around the house. The place he'd keep his drill and plumbing snake. Despite the fact that most of his tools were packed, she could see that wasn't the kind of workshop he had.

For one thing, the table saw—or radial arm saw, or whatever it was—was world's away from any household tool she'd ever seen. What's more, it was cleaner than her kitchen stove. Along one wall, built-in bins still held lumber, but not the average, rough two-by-fours; instead, each section corraled planks and rounds and big chunks of wood distinctive from that in any other section. Cherry and bird's eye maple and oak and others she didn't recognize. She picked up a chunk that was dark and unexpectedly heavy.

"Ebony," Michael said.

Colleen set it down and looked around. "You made the cherry secretary in the living room," she said in astonishment. "And the hall table. They're exquisite! I had no idea—"

"Uh-huh." He was clearly uncomfortable with the praise. "Right now I'm making a toy chest. I'll finish it once we're moved." He showed them the box, the corners smoothly fitted and rounded, the lid not yet hinged. "I'll carve 'Cameron' here on top. Maybe paint the letters."

"It's absolutely gorgeous," Colleen said, still in a state of shock. She held Cam up and said softly, "What do you think, sweetie? Look what your daddy made for you." Smiling at Michael, she said, "Why don't you throw over that bank work and open a cabinet shop?"

"I've thought about it, believe me." He seemed unaware that his hand was sliding lovingly over the richly grained wood. "But I don't know if you can make a living at it. I'm a perfectionist. I spend forever on one piece. Besides, I'm not sure both of us should be in high-risk, low-profit businesses."

Kim was visibly torn between passionate jealousy and

admiration. Shyly she reached out and stroked the side of the toy box.

With one perceptive glance, Michael took in her struggle. Sounding diffident, he said, "Would you like me to build you something next, Kim? You could even help, if you'd like."

Her lashes lifted to reveal brown eyes filled with hope. "Really? You'd make me something? And...and show me how to do it?"

"You bet." Michael's smile, slow and warm and maybe a little relieved that she hadn't thrown his offer back in his face, was just for Kim. It showed a side of him Colleen hadn't seen before. "Think about what you'd like. I could build a bookcase or a jewelry box." He shrugged. "Even a desk, if you'd like."

Eagerly Kim said, "With little places to put stuff? You know, all those nooks and tiny drawers?"

"You mean, like a rolltop?" Michael reached for a pencil and tablet of paper out on the workbench. "But smaller. Like this?"

"Neat." Kim edged up to him and pointed as he sketched. "Maybe put little drawers there. In the middle."

With peculiar, mixed feelings, Colleen realized she'd been forgotten. Kim was now hanging over his shoulder, abandoning both shyness and her stiff rejection of him.

Damn it, Colleen thought, here she went again! Jealous of her own daughter. Jealous because Michael never relaxed like that with her. He'd never even told her about his woodworking. Why hadn't he when they were talking about her quilt-making?

Stranger yet, Colleen thought, was why Sheila had never mentioned it, beyond snippets—"Oh, Michael's hiding in the workshop. I don't dare try to drag him out." Or an amused, "Michael feels about lumberyards the way I feel about Nordstrom's."

The truth was, Sheila hadn't talked about Michael much at all. Until this minute, Colleen hadn't realized how little. No wonder he seemed like a stranger to her.

Her mind jumped to the obvious corollary. Had *she* talked about Ben much in those endless conversations with her sister? The kids, of course; Sheila had always been hungry for news about them. But Ben—Colleen genuinely couldn't remember, which alarmed her.

She could see the pattern now, a legacy from their mother. The men in their lives didn't really matter. Couldn't be allowed to matter. After all, men upped and left when they felt like it. They didn't feel the same about their children as women did.

Why had she never seen it before? She was ashamed to realize how much of her behavior had been formed unconsciously, how destructive, as well as comforting, that loving circle had been.

These past months she'd been lost without her mother's and sister's love and support, but she knew suddenly that, on her own, she was freer than she'd ever been in her life. Their loving grip had brought comfort, but had also held her back. She was almost light-headed with an odd kind of relief. She didn't understand the strength of her reaction until her gaze, unbidden, went straight to Michael, who was still explaining something to Kim.

That inner voice, recorded in childhood, would not have let her have the marriage she desperately wanted. It would not have let her unreservedly love any man, far less Michael, who would demand much more of her than Ben ever had.

She had no idea what her expression gave away, but Michael turned his head just then, and whatever he'd been saying trailed off. They looked at each other, only each other, with rare intensity. Colleen's dizziness increased. She suddenly existed in two dimensions: in the one, she felt Cam's wet diaper and his feet kicking her, knew Kim was turning in puzzlement to see why she'd lost Michael's attention—while in the other, she was falling down a tunnel like Alice into Wonderland, with Michael at the bottom. His eyes burned into hers, melting the icy core of resistance she had guarded so carefully.

He took a step toward her. Irresistibly drawn, she took a step toward him. And then, predictably, reality intruded. Cam started crying, and Kim said loudly, as though she sensed she was being excluded from something, "Remember, our pizza's getting cold."

Just like that, it was over, whatever had happened between them. Michael answered Kim, said he'd change Cam's diaper, why didn't Colleen and Kim go eat. Colleen nodded and handed over the baby, now squalling lustily. Shaken, she wondered, Had she imagined the searing heat in Michael's eyes?

Well, maybe she had, maybe she hadn't. But she needed to acknowledge, if only to herself, what she felt. What she had fought so hard against admitting. She wanted Michael. She wanted, as she had never wanted anything in her life, to know what it felt like to have his hands on her body, his mouth on hers, his control shattered by her. Only her.

If that was a betrayal of her sister's memory, then so be it.

WHAT IN HELL had she seen or understood to bring that look to her face? Yesterday in his workshop something had changed. Colleen had reached a conclusion. But what?

Michael turned restlessly on the couch, either bumping the back of it or hanging off the edge. He'd had more comfortable places to sleep. But it wasn't comfort that made him wish he were upstairs in Colleen's bed.

Staring into the darkness, he wondered what she looked like sleeping. Did she curl in on herself like a cat, or sprawl extravagantly over the width of her bed? What if her husband reached for her and kissed her awake? Would she be grumpy or softly accepting?

Okay, admit it, Michael thought in disgust. What he really wanted to know was how passionate she could be. Would her eyes be dreamy? Did she whimper or cry out or whisper her love? Did she grab for what she wanted or wait passively for it to come to her?

Michael groaned and flipped onto his back. He was an idiot to torture himself. He wasn't going to find out what kind of lover Colleen was until they trusted each other in a hundred other ways. He had a feeling that wouldn't be any easier for her than it would be for him.

Like yesterday. In the months that came before, he had been tempted a dozen times to show her the chest he was making for Cam, but his woodworking had always been for him alone. It was his escape, his release. Private. Not that Sheila had ever resented the time he spent in his shop or given a damn either way. She liked the pieces he'd made for the house, but they were just furniture to her. She'd never seemed to realize how much of himself went into them. He'd always thought he preferred it that way. In the predictability of wood, in the precision of working it, in the beauty he could release when his skill was great enough, he found analogies to his inner self. When he stepped into his shop and shut the door behind him, he was himself in a way he couldn't be anywhere else.

From the beginning, he had seen a parallel in Colleen's quilt-making. Her craft demanded the same precision, and she was equally a perfectionist. Yet he'd seen the pleasure the simple combination of colors gave her; he'd seen her finger her quilts, absentmindedly but joyfully. Clearly she did it for herself, though the quilts themselves were sometimes made for other people. But the process itself satisfied her.

Because she understood her own motivations, he'd known she would look below the surface. He hadn't been sure he wanted that. But he had doomed himself the day he married her. Today he'd thought, why not now?

But that dazed look on her face—what could that possibly have had to do with his hobby? He'd have sworn she was in shock, as though he'd changed in some radical way right before her eyes. Either that, or she had.

He hadn't overlooked the battles Colleen was waging with herself. Something about the fact that they were now married had made her retreat. Generous enough to let him lay his hands on her bare stomach so he could feel his son move, Colleen was now going to ridiculous extremes to avoid his touch. And she'd become fiercely possessive of her children.

Most telling of all was that she had not even started to piece a wedding quilt. She was a woman who marked all of life's landmarks with quilts—quilts that celebrated and stored memories. He'd been stunned by the work and the love that had gone into the quilt she'd made for her sister's wedding to a man Colleen had never met. But thus far her own marriage did not, in her eyes, deserve a quilt. That scared him, as nothing else did.

But he couldn't blame her for everything. She couldn't trust somebody she didn't know, and he hadn't let her know him. Not deep down inside, where he felt unlovable. Not the Michael who had been an outsider in his own house and who felt like one all over again now.

But he had another chance. Colleen was as different from

Sheila as maple was from alder. She was a woman who loved easily, who touched easily, who might take his hand if only he reached out first. He couldn't live with himself if the failure this time was because of his own cowardice.

He had to take the chance that Colleen just plain wouldn't like him once she discovered who he really was.

CHAPTER THIRTEEN

THE LONG TELEPHONE CORD allowed Colleen to carry food to the table as she listened with half her attention to the man on the other end.

"I have to tell you, you're the seventh parent I've called, and none of the other six are willing to consider coaching the boys' soccer team. I have only two more to call, so the odds aren't good. Unfortunately the kids can't play without a coach. We hate to disappoint them, but we won't have any choice but to cancel."

He had all her attention now. "Drew would be so disappointed," she said unhappily. "But there's just no way I can volunteer. I just had a baby. Five weeks old."

The man from the soccer club sounded philosophical. "Well, that's a heck of an excuse. I don't suppose you can think of anyone else? An aunt or uncle, grandparent...?"

Colleen made a slow half turn to face the dinner table, where her family was already seated. Drew and Kim were listening, her son with alarm. But it was to Michael that she looked. Michael, who wanted to be a parent to her children. He met her gaze and raised an eyebrow.

"Just a moment, Mr. Lloyd." Colleen covered the receiver. "Drew, they can't find a soccer coach for your age level."

"Will you coach, Mom?" He fixed her with pleading eyes. "Please?"

"Drew—" she shook her head "—I can't. I'm sorry."

"You mean, I won't be able to play?"

Colleen looked back at Michael. His expression was ironic. He knew darned well she was setting him up. But he'd asked for it, hadn't he?

"I'll coach," he said.

"Mom," Drew begged. "I really want—" He stopped, then said incredulously, "*You'll* coach?"

"If you want me to."

Colleen couldn't help but notice how expressionless Michael's face was, how unemphatic his voice. He was braced for rejection, and no wonder. Neither Kim nor Drew had welcomed him with open arms. She held her breath herself, waiting for Drew's response.

"You'd really do that?" Drew asked doubtfully.

"I said I would, didn't I?"

"Do you know how to play?" His tone was still grudging.

"Uh-huh." Michael took a roll and passed the basket to Kim. "I played in college."

Drew's eyes got big. "Hey, that's cool! Ian's dad never played. Sometimes he has to look up rules in this little book he carries around. That's what Ian says, anyhow."

Growing impatient, Colleen prodded him. "Is that a yes?"

Her son glanced at her as though she were an idiot. "Well, sure." He turned back eagerly to Michael. "Will you let me be striker since I'm your kid? Well, sort of your kid? The striker gets to score all the points, you know."

Michael laughed and stood, pushing back his chair. "At your age, everybody should get turns to play all the positions. You don't really want me to treat you differently from the others, do you?"

Her son scrunched up his nose. "I guess not."

"Yes, he does," Kim said, rolling her eyes.

"What do *you* know?" her little brother snapped. "Don't tell *me*—"

Colleen squelched them both with a look. When Michael smiled ruefully down at her and took the phone, she mouthed, "Thank you."

He inclined his head, his eyes amused. Into the phone he said, "Mr. Lloyd? My name's Michael Delaney. I'm Drew's stepfather. I've just been talked into coaching soccer."

As they discussed times and places, Colleen put the last bowl on the table and sat down. "Let's start," she said. "Kim, will you pass the peas?"

When Michael came to the dinner table at last he said, "Well, the coaching clinic is next week. We'll start practice the week after that."

Through dinner he and Drew dominated talk with a discussion of what boys were on the team and what drills they would run in practices. Colleen had no sooner finished eating than she heard Cam crying. She sighed. "Kim, can you start cleaning up?"

"Drew and I'll do it," Michael offered.

Colleen waited for a rebellion that didn't come.

"Sure," Drew said. "Can I call Ian first to tell him you're coaching?"

"I don't see why not," Michael conceded.

"Then I'll make good my escape." Colleen smiled at Michael. "I don't know what I'd do without you." She tried to say it lightly so that he wouldn't necessarily think she meant anything special. But she's been trying to find small ways to let him know her attitude toward their marriage had changed. She was discovering how hard that was. She was ridiculously shy, feeling like a thirteen-year-old girl working up the nerve to flirt with a boy she liked. A boy who might not be the slightest bit interested in her.

But Michael gave her a look that was half thoughtful, half something that set her heart to pounding. In a voice that didn't slow her pulse any he said, "Good."

Blushing, Colleen hurried upstairs. Cam had kicked all his covers off and his diaper had leaked enough that she was going to have to change his crib sheet. At the sight of her, he quit crying.

Colleen reached for him. "What a messy boy," she said in the same voice she would have used to tell him how incredibly handsome he was. "Are you hungry? I think you need a dry bottom first. What do you say?"

He didn't *say* anything. He smiled. Really smiled, his whole body wriggling with delight because Mommy was here.

Grinning foolishly back, she said, "Oh, pumpkin. If I call Daddy, will you smile again?"

His short legs kicked happily, and she carried him to the bedroom door. "Michael!" she called. "Michael, can you come here?"

"Is something wrong?" He took the stairs two at a time.

"Nope." Her own smile was so huge she couldn't hide it. "I want you to see something." Her voice gentled. "Hey, big boy, look who's here." She turned Cameron so that he could see his daddy.

Thank goodness, he obliged. He gave Dad a happy, toothless grin. Michael cooed and tickled him, then looked up at Colleen with as much wonder and pride as any father had ever felt. "Isn't this a little early?"

"Well, reasonably." Secretly amused, she said, "But he's a big, strong boy. He'll be toddling along after you before you know it."

"He will be, won't he?" Michael gazed at his son with an expression of bemusement that tugged at Colleen's heart. "It's funny," he said. "I could have lived without having a child. Sometimes I was impatient with Sheila because she couldn't resign herself the way I had. But now..." He shook his head, as though he'd run out of the right words. But then he said them. "Already I can't imagine life without Cam."

"I know," Colleen said softly. Not once—not once!—had Ben ever shared her joy so explicitly. Moved by instinct greater than her inhibitions, she touched Michael's hard jaw, bristly with a Saturday's growth of beard. She whispered, "You don't expect to feel so strongly."

His hand caught hers and held it against his cheek; his eyes had darkened to navy when they met hers. For a wordless moment they looked at each other, even Cam forgotten, before Michael let her hand go. His voice had a rich, dark texture. "No," he said. "You don't expect it." Something told her he wasn't talking anymore about being a parent.

Behind him, Kim said, "Mom, what are you— Oh. I didn't know Michael— Forget it." The last sounded almost sullen.

"She's all yours," Michael said so easily Colleen was left wondering if she'd imagined the way he'd just spoken to her.

You don't expect it. No, she decided, half terrified, half exhilarated. She hadn't imagined anything.

"I've got to change Cam," Colleen told her daughter. A little regretfully she watched Michael head down the stairs without a backward glance. "And nurse him. Did you have a question?"

Kim hung her head. "I just wanted to talk."

"This is the perfect time." Hoping her cheeks weren't bright pink, Colleen smiled at Kim. "Come on."

Kim sat on one side of the queen-size bed while Colleen changed Cam's diaper at the foot. "Is something bothering you?" she asked gently.

"Not really." Kim watched Cam kicking and waving his hands.

Colleen let the silence grow, waiting her daughter out.

"When are we going to move?" Kim asked suddenly.

"We think the weekend after next. Thank heavens. I'm going to be glad to have Cam in his own room. This one's a squeeze." Which was putting it mildly. The crib blocked her approach to her chest of drawers. Now she had to climb over the bed to get a clean pair of underwear. "We'll barely be moved before you start school. Just think, you'll be able to walk. No bus."

"Is Michael going to sleep with you after we move?"

Question of the year. But not one she wanted to discuss with a twelve-year-old. "Probably," she said. "Although maybe not at first. We'll see." She straightened, lifting Cam high into the air and then bringing him down for a big kiss. "Mealtime," she announced.

Kim scooted over and Colleen sat on the bed, leaning against the headboard and unbuttoning her shirt enough to free the flap on her bra.

Out of the blue Kim said, "I called Dad last week."

"I remember. But he wasn't home, was he?"

Kim shook her head. A curtain of hair shielded her face and she tried to sound careless. "He never called me back."

Damn him, Colleen thought, with easily aroused fury. But she didn't let it sound in her voice. "Have you called again?" she asked gently. "You know how absentminded he can be."

Still hiding behind her shiny brown hair, Kim didn't answer for a moment. Then she burst out, "It's not fair! How come Michael has to coach Drew's soccer?"

Colleen turned her head to stare at her daughter. "What

on earth does Drew's soccer have to do with your dad? What does it have to do with *anything?*''

Kim mumbled, ''I'll bet if I played, he wouldn't coach my team.''

Naively Colleen tried logic. ''Honey, you didn't *like* soccer the time you tried it. You hated getting kicked, remember?''

''I *know* I didn't like soccer!'' Kim flared. ''But I'll bet if I did some other sport, he wouldn't coach that, either.''

Oh, boy. Colleen shifted Cam to her other breast. Then, carefully choosing her words, she said, ''In the first place, I'll bet he would. Michael's trying to be friends with you guys. In the second place… I thought you didn't *want* him doing things for you as if he were your father.''

''Yeah, well, Drew's a traitor. *He* said that, too, but look at him now.'' She heaved a huge sigh. ''Once the kitchen is clean, they're going to go out in the backyard and kick the soccer ball around.''

''Didn't they invite you?''

''I didn't want to go.''

This time the silence was a long one. Colleen contemplated her daughter, noticing subtle changes. She was definitely getting breasts. And though her legs were still long and skinny, her hips weren't boyishly narrow anymore. Even her face had filled out a little. Colleen had once thought Kim looked like Ben, but now she wasn't so sure. Kim's cheekbones had more in common with Colleen's mother, as did her beautiful brown eyes. She'd been acting almost like a teenager; Colleen now had to face the fact that her daughter almost looked like one, too.

''Mom?'' Kim said.

Cam drew back from Colleen's breast and smiled up at her. Tickling his toes, she laid him on the bed and then buttoned up. ''Yes?''

In a rush Kim asked, "Do you think Michael's cute?"

Shocked despite herself, Colleen hesitated. *Don't blow it,* she warned herself. *Or she may never talk to you again.* Taking a deep breath, she admitted, "Yeah. I think he's cute."

Kim went back into hiding behind her hair. Colleen had to strain to hear her next words. "I, um, well, I kind of think so, too."

Oh, boy, Colleen thought. She didn't know how to deal with this. She hadn't *had* a father or a stepfather! But almost immediately she remembered spending the night at a friend's house what seemed like a century ago. Had they been about Kim's age? Colleen couldn't even recall the girl's name, but she did remember the crush her friend had had on her stepfather. Hard to forget, when she had gone on and on about him, stopping herself every couple of minutes to exclaim, "I'd *die* if he knew! Or if *my mother* knew. That would be even worse!"

Funny the way things came back to you. The memory was enough to let her reach for Kim's hand and give it a squeeze. "You know what? That's perfectly normal. He's a very attractive man, and here he is living with us. I think lots of girls even have crushes on their own fathers without exactly realizing it. After all, dads are safe."

Kim looked up, her expression shy and painfully hopeful. "The boys my age are all such *nerds.*"

Colleen realized that Kim must really have been worrying about her feelings toward Michael. So she wrinkled her nose. "I know what you mean. At your age, they're all shrimps, too." More seriously she added, "I think maybe for a girl her father—or a stepfather—sets a standard for her. Something boys and eventually men she dates have to measure up to. You know what I mean?"

Kim was frowning in concentration. "Do you think Dad's a better standard, or Michael?"

Colleen opened her mouth, closed it, opened it again—and then had to laugh at herself. Giving Kim a quick hug, she said, "I've got to tell you the truth. There's no way I can fairly answer that. Mostly I'm not mad at your father anymore, but I can't look at him objectively, either. It makes me angry when he doesn't call you back, or on visits when he didn't pay any attention to you. It's too easy for me to see the bad things about him and not the good. But here I've just married Michael, so I'm still noticing the good, instead of the bad. I guess you've got to think this one out for yourself, kiddo."

"Even though I really love Dad—" Kim's face twisted, belying her exaggeratedly casual tone "—I think, well, that maybe Michael's a better husband. I mean, he's always here helping and stuff. He doesn't make excuses. So, even though I don't know whether he'll be a good father yet, I guess maybe I'll sort of think of him as what I want. Someday."

Colleen hadn't cried in weeks, but right this minute she had to bite her lip hard to keep tears from falling. She waited a moment for the stinging in her eyes and the tightness in her throat to go away before she answered.

"Well," she said, not quite lightly enough to fool her daughter, "you'll change your mind about fifty times before you really and truly fall in love and get married, but it sure wouldn't hurt to keep an eye out for somebody like Michael."

Kim had quit listening. At a yell of triumph coming through the open bedroom window, she bounced up and went to look out. "Drew can't kick worth beans," she announced. "And he thinks he's good enough to be striker! Maybe I will go out and play."

"Have fun," Colleen called after her daughter, who was already dancing out of the room. Smiling, Colleen held her hands for Cam to grab her thumbs. Softly she sang, "The itsy, bitsy spider went up a water spout." She lifted and lowered his arms in time with the tune. "And down came the rain and washed the spider out."

At Cam's round-eyed wonder and slowly dawning smile, she leaned down and kissed him, savoring his baby scent. "You know what, little spider?" Colleen whispered. "I think I love your daddy."

IT WAS GETTING EASIER to smile at Michael, even to touch him. Especially to touch him. Easier, at least, when other people were around, when the casual hand she laid on her husband's arm looked perfectly natural. She hadn't quite worked up the nerve yet to do the same when they were alone.

But, oh, how tempted she was. Lots of evenings, of course, she quilted at her frame once the kids were in bed, or packed what little wasn't already in boxes. She hadn't made as much progress on the Burgoyne Surrounded quilt as she would have liked, but then she wasn't as desperate for money, either. Michael was busy packing, too, or working at the computer he'd set up in the living room.

But other times, like now, they would both sit on the couch, each reading or Colleen quilting a smaller piece in a hoop, a safe distance between them, but not so safe that she couldn't have reached across it. Tonight she was working on a wall-size Fan quilt, embellished with bits of lace, which would be an entry into a regional show. She packed five stitches onto the tiny needle, then sneaked a peek at Michael.

His feet were on the coffee table and the newspaper was spread out on his lap. The pages rustled as he shifted slightly, and he frowned at something he was reading. His left hand lay on the couch not far from her. Colleen studied it sidelong, guiltily enjoying the perilous and therefore exhilarating experience of watching Michael unobserved. In the suits he wore to work, he was sleek and sophisticated, all except his strong, brown hands, with the scars and rough fingertips she had noticed and wondered about before. Now she'd seen those same fingertips stroking the wood in his shop, and she knew.

So she wondered something else. What would happen if she just slipped her fingers into the curve of his? Would they tighten? Might he even lift her hand to his mouth, or maybe tug until she scooted across the distance separating them? She hadn't moved the needle in a full minute; she scarcely breathed, watching her husband out of the corner of her eye and wondering.

He caught her that way, looking up so swiftly she couldn't evade the disturbing intensity in his blue eyes. Just like that, the very air was charged with nameless tension. Colleen was paralyzed, pinned by his piercing gaze.

She swallowed, moistened dry lips. His fingers uncurled and he slowly lifted his hand as though he was going to touch her, cup her cheek in his palm, run a rough fingertip over her lips… Oh, Lord, how she wanted him to!

But like an idiot, she leapt to her feet and babbled, "Oh, dear! I think I hear Cam," before bolting. Upstairs she hid in the bathroom and stared at her flushed face in the mirror, disgusted with herself. How could she want something so badly and yet be afraid for it to happen?

Or was she afraid it *wouldn't* happen?

Well, the moment of truth would soon be at hand, Colleen realized the next day. She lay on her back on the examining table at her doctor's office, contemplating the poster on the ceiling that depicted a hippopotamus lovingly nuzzling her stout offspring. Colleen liked the poster better now than she had when she'd been shaped like the hippo. To one side the nurse was cuddling Cam and telling him what a sweetheart he was, while Dr. Kjorsvik did an exam.

At last the doctor straightened, peeling off her plastic gloves. With her usual briskness, she said, "Everything looks good. No more restrictions on sexual intercourse. There may be a little soreness at first, but you know that. You have two other children, don't you?"

It wasn't really a question, but Colleen was glad to have something to talk about as she sat up, meanwhile trying to cover herself with that ridiculous hospital gown. "Yes, in another year my daughter will be able to baby-sit. Sometimes I think I'm too old for this." She couldn't help smiling at Cam, who was keeping an anxious eye on her as the nurse cooed to him. "But only in the middle of the night."

A glimmer of humor showed in Dr. Kjorsvik's slate blue eyes. "He'll be sleeping through the night soon. Then you'll be freer to enjoy—" she paused ever so slightly "—your own night's sleep."

On that note a flustered Colleen departed, collecting Kim from the waiting room. As she strapped Cam into his car seat, she wondered whether Michael knew that a woman usually was discouraged from having sex for the six weeks after birth. Would *he* be thinking about the fact that his son was, as of today, six weeks old?

"Let's go see how soccer practice is going," she suggested to Kim.

Her daughter sighed and let out a puff of air that fluttered her bangs. "It's *hot*."

Colleen didn't even bother to agree. After leaving the air-conditioned building, she already felt sweat trickling down her temples. Her legs, bare in shorts, stuck to the car seat. Early summer here had been gorgeous, with the vast blue sky and the streets shady with huge old maples. But now the broad leaves hung limply and the wheat had been harvested to leave stubble. The only saving grace was the dryness, which made the heat more endurable than it would have been in a humid climate.

The soccer fields, donated by a local wheat farmer, bordered an apple orchard. Painted white goalposts and lines on the grass delineated the several playing fields. The gravel parking lot was half-full, and she spotted five separate practices going on.

Michael was down at the far end, surrounded by a herd of little boys. She parked as close as possible, and Kim followed reluctantly when she tied Cam's sun hat on and headed across the close-mown grass toward the sideline.

Colleen smiled at Michael, who grinned a little ruefully at her over the boys' heads. "Hey, Kim," he called. "How would you like to be the goalie so we can have even sides?"

"Sure," she said, looking happier immediately. She loped toward the goal and leapt up to touch the cross-piece.

Colleen found a shady spot under a maple and settled down on the grass to watch. It was oddly peaceful here, the shouts of the players and coaches muted in the still air, the buzz of a passing bee a pleasant counterpoint. She spread out a small quilt and Cam fell asleep immediately. Colleen blinked a little sleepily herself and watched as the boys, divided into two teams, swarmed the ball the moment Michael tossed it into play. He let them go for a few minutes, then blew his whistle, freezing them.

"Okay, don't move! Take a look around. Ian, what's your position?"

"Um..." Wide-eyed, Ian pointed off toward one side.

"That's right. Wing. Jacob, you're a wing, too. What are you doing in the middle?"

The boys grinned sheepishly and retreated to their places. Michael went down the roster, sorting them out again. "Remember, sometimes you've got to help out, but most of the time you trust your teammates to play their positions and to pass. They can't pass to you if you're not where you're supposed to be. If you're all clumped up in the middle, you trip over each other. Okay." He gave another blast on the whistle. "Let's go!"

Colleen could see improvement over a week ago, when they'd either been stepping back to politely let someone else have the ball, or kicking it without paying any attention to where the goal or a teammate was. Drew seemed to be having the time of his life, charging into the fray and kicking wildly without any of Kim's timidity. That set her to thinking about differences between the sexes, and before she knew it she was watching Michael.

Which, if she were honest with herself, was what she'd come for. He had changed after work into athletic shorts, and she admired his muscular, tanned legs dusted with dark hair. Even better, he wore a tank top that left bare sleek, powerful shoulders. Damp with sweat, the fabric clung to his chest and back. He kept wiping his face on his forearm or the hem of his shirt, and his hair was tousled. He moved lightly on the balls of his feet, staying just ahead of the boys, his attention always on them. He was quick to stop them and point out mistakes, but just as quick to grin, with a flash of white teeth, and clap a boy on the back for a good pass or great defense.

It made Colleen's heart ache to watch him. How close she had come to robbing Cam, and Drew and Kim, too, of Michael. But the intensity of her own feelings scared her. She was finding it so easy to forget that theirs was a marriage of convenience; that Michael might still be grieving for Sheila to the point where he wasn't ready to love again.

Colleen heaved a deep sigh and touched Cam's flushed cheek. Time to quit dreaming and go home to start dinner.

The rest of her family showed up just as she finished slicing vegetables for a stir-fry. At the table, Drew chattered happily about soccer practice and the goal he'd almost scored on his sister. Kim was obviously feeling pretty good about having stopped the ball. Michael listened and commented without correcting any of Drew's more extravagant claims.

Leaving the kids to clean up the kitchen, Michael and Colleen moved into the living room. He sat on the couch and began unlacing his athletic shoes. "How was your day?"

Here was her big chance. Colleen's heart began to drum, but she picked up her sewing basket and opened it, answering casually, "Oh, fine. I had a doctor's appointment today."

Michael dropped his shoes and looked up. "What for?"

"Just a six-week checkup." Colleen automatically measured out a strand of thread and snipped it off.

"And?" he probed. Being the subject of his complete attention made her sympathize with microbes in a lab. Except, of course, that she *wanted* him to be interested. Very interested.

"Dr. Kjorsvik says I'm fine."

"Did you think you weren't fine?"

It took every bit of acting ability she possessed to glance up at him with an expression of vague surprise. "No, it's just routine. Before you go back to..." *Sex.* Colleen frantically sought for an alternative. "Um, normal life."

"Normal life," he echoed. His eyes were unreadable.

By this time, her cheeks no doubt glowed. She might as well have lit neon signs that said, *Yes, that's right. Sex.*

"I...well, I guess I have a few more pounds to lose, but

that's normal." She shouldn't have used that word again. "I mean, after all, it's only been six weeks. And when you're nursing, you lose quickly, thank goodness. All those calories going into Cam, you know."

Michael just sat there looking at her. Probably in disbelief that she was rattling on this way.

Even so, she'd have kept going if she could have thought of a single more thing to say. But unless she planned to give him her hip and bust measurements, she wound down.

"Well, anyway, other than that the day was..." Not normal. Anything but normal. "...pretty much like always."

He was still contemplating her, his eyes a dark blue, which usually meant he was doing some concentrated thinking. "Good," he said at last.

Good? What did that mean? Was he talking about her day or her body? Had he even received her clumsily sent message?

Kim stuck her head in the living room. "I'm done, Mom."

"Thanks, hon," Colleen said absently. Where the heck had she put her needle?

"I'm bored. Can I go ride my bike?"

Michael turned his head. "I have a suggestion. How about if we all go to a movie? We're all packed, and once we've moved it'll take us weeks to unpack. I thought this might be a good night."

"Wow! Can we? Please, Mom?"

Colleen was a little ashamed that they'd done so few things this summer that were fun. Kim didn't have much to look forward to these days. With the move tomorrow, probably they should stay home and get a good night's sleep. And, of course...

"What about Cam?"

"I'll bet Jennifer would watch him," Michael suggested. "Maybe Stacey could come with us."

Colleen hadn't left Cam yet. It was always hard the first time. Even so, the hopeful look in her daughter's eyes decided her. "Let's give her a call."

His sister-in-law agreed, and half an hour later they dropped off Cam, two bottles and his playpen. The ranch house was a handsome one, separated from the fields, golden with wheat not yet harvested, by a windbreak of poplars. The hill was crowned by long irrigation pipes on huge wheels that allowed them to be moved around.

Colleen had been here only once, when Stephen and Jennifer had invited them for dinner. Kim hadn't had a chance that time to get to know Stacey, who had been at a friend's that evening.

Now Michael didn't give Colleen more than a brief chance to chat with Jennifer. "We'd better get this show on the road if we're going to have time to buy popcorn first." He was already herding the kids back to the car. Stacey went, but shyly.

"Thanks for taking Stace," Jennifer said. "They always want summer to come, and then they're so bored. Thank goodness school's starting Tuesday." She accepted Cam with a smile. "And don't worry. I'll take good care of this gorgeous boy."

"I know you will." Even so, Colleen had to tear herself away.

The movie was the latest sci-fi epic, with enough laser guns to make Drew happy and enough adventure and romance for the two girls. Colleen and Michael shared a popcorn, and in the dark they kept reaching for a handful at the same time. Each touch sent a brief thrill through her. She was as self-conscious as a girl on her first date, painfully aware of Michael's every shift in his seat.

She jumped when he nudged her and held out the pop-corn bucket. "More?" he asked in a low voice.

Colleen shook her head, and he leaned forward to set it on the floor. When he sat back, he laid his arm on the back of her seat, so that her neck brushed it. Her heart stepped up its pace, and she sneaked a glance at his profile. His whole attention appeared to be on the screen.

Colleen's tiny sigh of disappointment must have been audible, because Michael wrapped his hand around her shoulder and squeezed. "Don't worry," he whispered. "Cam's fine."

"I know," she whispered back.

It figured, she thought morosely. She was having roman-tic fantasies, and *he* was looking at her as the mother of his son.

On the other hand, she realized an instant later, he hadn't removed his hand. It rested loosely on her shoulder, not all that many inches away from her breast. He was definitely cuddling her, if in an absentminded way. Surely he couldn't be unaware that his arm was around her.

No, because his hand tightened again and gently mas-saged her shoulder and upper arm. Colleen totally lost track of what was happening on the screen. She was awash in a sea of pleasurable sensation. For the first time in her life, she passionately wished her children were elsewhere. She hadn't necked at the movies since... She couldn't remem-ber. High school, anyway. She very much wished she could tonight.

But no, Drew sat right next to her, and Stacey and Kim were on the other side of Michael. If Drew even noticed that Michael's arm was around her, he'd probably pretend he was gagging.

Just before the lights came up, Michael casually removed his arm. She glanced at him as they stood, but he was listening to Stacey on his other side. The talk on the way out was about the movie, which the kids all thought was the greatest. By the time they reached the car, Colleen gave up expecting some significant look from Michael. He was treating her just as he always did. In the car, Stacey and Kim got far enough to discover they would have the same homeroom teacher this year, Mr. Griggs.

They returned Stacey and picked up Cam, who Jennifer claimed had been a sweetheart for her. At the sight of his mother, he began to sob as though his heart was broken.

"He's already laying a guilt trip on you," Jennifer said cheerfully.

Colleen had to laugh. At home she carried Cam upstairs, where he latched eagerly on to her breast. The bottle he'd emptied just wasn't the same, he seemed to be telling her. She tenderly rubbed his back and whispered, "You sleepy, pumpkin?"

He pulled back from her breast and patted it before making a happy, gurgling sound. Definitely wide-eyed. Colleen burped him and felt his head wavering only a little as he looked around. Just when she would have liked him to go down early. She could hear Michael supervising teeth-brushing and apparently even braiding Kim's hair. Dared she hope he was hurrying them to bed for a reason?

Colleen boosted Cam into the air and then eased him close enough for them to rub noses. "Are you sure you're not sleepy?" she asked hopefully.

He grinned. Despite everything, she grinned back.

So much for true romance.

So much, anyway, she discovered when she went back downstairs after kissing Drew and Kim good-night. Michael was in front of his computer, frowning at the numbers on the screen. When she ventured a hello, he barely glanced at her.

Unnoticed, she stood there behind him, stunned at the change from charming date to indifferent stranger. She felt like a child who had just had somebody pop her first helium balloon. She wanted to cry, scream, plead. But she wasn't a child, and she had her pride. Her pride, and a husband who wasn't interested.

Quietly she turned and went back upstairs.

MORNING BROUGHT no time for self-consciousness. It was the beginning of Labor Day weekend—and moving day. Thanks to their excitement, the kids were amazingly cooperative, and the whole thing went reasonably smoothly. Even so, Colleen barely had the kitchen in working order by Tuesday, the first day of school.

Drew liked his teachers "okay," he announced, bursting in the door at the end of the day. If Kim found middle school, with six different classrooms and teachers, confusing, she wasn't about to let on. "They treat us like grown-ups," she told her family at dinner. "It's cool."

Colleen went back to work full-time that week, taking Cam with her. She'd set up his playpen right beside the counter. She was still letting him nap whenever it suited him, even though he wasn't sleeping through the night.

The first two weeks in the new house were exhausting. Colleen would hustle the kids out the door mornings, lunches packed, then get Cam and herself ready. At five-thirty in the afternoon, she walked back in. Some evenings, Michael made dinner; others, he and Drew had soccer practice and she had to manage. Then, in addition to helping the kids with their homework, she and Michael unpacked and rearranged furniture. Cam usually went down for the night at around nine, and even at eight weeks was still insisting on a feeding at two or three in the morning.

Usually the first thin cries were enough to penetrate Colleen's sleep. One night Cam had worked up to a full-fledged temper tantrum by the time she struggled to wake up enough to understand who wanted her.

She opened one eyelid and saw the fuzzy green numbers on her clock: 2:15. He'd only been asleep an hour. Colleen groaned and longingly closed her eyes again. But of course Cam went right on, sounding like a fire engine parked in the hall.

Putting him in his own bedroom was supposed to have made it easier for him to sleep. For *her* to sleep. So far, no cigar. Maybe before he'd been comforted by the small sounds of his mother sleeping only a few feet away. Whatever. He hated his bedroom in this new house.

Colleen was just bleary enough to stop in confusion when she found the hall light already on. As she stood there swaying, the high-pitched screaming abruptly ended.

She stumbled to the door of the nursery. Light from the hall let her see Michael sitting in the rocking chair with Cam nestled against his bare shoulder. They were rocking back and forth rhythmically, Michael murmuring a song of which she caught only a whisper. His eyes were closed and his cheek rested against Cam's fuzzy head. Even as tired as she was, the picture her husband and son made brought a painful, joyous lump to her throat.

Cam was so tiny with his knees drawn up, dwarfed by the breadth of his daddy's shoulders. Oh, God, she thought, Michael was beautiful, a lock of dark hair falling over his forehead, the golden light from the hall casting shadows beneath high cheekbones, muscles supple under his skin, another shadow where hair formed a V on his chest. And his tenderness, his patience...

The vicious knife blade of pain was deep inside her, stealing her breath, before she even saw it coming. Why can't he love *me?* she asked in silent agony.

Colleen was still frozen there in the doorway when Michael opened his eyes. They stared at each other, though his rocking didn't change rhythm. Nor did he look away from her when, still cradling Cam, still murmuring, "Rock a bye baby," Michael eased to his feet. Cam never lifted his head and stirred only slightly when Michael laid him in the crib and gently covered him with the soft weight of his Carousel Horses quilt.

Her husband came silently toward her on bare feet. Colleen retreated into the hall until her back was against the wall. Michael paused to pull the nursery door almost closed behind him, leaving just a crack for light to spill in. Then he faced her, wearing only pajama bottoms, his body lean and very male.

Colleen was suddenly aware of how quiet the house was, of the darkness in her bedroom and down the stairwell. She couldn't tear her eyes away from Michael's bare chest and knew in the same instant how little her thin, cotton nightgown covered. Goose bumps rippled over her skin and she hugged herself, trying absurdly to cover as much as possible.

His voice was low and just a little rough, as she imagined his fingertips would be. "You could have stayed in bed."

Or had he said, "You *should* have stayed in bed"?

"I—" she moistened dry lips "—didn't realize…"

His mouth twisted and he looked at her—really looked, openly, hungrily. And when his eyes met hers again, the molten glow in them came close to shocking her. Did shock her.

"I guess—" her lips formed the words, but they were soundless "—I'll go back to bed." She took a step sideways, bumped the molding on Kim's closed door. Colleen's bare foot was feeling for another step when Michael took one stride and swung her up into his arms. She caught a glimpse of his face, skin stretched taut across strong bones, eyes smoldering and teeth clenched, before he nudged off the hall light with his elbow and swept her across the threshold into her bedroom, a bride to her belated wedding night.

CHAPTER FOURTEEN

COLLEEN REGRETTED the darkness even while she was grateful for it. She wanted to see Michael, but was glad he couldn't see her. What if he was disappointed?

He hadn't said a word yet, just carried her into her bedroom. Beside the bed, he lowered her to her feet without releasing her. Knowing she couldn't be seen let Colleen be bold. Leaning forward, she pressed her parted lips to his chest, moved her hands tentatively on his bare, smooth shoulders and felt a ripple of reaction, heard a swift intake of breath. Then his mouth captured hers in a way nothing like those dutiful kisses that had been part of becoming Michael's wife.

This one was almost savage. His formidable control was shattered. He devoured her mouth, demanded entrance until his tongue found hers in long, erotic strokes. Already her bones were dissolving. She answered him in kind, kissing him as frantically as he kissed her. She had waited so long, dreamed so many nights of this, of Michael's lean, tough body pressing her back against the bed until her knees began to buckle. But he held her up, too, one hand moving restlessly over the small of her back, the curve of her hip, exploring, kneading. The other he'd plunged into her loose hair, gripping it to angle her head for his mouth to ravish hers.

Colleen needed to breathe, didn't care if she ever did again. But she sucked in air greedily when Michael's mouth left hers to travel, hot and damp, along her jaw, down her neck, to nip at her shoulder. Was she the one whimpering, making tiny sounds of need? She was shaking, he was shaking. Now he'd gripped her nightgown and was gathering it, pausing long enough to cup her breasts and squeeze, before he pulled the gown over her head and tossed it over his shoulder. He kicked off his pajama bottoms in one move. And then he lifted her again, sliding her body along his in an exquisite, slow caress until she wrapped her legs around his waist and he let them both fall onto the bed.

Every sensation was heightened. She no longer knew where she ended and he began, which texture was covers beneath her naked back and which the feel of his leg between hers. The heated need inside her was a tightening thread that might snap if he thrummed it with a careless hand. But he was never careless; he touched her, stroked her, as he had stroked the wood he loved, creating the satin finish that showed the richness beneath.

And, oh, Lord, she touched him, found the contours of muscles and the tendons that were tight, wrenched rough groans from him and used fingernails to tell him what she needed.

The darkness wrapped them like a quilt, muffling the small, frantic sounds of lovemaking. The urgency had snatched her so quickly, driven by touch and the one glimpse of his face, that all of this must have been happening fast, yet it might have taken forever. He entered her with a thrust that brought a shudder of pleasure in its wake. Michael was trying to slow down, she could feel the strain in the quivering muscles of his arms and back, but she didn't want slow, not this time.

With distant astonishment Colleen heard herself whispering, crying, "Please, please, please," and Michael drove into her faster and faster. The bed shook, the covers tangled beneath her, he rolled onto his back so that she could sink onto him as the convulsions started and multiplied, sending out ripples of feelings so intense she couldn't name them.

His own release was as violent; he gave a ragged cry against her neck, his body arching into one last spasm before he sagged back into the covers. Collapsing, Colleen lay sprawled atop him, pleasurably weak, momentarily at peace, her thoughts unfocused.

Only slowly did bits of awareness surface—the sandpaper texture of his jaw against her cheek, the hard, swift beat of his heart beneath her breast, his hand moving almost idly up and down her spine, the way their legs were tangled together and her undignified position.

She hesitated, lifted her head. Although her eyes had adjusted to the dark, she still couldn't make out Michael's features. If only he would say something, pull her mouth down to his for another kiss, one of tenderness, instead of passion.

As swiftly as passion had risen, icy doubt was chilling her. If only just once he had called her name. How could she know in the darkness what Michael thought or felt? What if he had never wanted *her?* Tiredness lowered inhibitions; night brought dreams hard to separate from reality. The possibility lodged in Colleen's throat: *I look like Sheila.*

Which sister had Michael made love to?

On the thought of Sheila, shame washed over Colleen. "Oh, Col!" her sister had exulted not so many years ago. "I've met the most incredible man." And another time, "When he touches me, I just become a mass of little shivery atoms. It's so amazing." Her voice had had a funny little catch, perplexity and wonder and delight. "I never knew I had it in me. Or that some man could find it in me."

Colleen had always believed that she and Sheila were very different beneath the surface. But maybe not. Maybe they had been genetically programmed to be attracted to the same man. A man who could substitute one sister for the other? she wondered.

Trying not to overreact, she disentangled herself. Michael let her go. Too easily? *Say my name,* she begged silently. *Tell me what you feel.*

But instead, he swore.

Colleen turned her head. "What?"

"Cam."

And she heard it, too, the first snuffling whimpers that presaged another storm.

She moaned, but Michael was already rolling away from her. "He can't be hungry. I'll take care of him. You go back to sleep."

Her mouth silently framed the words *come back.* But he couldn't hear what she didn't say. She felt his weight leave the bed, heard the rustles as he searched for and put on his pajama bottoms, the creak of a floorboard under bare feet. When he turned on the hall light, she blinked against the brightness, her eyes registering only his dark silhouette.

Wide-awake, Colleen lay there, torn between a terrible feeling that she had just betrayed her beloved sister and a yearning equally as powerful for Michael to return, to whisper her name, to kiss her again. To want *her,* not Sheila.

And she lay there awake long after the hall light went out, long after she heard his door down the hall close.

HEAVEN AND HELL, wrapped up in one night.

Everything Michael had ever wanted except a few small words had been his—the weight of Colleen's breasts in his hands, her breathless, throaty cries, her shivers and her legs opening to receive him, her arms holding him tight.

But afterward she'd scrambled away as if she'd discovered herself in bed with the wrong man. He'd felt her flood of realization and the subtle tension in the body so intimately in contact with his.

What did he do so terribly wrong that the women he loved wanted passion but nothing that cut deeper? He and Sheila had called what they felt love, but the gut-wrenching vulnerability he'd imagined between husband and wife, the baring of secret fears and hopes, had never materialized.

His fault, Michael thought, as he stared at his own face in the bathroom mirror and adjusted his tie. Last night, why hadn't he said, *I've never touched anything as soft as your skin?* Or, *I need you?* Or even, *I thought I might die if I didn't have you soon?* Why were simple words—the ones that really meant something—so hard for him to say?

But they hadn't flowed out of her, either, he reminded himself grimly, giving his tie a last tug. She'd been straightforward enough about her motives in marrying him: her children. And last night's passion...well, she hadn't had a man in her bed for a long time; years, probably. She'd needed him last night, but he wondered if she had blocked out who he was.

But at some point she had remembered.

He turned away from the mirror. He didn't want to think about Sheila, didn't want to acknowledge that, although he had claimed to love her, he had never felt for her a fraction of last night's desperate hunger and intense satisfaction.

Downstairs he found Colleen already in the kitchen and Cam in the playpen. She gave Michael a quick, almost shy glance from where she was unloading the dishwasher.

"Good morning."

"Good morning," he said gruffly. He stopped at the playpen. Cam lay on his back, staring wide-eyed at his own hands, which he was slowly bringing together and then separating. Michael shook his head. "How come he doesn't have bags under his eyes?"

He'd surprised a chuckle out of her. "Are you kidding? With all the naps he takes?"

"I wonder how well it would go over if the bank closed for a siesta?"

"Oh, dear." She straightened, looking the way she would if Drew had announced he had an earache. "I'm sorry. You must be dreadfully tired."

The truth came more easily than he'd expected. "Some things are worth it."

Her lashes fluttered and her cheeks pinkened. "Well, Cam—"

"I'm not talking about Cam."

Her face was always expressive. Anxiety and pleasure and feminine vanity warred briefly. But at last she offered a small, tentative smile. "Oh, good."

Michael crossed the kitchen and threaded the fingers of one hand into her vibrant hair. He closed his eyes and kissed her, savoring her soft mouth, her morning taste of mint and tea, the way her lips parted and she leaned toward him.

Lifting his head and releasing her, stepping back, was agonizing. Michael flexed his fingers and curled them into fists before shoving them in his pockets.

Colleen looked as shell-shocked as he felt. The tremble in her soft, lower lip and the cloudiness in her moss green eyes made him wish he'd been able to see her face last night as he made love to her. Right as he entered her, and then at the end. Next time...

But he tamped down on the thought. Last night it had just happened, too quickly for reflection or guilt, taking them both by surprise. But if he deliberately went to Colleen's bed...

Her thoughts had obviously paralleled his, because Colleen said quietly, "Last night…it was wonderful. And now I feel so guilty, as though I've done something wrong." She drew a shaky breath. "Tell me…"

"That I feel the same?" His voice was raw.

She quivered as though he'd struck her. "I was going to say, tell me what an idiot I'm being."

His own guilt was magnified tenfold by hers. Michael felt as though his chest had been scalded. "Who am I to tell you that?" To his own ears, he sounded as though he was speaking from a great distance away. "I promised Sheila eternity. I didn't even stay in mourning for ten months."

He didn't wait for a response, didn't want to see any more pain in Colleen's eyes. He left without breakfast, without finding out whether he was supposed to take Drew or Kim somewhere. Right this second, he couldn't deal with anybody else's expectations.

How could he when he knew how selfish he really was? The taste of heaven last night had been too sweet. Whether Colleen was ready or not, Michael wasn't going to be able to stay away from her for long.

BY THE TIME he got home from work, Michael had pulled himself together enough to draw Colleen aside. "I'm sorry," he said roughly. "Talking about Sheila this morning, it just got to me. I, uh, I don't know…"

Colleen laid a hand over his mouth and shook her head. "No, don't say anything. I wanted reassurance, and I didn't stop to think that I might make you feel as bad."

A muscle in his jaw jerked. "Don't worry. I felt guilty as hell all on my own."

Colleen pressed her lips together and turned quickly away. "Dinner's almost ready."

Dinner. Kids. An evening meeting of the soccer coaches to set a game schedule. The mundane in the midst of melodrama.

Michael came home from the meeting inexpressibly weary. He felt a little better the minute he parked in front of the barn. The old house was lit and welcoming; in seeing generations come and go, it fit perfectly his idea of a real home.

He let himself in quietly, locking the front door behind him, then paused to glance into the living room. Colleen was there, quilting at the large frame they'd decided to set up there so she could be with the family while she worked.

Lamplight cast a warm glow over her; her reflection in the small panes of the bay window was timeless. How many women had quilted in this house, making bed covers to keep their families warm?

Colleen wore a loose cotton dress that exposed a delicate collarbone and a long, graceful neck. Her heavy, auburn hair was bundled at her nape, and her arms were slender and pale in what should have been an awkward pose, but was utterly natural for her. She seemed absorbed in her work, and patient beyond his understanding.

Would she be as patient with him?

"Hello," he said.

She started and lifted her head. "Oh, Michael. How was the meeting?"

"Eight Saturday games, two Sunday. Most of the boys' coaches wanted to stick the girls' teams with the Sunday games."

She made a face. "Figures."

Michael leaned against the arched opening. "A few of us thought the inconvenience should be spread around equally. We won."

"A small victory for the rights of women."

He let himself smile back. "You bet."

Her face was soft, her eyes enigmatic. "Can you sit down?"

Go slowly, give her time to think, Michael told himself. He shook his head. "I have work to do."

"Oh. Fine."

He wanted to believe she was disappointed, but she could just as well be relieved. "Kids in bed?"

"Yes, but reading. Although to tell you the truth—" her nose crinkled "—I think Drew has that wretched hand-held electronic game he borrowed from Ian under the bed covers. I could swear I heard a beep before I stuck my head in."

"I don't think it'll warp him for life," Michael said mildly.

Colleen made a face. "No, of course not. But as a mother, I have a duty to make him feel guilty for..." Her voice died, and they stared at each other.

God, he wanted her. Wanted to put his lips to her throat, his hands on her lush breasts. He wanted to rip that dress over her head and see her milky, pale skin and the pink-brown areolae of her nipples, the silky hair that must be as richly colored as that on her head. He'd dreamed a million times...

But when had the dreams started? Had he wanted Colleen even when Sheila was alive?

That was the question he couldn't afford to ask. Even now, he flinched away from it.

"I'll say good-night to the kids." He sounded hoarse. "And see you in the morning."

Colleen gave a tiny nod. Her stricken expression stayed with him even after he booted the computer in his office. Could she possibly be hurt that he'd made clear he wasn't coming to her bed? Had he misunderstood her completely?

She was so reserved the next day he had to wonder again. For the first time in weeks she was prickly when he asked Kim to do a chore and a minor scene erupted. He was just ticked off enough to decide that if Colleen couldn't take steps to do something about Kim's unhappiness, he would, and why the hell should he consult her, anyway?

At dinnertime even the kids picked up on the tension. He caught a few speculative looks, but Kim apparently was old enough to keep her thoughts to herself—or to wait and talk to her mother, rather than him. Actually, Michael was surprised when Drew trailed him outside.

"What are you doing?"

"Trying to decide where we should have the garage built. I don't want my car outside when winter comes."

"Oh." Drew hoisted himself onto the porch railing. "Are you and Mom mad at each other?"

Michael's first instinct was to lie. He ignored it. "Yeah, I guess we are. Grown-ups get mad, too, you know."

"Are you going to get divorced?" The boy was trying hard to sound untroubled. He didn't quite succeed.

"Afraid you'll lose your soccer coach?"

"Well, yeah." Drew swung his legs, and his eyes wouldn't meet Michael's. "But, um, it's been kind of cool having, well, almost a dad. You know?"

The kid might as well have reached right into Michael's chest and given his heart a little twist. "Yeah." He cleared his throat. "It's been cool having almost a son, too."

Drew looked up anxiously. "But you have a real son."

Michael gave him a crooked grin. "He's no fun yet."

The boy's face cleared. "Mom says he won't even be able to *walk* for a year! Walking's easy!"

"So will pitching be for you when you're a foot taller."

"I guess," Drew conceded. He kept swinging his legs. "*Are* you getting divorced?"

"No divorce."

"Well, then, I've been thinking. Could we get a puppy?"

Michael coughed to hide his smile. "Uh...have you talked to your mom about this?"

Drew's brown eyes were wide and innocent. "No. I thought I'd ask you first."

"Ah. Well, why don't you see what she says?"

"Right now?" He jumped down from the railing. "Cool!"

Michael opened his mouth to suggest he wait until his mother was in a better mood, but he was too late. The screen door was already slamming shut and Drew was bellowing, "Mom!"

Five minutes later, Colleen stalked out onto the porch. "You said he could have a dog."

Michael crossed his arms. "Actually, no, I didn't. But is there any reason he can't?"

Her mouth opened and then she snapped it shut. "He lied."

Michael was momentarily able to see the humor in all this. "Would you put it that strongly?"

"Yes!" Colleen gave an exasperated sigh. "No. I'm just not used to them going behind my back."

He gave her a minute before suggesting calmly, "You know, I suspect kids in any family play one parent off against the other. Didn't they try that with Ben?"

She frowned. "Drew wasn't old enough. Kim...maybe." It was grudging. "But Ben didn't do a heck of a lot of parenting." Some emotion Michael wished he could decipher flickered across her face. "You're right," she said shortly, and went back into the house.

"Damn it to hell," Michael muttered, and turned to stare out at the yard. Dusk was slipping over the eastern hills, purple and gray and cool. The leaves were turning brilliant shades of scarlet and yellow.

Were he and Colleen getting anywhere? he wondered. Or were they being pulled back by the undertow?

On the positive side: she was being honest with herself, even though her insight was obviously unwelcome some of the time. Positive: the kids seemed to be learning to accept him. Positive: he and Colleen had made love and been compatible—a pallid word for what they had actually felt.

Negative: they were both ridden with guilt. Negative: he didn't know whether she wanted him back in her bed or not. Negative: he didn't know what she felt, and she didn't know what he felt.

To both the last two points, there was only one way to find out. And to hell with Sheila's ghost.

For a change Cam went down for the night at about the same time as Drew and Kim. Michael hung around downstairs, pretending to read the paper, while Colleen quilted. When she finally announced she was going to bed, he promptly rose to his feet.

"I think I will, too."

Her eyes rolled like those of a spooked horse, but she sounded only a little breathless when she said, "Do you want to lock up?"

"Sure."

Upstairs he brushed his teeth, shaved for a second time in the day and, in the office where he was also sleeping, stripped down to his jeans. Then, as nervous and excited as a sixteen-year-old kid his first time, Michael went down the hall to Colleen's bedroom.

Her door stood half-open, as it always did so she could hear Cam in the night; the lamp beside her bed was still on. Under his hand, her door opened silently, but she was waiting for him, sitting up in bed, ramrod straight, her eyes huge and dark.

Just as silently, Michael closed the door behind him. She watched wordlessly as he went around to the other side of the bed, but she flushed and looked away when he reached for the snap on his jeans. He stepped out of them and tossed them onto a chair, then slipped quickly into bed. Lying on his side, braced on one elbow, he looked at her.

Colleen's silken, heavy mass of hair was confined in a fat braid. Her nightgown was different from the other night's, but the white smocked fabric was as thin, and this one, too, was sleeveless and scoop-necked.

Michael reached out and cupped her cheek in one hand, turning her head to face him. Her lips were compressed, her lashes lowered. But she was no coward; after a bare moment they lifted to reveal eyes as deep and mysterious as that deep, green pool to which he had once compared her.

He knew he should say something; he knew he shouldn't have walked in here and climbed into her bed without asking tacitly or otherwise for permission. But words never had been his strong suit.

With his thumb he traced the line of her lips, felt them soften, part, her breathing quicken. Suddenly she sucked in a breath and turned to reach for her lamp switch.

"No," he said quickly. She hesitated, but didn't turn back to him. His voice was scratchy. "I want to see you."

"But I'm—" She clamped down on whatever she'd been going to say, but she still wasn't looking at him.

"Beautiful." He didn't sound like himself.

"Thirty-five years old. I've had three children."

"You're a woman, not a teenage girl. I don't want a girl."

"But Sheila—" Colleen stopped again.

He didn't want to think about Sheila, but this was one time he was going to have to. "Sheila?"

"She was younger. And slimmer. And she'd never had a baby."

Michael had her flat under him before she could think twice. He bent his head and kissed her until she began to shiver. When he lifted his head he said grittily, "You are not Sheila, and I never thought you were. Your faces looked a little alike to people who didn't know you well. The rest of you doesn't."

"But...you've never seen..."

"I've touched you." He raised himself on his elbows. "Your breasts are bigger..."

"Because I'm nursing."

"All the time." Her nipples were tight and hard. Michael rubbed his mouth against them through the fine cotton of her gown and felt another little quiver in the body waiting quiescently under him. "You only have freckles on your nose." He scooted her nightgown up and rejoiced in the way her hips rose to help him take it off. Her skin was just as pale and creamy as he'd imagined, her curves as gentle. Her belly was a little soft under his hand, but to each side were the peaks of pelvic bone. And her hair... Michael sat up. "It's like licks of flame," he said, tangling his fingers in the curls, feeling the heat and damp beneath.

Now her eyes were so dark he couldn't have seen their color. She was breathing in tiny gasps, her hands clutching the covers. Shyly she said, "You have a nice body yourself."

"But not a boy's."

Her gaze dropped to the forceful evidence of his arousal. "No, thank goodness," she said, that little bit of huskiness in her voice an aphrodisiac. As if he needed one.

"I want *you*," he said straight out, and braced himself for her answer.

"I don't suppose you'd believe me if I said I didn't want you." She was trying to tease him, and he knew she was thinking about that unmistakable dampness his fingers had discovered.

But he said, almost grimly, "I'd believe you," and hoped she knew what he was trying to tell her.

Apparently she did, because her lashes lifted and she studied him inscrutably for a moment long enough to scare the hell out of him. And then she smiled, still shyly, and held her arms out to him. A simple gesture, and a powerful one. One a man could wait his whole life for.

He went into her arms and closed his mind to anything outside the circle of her embrace. They would have to talk soon; passion couldn't vanquish guilt. But tonight he was going to take what she offered, and not wish he deserved more.

ONE MINUTE Michael's eyes were molten with hunger for her, and he made her feel sexy and womanly and maybe even loved. And the next he damn near shut her fingers in the doors he used to guard himself, he slammed them shut with so little warning.

One *minute* wasn't quite right, though; one *night* he made love to her until she had no more identity or resistance than a little pool of amoebas, happy in their simplicity. But come morning he was back to his silent, frowning self. Which he'd been ever since. Polite, helpful—and distant. Two nights now she had waited for him to come to her bed. But no, he'd apparently felt strong and able to resist her feeble lures. And she didn't have the guts to stalk down the hall and climb into *his* bed.

Maybe she should be flattered that he regarded her as a

forbidden fruit. No man had ever found her that exotic before. But she had always valued calm, a life of security and confidence and tranquillity.

Tranquillity. Colleen almost snorted, which startled a customer who turned from the bolts of solid-color cotton. "Pardon me?"

"Just mumbling to myself," Colleen admitted.

The older woman smiled. "I do it all the time."

"Do you need any help?"

"Um—" she tilted her head "—well, I like this pale green with the sunflower print, but then the brown doesn't look right. What do you think?"

"Are you determined to have the green?"

"Heavens, no."

"Well, then, how about a pale yellow or cream?" She reached unerringly for the bolt she wanted. "Like this."

The woman blinked. "Perfect! Bless you. Cut them before I change my mind."

Colleen was still brooding about her marriage on the way home at five-thirty. Maybe that was why she suddenly found herself headed for the rental that had been home the past year. In the absence of conscious direction, habit had taken over. On impulse, instead of turning at the next intersection, she decided to drive by the house.

New renters had already moved in. A tricycle sat on the sidewalk, a teenage boy was dribbling a basketball in the driveway and eyeing the hoop above the neighbor's garage. Colleen stopped on the other side of the street and just sat looking for a minute, trying to find inside herself the woman who had lived contentedly here.

All she discovered was that she wouldn't go back even if she could. Back before Cam, back when Michael was her sister's husband, a remote man she'd always felt a little uncomfortable around...

Back before Sheila had died.

But the reminder didn't have the impact it once had.

"We have to go on," she said softly. This time she didn't expect an answer. Sheila was gone, alive only in their memories. Which was as it ought to be.

Ten minutes later, Colleen turned into her own driveway. She had parked and was getting out when two girls came tearing around the corner of the house.

"Hey, Mom!" Kim called. "Stacey's here."

"So I see," Colleen said, smiling at the other girl. "Is your mom or dad here, Stacey?"

"No, I just came over to hang out with Kim." She shrugged nonchalantly. "What a neat house. And barn."

Kim was fairly dancing with excitement. "Mom, Stacey's parents say she can take horseback-riding lessons. Can I take them, too? Michael says it's up to you."

"Honey, they're expensive."

Her daughter's joy dimmed. "But you said maybe I could get a horse. I mean, why else did you buy a place with a barn and pasture?"

"Because we liked the house." Colleen closed her eyes. "Kim, I'll think about it. Do you suppose I can take Cam out of his car seat and have something cold to drink before we make any decisions?"

"Sure." Kim's voice went flat and her shoulders had sagged. "You'll say no, anyway."

"I haven't yet." Aware of Stacey's presence, Colleen didn't add, "But I will if you go on this way."

Inside, Colleen deposited Cam in the playpen and went to the refrigerator. Behind her, Michael said, "Hi. How was your day?"

"Fine." She grabbed a can of soda pop and flipped open the top, bumping the refrigerator door shut with her hip. "Yours?"

Damn, just the sight of him, arms crossed, shoulders filling the doorway, was enough to make her weak. Where was her pride?

"Did you see Kim?" His voice was slow and deep.

"I gather she's acquired a bosom buddy."

His dark brows went up. "Is that bad?"

"Don't be silly. I like Stacey. If their friendship amounts to anything, I'll go down on bended knee." Colleen tried to ignore the tension creeping up her neck, tightening around her forehead. "Was this your idea?"

"Um-huh." He was using that calm, neutral tone he had undoubtedly perfected for business negotiations. The one designed to smooth feathers, to keep emotion out of the discussion. "I figured if they were stuck with each other for the day, something might come of it."

He expected her to be jealous, she realized; jealous because he'd been able to do something for Kim that she hadn't. And she'd asked for it, after the way she'd acted the first few times he took some initiative with the kids.

Colleen took care to keep her own tone as deliberately calm. "She said something about riding lessons."

He just watched her with those vivid eyes. "Seems like a good idea to me."

"Michael...do you know what they cost?"

He shrugged. "We can afford them."

Now, when she least needed it, was when her pride reared its ugly head. She'd gladly have accepted everything he could do for her children if only he had married her for love, which she could return in equal measure. But theirs had been a bargain—and an unequal one. At moments like this, she felt like a kept woman.

Her hesitation was brief, but even that was too long.

Just like that, his teeth clenched. "You'd rather live on what you make, wouldn't you?"

She felt she owed him honesty. "Michael, being able to support myself was important to me. These days I feel a little like the beggar maid. Anyway, you shouldn't have to fork over money for everything my kids want."

"I gather," he said, his tone remote, "that you don't exactly feel married. At least, not 'for richer or for poorer.'"

"Michael—"

His eyes glittered. "Or are you in this marriage at all?"

"Michael—"

CHAPTER FIFTEEN

ANGER RUSHED through Colleen. It came easily, a wave breaking over her head. "Maybe that's a question you should ask yourself," she snapped.

Michael loomed over her like a thunderhead. "What's that supposed to mean?"

It means, do you love me or don't you? She couldn't say that. But she could come close.

"One night you're in my bed telling me I'm beautiful, and the next night you can't go into hiding fast enough!"

His voice rose. "You haven't exactly been handing me an invitation!"

"Well, I won't be tonight, either!"

Michael leaned toward her, his teeth set. "According to you," he said silkily, "it's *my* money that bought your bedroom. That makes it mine."

Colleen inhaled sharply. "Do you think you've bought me?"

They stared at each other. Suddenly Michael bowed his head. He was breathing as though he'd been running. "You know I don't," he said quietly. "Colleen—"

"No." She shook her head and backed away. "I don't want to talk about it right now."

"Uncle Michael..." Stacey stopped in the doorway and looked wide-eyed from one to the other. "I'm sorry." She started to retreat, stopped, bit her lip. "Um, my mom's here to get me."

"I'll go out," Colleen said quickly. She made a distinct circle around Michael. She hoped the smile she gave her niece by marriage didn't look as faked as it was. "So, Stacey, do you like middle school?"

"Yeah, it's okay. I'm glad Kim and I have classes together."

They found Kim outside talking to Jennifer, who smiled at Colleen. "Sounds like the girls had a good time today."

"Looks like it," Colleen agreed. "We'll have to do this again."

"Mom, can Kim come over after school Monday?" Stacey asked. She gave Kim a shy glance. "If she wants to."

Kim turned pleading eyes on Colleen. "Can I, Mom?"

The two mothers agreed that, yes, that would be fine, and Colleen promised to pick Kim up at six.

When the station wagon backed out, Colleen glanced at her daughter to find her face averted. "Honey…" Colleen sighed. "I'm sorry. I was cranky today."

"I know we don't have the money," Kim said unexpectedly. "I shouldn't have asked you. I just thought…well, that maybe we did now, since you're married."

"I guess we do," Colleen admitted. "I'm just so used to thinking one way, I'm having trouble readjusting. But Michael and I talked about it, and lessons would be fine."

"Really?" Kim breathed, instantly up from the depths. "With Stacey?"

"Sure. I'll talk to her mom."

"Oh, thank you, thank you, thank you!" Kim gave her a quick squeeze. "Where's Michael?"

"In the house…" Kim was already on her way. Colleen stood in the middle of the yard, reluctant to go back in herself. Michael was right; they did have to talk. But she didn't look forward to it. She didn't want to hear him admit how he really felt about her and the marriage.

They succeeded in getting through the evening without the kids noticing anything wrong. Colleen was very careful not to give signals Michael might have taken as an invitation—not because she didn't want him to come to her bed, she admitted rather unhappily to herself, but because of her pride.

Michael came, anyway, silently in the dark. This time she didn't know he was there until she felt the bed give under his weight. To her shame, she didn't protest. Instead, at the first touch of his hand, need clenched inside her and she went willingly, even eagerly, into his arms. Neither spoke, though they sighed and moaned and sobbed for breath. The time might come when their lovemaking could be sweet and lingering, when they could laugh or tease or tantalize. But not yet; stark hunger drove them to snatch desperately at these rare moments, at the sensual stroke of rough fingertips on her breasts, at the shiver of muscles under her palms, at the shudder of pleasure when they came together. In the dark they had to admit nothing; passion was enough.

It held Michael there when Colleen got up once in the middle of the night to nurse Cam; it brought them together again in another feverish coupling. But when she awakened in the morning to find herself alone, the emptiness that clutched at her was greater than this bed or this room.

She needed more than the coming together of their bodies, more than physical release. And she was terribly afraid that that was all either had sought or found in each other's arms. She wasn't even sure how to name what they'd done last night. Was it lovemaking? Colleen wondered with self-loathing, or just plain sex?

MICHAEL HAD just discovered the difference between having sex and making love. He had made love to a woman for only the fourth time in his life last night. The knowledge was like an ulcer, eating away at him from the inside out.

Michael dipped the sponge into the bucket of warm, soapy water and sloshed it over the hood of Colleen's car. The activity was just about right for his state of mind today. The kids were washing his car at the same time so he could supervise, though as attentive as he was, they could have been using it as a water slide.

No, his mind was mired in the past, trying to understand how he could have made such a mistake in his first marriage and wondering whether, if Sheila hadn't died, he would ever have recognized quite how fundamental that mistake had been.

Because the truth was, he had married the wrong sister. Lifting the wiper blades to get at the windshield, Michael had a flash of remembering the dreams he'd had shortly after Sheila died, the ones in which he hadn't been able to tell which sister he was with. He hadn't had the dreams in a long time. And for a good reason. He doubted he would even see a resemblance between the two now if they were standing side by side.

If he'd met Colleen first, he would never have looked twice at Sheila. It was the ways in which they were similar that had attracted him to Sheila; but it was the ways in which Colleen was different that reached him most powerfully.

He didn't feel guilty anymore because Sheila was dead and he wasn't; he didn't even feel guilty because he had married Colleen. No, what got to him was the fact that on some gut level he couldn't help rejoicing, because only Sheila's death would have let him find and have the woman he loved.

But he was going to lose her if he didn't soon come to terms with his self-knowledge.

He made a sound of disgust and reached for the hose. Maybe he already had come to terms and just hadn't yet figured out a way to make it palatable for Colleen.

On Monday, as much to corner himself as to corner her, Michael left the bank early and drove over to her shop. Here they couldn't be interrupted by the kids. If she had customers, he'd just wait until closing time. But the only car in the gravel parking lot out front was Colleen's.

She was perched on a stool behind the tall front counter, her head bent, contemplating a fan of fabric swatches. When the bell over the door rang, she looked up, smiling automatically. "Hello...oh, hi, Michael." With a mother's quick alarm, she added, "Something wrong?"

"Nope." He let the door close behind him and the bell tinkled again. "Busy?"

"Heavens, no. Cam's sleeping." She nodded at the play-pen, then made a face. "Actually, the place was dead today. House of Fabrics is having a forty percent off sale this week."

"Your customers will all show up Monday to buy more fabric to go with whatever they bought there."

This time her smile was grateful. "I hope so. What's up?"

"I thought this might be a good chance for us to talk."

Colleen studied him gravely. After a moment she nodded.

Michael paced the length of the small room and stopped in front of the window. He turned to face her and pushed his hands into his pockets.

"I should start," he said abruptly. "I always figured that Sheila told you everything. That she talked about our marriage and our problems."

Her voice was whisper soft. "I suppose that didn't make you feel any too happy. I never realized... I guess Sheila didn't, either."

"No." He moved his shoulders to loosen tight muscles. "And, yeah, it bothered me. I, uh... Hell, this sounds petty." He made himself say it, anyway. "I was jealous of you before I ever met you. A couple of times I overheard the tail end of one of Sheila's conversations with you. She didn't talk like that to me. She claimed to love me, but I don't think she ever trusted me. She didn't have to, because she had you."

He caught a glimpse of the odd expression on Colleen's face before she bowed her head. Her voice was strained. "There's something I should tell you."

"Wait. Let me finish." Michael swung away again and gazed, unseeing, out the window. "Our marriage was in trouble years ago." He made a rough sound in his throat. "No, that's not right. It wasn't that we fought or either of us took up with someone else. I just...felt empty, and I think Sheila did, too. Or maybe she didn't, God, I don't know. She had you to talk to. She didn't need me."

The compassion in Colleen's eyes was too close to pity. "Sheila never said a word of this to me. I'd have sworn she was in love with you. Only once..."

"What?"

"I told you about it. That once, she sounded angry because you didn't seem to understand why she kept trying to get pregnant despite her miscarriages."

"No, I didn't understand. It was crazy. She might as well have been rubbing sandpaper over raw skin. I figured..." He let out a long breath. "I figured she was desperate to fill the emptiness we both felt. I wasn't enough for her. Never had been enough. I used to wonder..." God, it was hard to bare himself. He felt Colleen's gaze even though his face was averted. "I wondered why she didn't leave me, why she didn't find a man who could love her the way she wanted to be loved. But I don't think she ever even looked. All she wanted was a baby. For that, she needed me. I used to think that was all she kept me for."

"I...really don't think it was that simple," Colleen said with seeming difficulty. "I've been doing a lot of thinking lately myself."

Now he did look at her, expecting to see open pity. Instead, her luminous eyes held distress and weariness and even guilt.

"You know that our own father walked out on us when we were young."

Michael nodded.

"Even though I still have a few memories of him, I've always told everybody I didn't really miss him. Now I think that Mom was so determined to make sure we didn't, she overdid it. Probably it wasn't on purpose, but I can still hear her voice, telling me we didn't need him. I thought she was brave and strong." Colleen gave a funny, twisted smile. Her eyes had a far-off look. "Maybe she was. For sure, Mom was just doing the best she could. But I think Sheila and I heard it so many times, neither of us were left with the ability to trust any man, much less admit to ourselves we needed him."

She kept talking, and Michael listened without interrupting. He wasn't the only one who had dammed up his emotions. But it developed that not all her guilt had to do with Sheila. Colleen had decided that she'd pushed Ben away, and though Michael never had thought all that highly of her ex-husband, he hadn't known the two of them together well enough to tell if there was any merit in her conclusion. The rest of it—her belief that Sheila had done the same to him—he didn't dare allow himself to buy one hundred percent. It would have let him off the hook, given him an excuse when he didn't deserve one.

But maybe there was something to her theory. Maybe it explained why Sheila never seemed to mind how shallow their relationship was. And maybe it explained why she hadn't looked for another man. According to Colleen, she wasn't programmed to need a man. She was programmed to have babies and raise them and be strong, to trust her mother and her sister, but never her husband.

But Michael knew damn well that the kind of man he was hadn't helped matters. Sheila had to have been hungry for love and tenderness and attention—all things he hadn't known how to give her. All needs she'd thought a child would fill.

On the heels of his sadness that she had never had that child was relief. Because the child was no longer an abstraction. It was Cam, small and vulnerable, who would have had to carry the burden of his mother's needs.

It was her husband who should have carried them.

And so he'd failed in his marriage, whatever his excuse. What scared him was that he'd fail again. He couldn't lose Colleen now that he'd found her. But he had no idea what she needed from him.

And he wasn't sure he was capable of letting her see how badly *he* needed her.

She had lapsed into silence, staring down at the fan of fabric samples on the counter in front of him. He moved his shoulders uncomfortably inside his suit jacket and looked away himself, scrutinizing bolts of calicos shading from navy to ice blue as though they could tell him something.

His voice sounded gravelly, and he made himself look back at Colleen. His wife. "I don't know if this got us anywhere, but I thought you should know. I won't say I haven't mourned Sheila, because I have. But...not the way you probably thought."

Colleen nodded. Her gaze touched his, shied away, came nervously back. "Then why—" She stopped.

"Why the guilt?" *Because I love you, and I didn't love her.* He might have had the nerve to say it if he'd had any reason to think Colleen loved him. Any reason except the way she responded to him sexually. He cleared his throat. "It just felt sometimes as though I picked up and moved on so quickly. One minute everything we did was for her. The next, she was gone, and you and I were haggling over the baby. Now here we are married, making the kind of family Sheila wanted, but we're doing it for us, not her." He rubbed a hand over his face. "And she hasn't been dead a year."

In a few stark sentences he'd destroyed any chance of saying, *I love you.* But Colleen surprised him.

"Not just for us," she said spiritedly. "For Cam, too. And Drew and Kim."

"True."

Her back was very straight, her cheeks pink. "You know, it would be easy to feel guilty forever because we're alive and Sheila's dead. But what's the point? We aren't doing her any good."

"True."

Colleen eyed him suspiciously. "Are you agreeing just so you don't hurt my feelings?"

"No." Was he smiling? "I do agree. Everything you say makes sense. I didn't say I was always rational."

"Emotions never are," Colleen told him with childlike solemnity. She made the conversion to being thoroughly adult when she added, "Thank heavens."

"Why thank heavens?"

She scrunched up her face. "Because I'm a gutless wonder. If I didn't follow my feelings sometimes, instead of thinking everything out, I'd be paralyzed by indecision.''

The difference between them was he never followed his feelings. Or at least, Michael amended in faint surprise, he never used to. Asking Colleen to marry him had been an impulse. Not entirely, though; he'd buttressed his decision with all sorts of rational reasons why it was the thing to do. But that wasn't why he'd asked her; he'd asked her because it had felt right.

And God knows he hadn't hauled her off to bed because calm reason had told him the time had come. Calm reason had been screaming, *Stop!* He'd told it to go to hell.

The idea amused him. It also made him wonder if there wasn't hope for him. If he could be swept away by passion, surely he could manage a few simple words. *I love you. I need you.*

"Well." Colleen stood up behind her barricade. "If I don't get going, I'll be late picking up Kim."

"I'll do that," Michael offered. "Do you want me to grab something for dinner on the way home? Chinese, maybe?"

"I put a roast out to defrost this morning. Besides—" she was lifting Cam from the playpen and making silly faces at him "—cooking dinner is about the only thing I do that makes me feel useful."

Michael stiffened. Why was money such a sticking point for her?

But she surprised him yet again with a pert smile. "Not that I mind having a cleaning woman. I can't say I want to go back to dusting and vacuuming. Or cleaning bathrooms, heaven forbid."

Generous to the end. He was a lucky man, even if Colleen never came to love him.

The thought was infinitely depressing.

*NOW HERE WE ARE MARRIED making the kind of family Sheila
wanted, but we're doing it for us, not her.*

Colleen went home feeling more optimistic than she had
since the day Michael asked her to marry him. He hadn't
just sought her out to talk to her, he'd sought her out to
send a message.

He'd wanted her to know that he hadn't been madly in
love with Sheila, that his heart hadn't been broken by her
death. Was there any chance at all, Colleen wondered, that
he'd been trying to say that he was free to love again? Free
to love her?

Well, then, her argumentative inner voice demanded,
why didn't he just *tell* you he loves you?

Maybe because he didn't have a clue how she felt? After
all, as far as he knew, she'd married him only to keep
Cam—and, of course, she thought ruefully, for his money.

Well, he'd taken the first step. She should be grateful for
that much, and patient. Besides, they had a lifetime together.

Michael came to her bed that night. As he made love to
her, he told her how beautiful she was, and he quivered at
her touch. But he said not a word about how he felt, and
as a result, neither did she. When she was dragged out of
a deep sleep by Cam's cries and Michael mumbled, "I'll
get him," before rolling away, Colleen reached after him.

"You know," she said sleepily, "you could come
back."

He went still. "Do you want me to?"

"Uh-huh," she murmured.

His hand smoothed her hair off her face, and she brushed
her lips against his wrist. "You could sleep here every
night," she said a little less sleepily. She held her breath
waiting for his answer.

"Is that what you want?" he asked again, his voice deep.

"I wouldn't have said it if I didn't." Her heart was pounding hard now at her boldness. "But if you're more comfortable having your own bedroom, that's okay."

"No." He bent down and kissed her, his mouth lingering even as Cam's cries escalated. "Oh, hell," Michael muttered. "Don't go anywhere."

"I won't," Colleen said breathlessly.

The very next day, he moved in, taking over the second closet. Colleen felt more secure in her marriage and less like someone who has an illicit lover slipping into her bedroom in the wee hours of the night.

But she still had to face the fact that Michael hadn't said a word about his feelings. His silence was unsettling. Would the kind of explosive passion they had endure if love wasn't part of it, sending down deep roots to anchor their marriage?

Her uneasiness came to a head that night when they went into their bedroom. Michael dropped his shirt on a ladder-back chair and sprawled on the bed wearing jeans and nothing else. Colleen grabbed her nightgown and headed for the bathroom.

"Why are you going in there to undress?" he asked her.

Colleen stopped with her back to him. "To protect you?" she ventured.

"I'm a big boy." His voice was husky. "I like to take risks."

"Michael..." As she turned to face him, excitement shivered in her, but also some primal terror. She didn't want him to see her body's every flaw, all exposed at once. If she stood before him naked, she would be painfully vulnerable.

"Come here."

"No, I... No." She shook her head hard. "I'd rather not."

He studied her from the bed, where he lay with the pillows bunched behind him. Lines were etched between his dark brows. Colleen held his gaze defiantly.

"What are you afraid of?"

She hardly knew the answer herself, except that she had to protect herself.

"I don't know." It wasn't as though he hadn't seen her, but somehow this was different. She clutched the nightgown in a death grip. "I just..."

"Never mind." His expression had closed. "I don't want you to do anything that makes you uncomfortable."

Yes, but why had it? Colleen spent the next day brooding about her own reaction. She hadn't been especially modest around Ben, and her third pregnancy hadn't wreaked such havoc with her body that she had to be ashamed of it. No, there was another explanation.

Probably she was afraid of losing Michael if he was disappointed; maybe more afraid of losing him because of the very strength of her feelings. And, after all, her first husband had walked out on her.

But Colleen knew in her heart that Michael wasn't the kind of man who would leave a woman because her body wasn't flawless. Still, it took such trust to stand naked, with nothing to hide behind, in front of a man. A woman had to be secure in her beauty or secure in his love. And she wasn't either.

She had begun to believe that he liked her. She knew he wanted her. But neither fact meant that this wasn't still a marriage of convenience as far as he was concerned. Neither fact meant that he would have chosen her out of all the women in the world.

The scary part was that she was driven to know one way or the other. The uncertainty was killing her. She had to ask. But it wasn't fair to expect him to reveal his innermost emotions without her doing so, as well. And if she did—if she told Michael she loved him and then he hesitated, or fumbled for an answer, or even admitted he didn't love her... Her heart squeezed at the thought. Oh, Lord, what would it do to them? Could they maintain even the kind of marriage they had if one was in love and the other wasn't?

She'd told him she was a coward, and now she discovered how much of one. After the kids went to bed, he sat down on the couch with the newspaper. Colleen sneaked a glance at him just as she had when she wondered what it would be like to have his hands touching her.

Suddenly she realized he was looking straight at her, one eyebrow lifted in faint surprise at whatever he saw in her expression.

"Is something wrong?" he asked.

Now, Colleen told herself, and opened her mouth. Incredulous, she felt herself shaking her head. "I was just thinking. I'm sorry. Was I staring blankly at you?"

His eyes narrowed for a heartbeat, but he didn't comment.

And in bed that night, under the antique nine-patch quilt that covered them, she tried to whisper, "I love you." But it stuck in her throat, and Colleen told herself she wanted to see the expression on his face when she made her declaration.

Three little words. Easy to say to the kids. Wrenchingly difficult to say to Michael.

DREW CAME TEARING into the kitchen, chanting, "Kim has boobies, Kim has boobies!"

His sister was in hot pursuit. "You're a brat, Andrew Deering!"

Colleen turned from the hot stove to find that Michael had just walked in the back door, suit jacket slung over his shoulder. He reached out a long arm and effortlessly snagged his stepson. "Let's have a little talk," he suggested. Only Colleen heard the suppressed amusement in his voice.

"Mo-om!" Kim wailed, stopping in the middle of the kitchen. "I'm so humiliated!"

Michael held Drew in a hammerlock. "You know," he said conversationally to Kim, "you'll have plenty of chances to get him back. I don't think it's occurred to him yet how humiliated *he'll* be when his voice starts cracking or when his friends are shaving and he's not, or when he's still a little shrimp and they're nudging six feet."

"Who says I'll be a little shrimp?" Drew protested.

Michael set him on his feet. "You may not be," he agreed. "But, hey, who knows? If you tease her about something she can't help, like her body, you're asking for it back."

Kim's cheeks were still bright pink, but her voice had moderated when she said, "Yeah, you ought to think about it."

Drew thought. For about five seconds. He gave a big grin. "Who cares if I can shave or not? That won't embarrass me. Not like *boobies* embarrass Kim."

"Aargh!" She lunged for him, he dodged, and they were off again, out of the kitchen.

Michael called after them, "Guys, keep it down," but the sounds of battle had moved into the living room. He shook his head, but he was laughing when he kissed Colleen on the cheek. "Sorry. I gave it my best."

What a peculiar moment to realize afresh how much she loved him. It had happened while he was holding Drew in the only way a nine-year-old boy would accept and talking to Kim as though she were an adult. Patiently. Kindly. He was the father her kids needed so desperately, and her heart suddenly felt as though it were being squeezed in a giant fist.

There she stood, wooden spoon dripping spaghetti sauce unheeded onto the stove top, wearing an apron and a sweat-shirt that said The One Who Dies with the Most Fabric...Wins!

And just like that, Colleen blurted, "I love you."

Michael's smile slowly died. He stared at her for so long she began to feel aghast at what she'd set in motion. Her heart pounded in her ears and she was on the verge of apologizing, of trying somehow to retreat, when he suddenly closed his eyes.

When he opened them again, they blazed with a fire so hot she was seared. He took a step toward her. "Say that again."

"Make him shut up, Mom!"

Her children exploded back into the kitchen, and behind them came Cam's thin cry. Michael backed away and gave his head a shake. By the time he looked at her again, the fire was banked. Colleen wanted to follow Cam's example and weep.

Michael said huskily, just for her ears, "You know how to pick your moment."

Colleen half laughed, half groaned. All those ideal times she could have chosen, and she had to declare her love right in the middle of Drew and Kim quarreling.

"Kim flushed my slime down the toilet! Just for that I'm going to—"

"Set the dinner table," Michael said. He grasped both kids by the upper arms and turned them toward the dining room. Over their heads, he gave Colleen one last look of near desperation before he marched them out. "Drew, do you believe every word your sister says? I seriously doubt she really flushed—" The swinging door cut off his voice.

Colleen sagged against the stove. Dear God. She'd done it. For better or worse. But which? He had to love her! How would she survive if he didn't? If what she had seen in his eyes had been pity and regret, not need that cut to the bone. Could she have deluded herself?

Her mind jumped like a grasshopper in dry grass. Cam. Was Michael taking care of him? Michael…

Something burned her hand and she yanked it back, straightening. The spaghetti sauce was bubbling furiously, spattering the stove and her.

"Damn," she muttered, and stuck her hand under cold water. It was shaking, she saw, and no wonder.

That evening was the single, longest of her life. Neither of the kids, still bickering, seemed to notice how quiet the two adults were. Michael answered Drew's questions, Colleen heard about the horseback-riding lesson to which Jennifer had chauffeured the two girls today. Every once in a while Michael's gaze met Colleen's, and though his expression didn't change, awareness flared in his eyes and her heart skipped a beat.

Ridiculous to be married and unable to find a moment to themselves, but it was as though even Cam had joined a conspiracy to keep Mom and Dad busy. When Drew and Kim settled down at the table with homework, the phone rang and the father of one of Michael's soccer players wanted to discuss—at length—the amount of playing time his boy was getting. And then, of course, Cam insisted on nursing, which Michael watched with a grimness that secretly pleased Colleen.

The kitchen had to be cleaned, Drew persuaded to take a bath, Cam's diaper changed. Colleen rocked him to sleep and laid him in his crib with the care she gave a soufflé. He stiffened, she held her breath—and then he relaxed and sucked noisily on his fist. Colleen tiptoed out.

Michael was waiting at the foot of the stairs. When he saw her, he straightened from where he leaned against the banister. His eyes didn't leave hers from the moment she started down.

All the way she looked at him: the shadow beneath his cheekbones, a mouth that could be astonishingly sexy, his straight, dark hair and dark brows that made his vivid blue eyes even more startling. He was large and solid and devastatingly handsome. And hers. For better or worse.

He didn't touch her when she reached the foot of the stairs, just stood there with his hands at his sides.

Colleen moistened dry lips. "Michael—"

"Did you mean it?"

Beyond pretense, she gave a small nod.

His voice was uneven. "Say it again."

"I love you," she whispered.

"God." He closed his eyes and blindly reached for her.

She stumbled into his arms and laid her head against his chest, where she could feel the slam of his heartbeat. He held her so tightly she knew he needed to be held just as much.

Against her hair Michael said roughly, "I never thought I'd hear you say that."

"I love you so much it scares me," she said, and waited for him to tell her the same.

Instead, she felt him take a long, shuddering breath, and then he held her away from him. A muscle jumped in his cheek, and his eyes searched hers. When he finally spoke, it was hoarsely. "Why?"

Her heart skipped a beat. "*Why?* Why what?"

His hands actually dropped from her arms; his face was set in lines of harsh restraint. "I know I'm not an easy man to love. Not even my own parents loved me." He said it almost indifferently, as a matter of fact. "I'm not taking the blame. They're the kind of people who should never have had kids. God knows why they did. I know it wasn't my fault, they were just as distant with Stephen, but somehow I never learned..." At last a spasm of pain twisted his face and he broke off. Colleen lifted one hand to his cheek, and he turned his mouth against her palm. His voice was muffled. "I didn't know how to make Sheila love me. I don't know how to make you."

Colleen's throat was thick with tears. "I already love you," she said in a voice that shook. "Michael, listen to me." She lifted her other hand and cradled his face, holding it so that he had to look at her. "Sheila did love you, as much as she could. And me...I spend every day wondering how I could have been so lucky. You're the father my kids deserved. You're patient and kind and gentle and sexy. Every time I look at you, my heart jumps and my stomach does a flip-flop and my knees get weak. I love you," she said again. "I'll spend the rest of my life convincing you, if...if you want me to."

He crushed her convulsively in his arms. "I need you," he whispered into her hair. "I love you. God, I love you."

And finally his mouth found hers in a kiss so achingly tender, so wondering, her cheeks were wet with tears by the time he lifted his head.

Michael wiped her cheeks gently with his thumb. "I've loved you since long before Cam was born. I think maybe I knew it the first time you lifted your shirt and let me put my hand on you. I never expected..." His voice had become ragged. "Never dreamed..."

One confession deserved another. "Do you want to know something really awful?" Colleen asked. She didn't wait for an answer. "I think maybe I was always attracted to you. I never liked being around you. It made me uncomfortable. I didn't let myself know why."

Huskily Michael said, "The first time I ever saw you, I felt as if somebody had punched me. I told myself it was surprise, because I'd expected you to look more like Sheila. I think even then I knew better." He was silent for a moment. Somehow Colleen knew what he was going to say even before he said it. "How do you think she would feel about us?"

Colleen thought of Cam, with his plump cheeks and downy hair, and she thought of her sister, whose joy for life had never been selfish. She had wanted a baby, but never at anybody else's expense. Her hand had held Colleen's through every hurt in both their lives, never slackening until the day she died. Maybe she hadn't learned to open their loving circle to others, but she would rejoice because Colleen had.

With sudden, unshakable certainty, Colleen said softly, "She'd be rooting for us all the way."

"I think she would be, too."

This kiss was sweet and passionate and mysterious, everything life with Michael would be. When he swung her into his arms and started up the stairs, she whispered against his throat, "I do believe I'm in the mood to undress in front of you. Slowly."

His laugh was husky. "I do believe I'm in the mood to enjoy that." And for the second time he carried her across the threshold of their bedroom door, a husband impatient to celebrate his marriage in the best of all possible ways.

Afterward Colleen snuggled up to Michael, reveling in his warmth and the strong beat of his heart and the idle way his fingers played with the curls at the nape of her neck.

Sleepily, contentedly, she said, "Did I tell you that some boy wants Kim to be his girlfriend?"

Michael's hand stopped. Colleen lifted her head. "I'm sorry. You were trying to sleep. I'll shut up."

"No!" She felt the bob of his Adam's apple, and then he said more moderately, "No, I'd like to hear about it. I'd like to hear anything you want to tell me."

Still she hesitated, but he pulled her head back down on his shoulder. "The kid must be some quick worker."

Reassured, Colleen gave him a quick kiss. "No kidding. He sent her a note the third day of school. Well, actually his friend sent Stacey a note in school. You know how it works. Kim says she thinks he's cute, but he's only the third-cutest boy in her class, so she isn't sure."

How she had missed having someone to talk to! Really talk to. She wasn't sure which she valued most—the desperate hunger in his eyes that only she could appease or the intimacy of this kind of talking.

But it hardly mattered, did it? In Michael, her husband, lover and friend, she had both.

NOT TWO DAYS LATER Colleen started piecing a traditional Wedding Ring quilt. She told Michael that it was the circles overlapping that held meaning for her.

"Loving circles," she said.

Looking at the tiny pieces she would stitch so patiently together to make a whole, symbolizing what her marriage meant to her, Michael believed at last that this woman would hold him and love him and, at night under this quilt, share her hopes and deepest heartaches with him. For a lifetime.

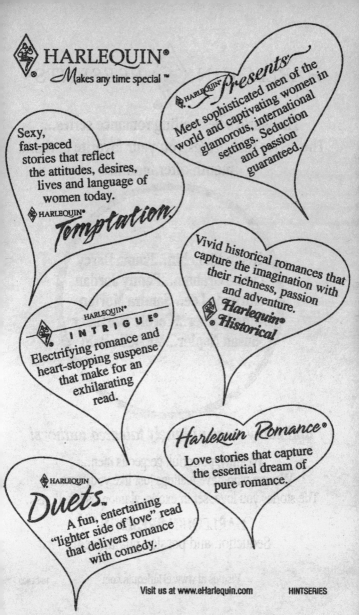

HARLEQUIN®
Makes any time special ™

HARLEQUIN *Presents~*

Meet sophisticated men of the world and captivating women in glamorous, international settings. Seduction and passion guaranteed.

Sexy, fast-paced stories that reflect the attitudes, desires, lives and language of women today.

HARLEQUIN®
Temptation.

Vivid historical romances that capture the imagination with their richness, passion and adventure.

Harlequin®
Historical

HARLEQUIN®
INTRIGUE®

Electrifying romance and heart-stopping suspense that make for an exhilarating read.

Harlequin Romance®

Love stories that capture the essential dream of pure romance.

HARLEQUIN
Duets.

A fun, entertaining "lighter side of love" read that delivers romance with comedy.

HARLEQUIN ◆ PRESENTS®

The world's bestselling romance series...
The series that brings you your favorite authors,
month after month:

Helen Bianchin...Emma Darcy
Lynne Graham...Penny Jordan
Miranda Lee...Sandra Morton
Anne Mather...Carole Mortimer
Susan Napier...Michelle Reid

and many more uniquely talented authors!

Wealthy, powerful, gorgeous men...
Women who have feelings just like your own...
The stories you love, set in exotic, glamorous locations...

HARLEQUIN PRESENTS,
Seduction and passion guaranteed!

Visit us at www.eHarlequin.com

HPGEN00

AMERICAN ✦ ROMANCE ®

Invites you to discover the fun!

HEART:

Heartwarming emotion, heart-pounding romance, heart-stopping heroes!
Every month we offer diverse stories such as marriages of convenience, secret babies and plain Jane gets her man!

HOME:

4 brand-new books every month with delightful American settings!
Our wonderful authors have created communities of unforgettable characters you'll want to read about again and again!

HAPPINESS:

Where happily-ever-after is 100% guaranteed!
Each American Romance novel fulfills our promise to bring you exceptional romance the way *you* want it—upbeat and lively!

AMERICAN ROMANCE—
the place for Heart, Home & Happiness

What are you looking for in your romance novels?

★ A *longer*, more satisfying read

★ Characters you can *identify* with and care about

★ Characters who are *realistic* and true to life

★ A compelling story that completely *involves* you—
a story you can really escape into

★ A story with a strong, believable and *positive* romance

★ Stories by some of the *best* romance authors writing
today—many of them award winners

★ Stories with *places and backgrounds* so real, you feel
as if you're there

★ A huge *variety* of stories—from family dramas to classic
romances, from suspense to comedy…and everything
in between

★ Stories with *more!*

**If these are the things you want in
your romance novels, welcome to**

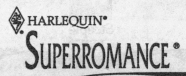

HARLEQUIN®

SUPERROMANCE®

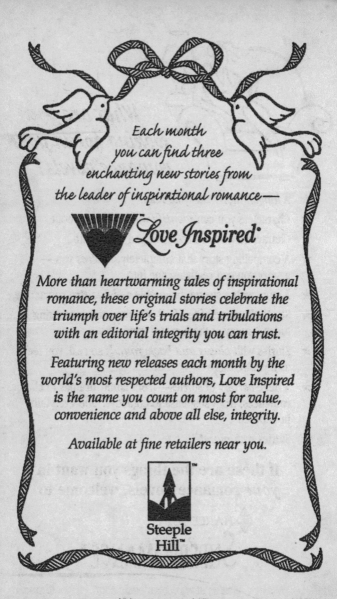

Each month
you can find three
enchanting new stories from
the leader of inspirational romance—

Love Inspired

More than heartwarming tales of inspirational
romance, these original stories celebrate the
triumph over life's trials and tribulations
with an editorial integrity you can trust.

Featuring new releases each month by the
world's most respected authors, Love Inspired
is the name you count on most for value,
convenience and above all else, integrity.

Available at fine retailers near you.

Steeple
Hill™

HARLEQUIN®
INTRIGUE

IS *THE* PLACE
FOR BREATHTAKING
ROMANTIC SUSPENSE!

Harlequin Intrigue brings you all that you
want in category romance—and more!
Four titles each month deliver the drama
of romance *plus* an explosive sense of
suspense for a thrilling reading experience
that will leave you breathless.
From whodunits to witness protection,
you get variety and the guarantee of
a happy ending—case closed!

So unlock the mystery of the heart
with Harlequin Intrigue.
You won't be disappointed.